THE RELUCTANT ASSASSIN

LEE JACKSON

Severn River Publishing
www.SevernRiverBooks.com

ISBN: 978-1-64875-569-9 (Paperback)

ALSO BY LEE JACKSON

The Reluctant Assassin Series

The Reluctant Assassin

Rasputin's Legacy

Vortex: Berlin

Fahrenheit Kuwait

Target: New York

The After Dunkirk Series

After Dunkirk

Eagles Over Britain

Turning the Storm

The Giant Awakens

Riding the Tempest

Driving the Tide

To my wife and best friend, Barbara:
"Ah Fifi."

And, to my father-in-law, the real-life Atcho:
Your courage was inspiring.

MAJOR CHARACTERS

Atcho: Eduardo Xiquez
Alias 1: José – Poses as own messenger
Alias 2: Tomas – Identity to US Intelligence
Alias 3: Manuel Lezcano – Prison identity

Isabel: Atcho's daughter
Juan: Atcho's best friend and deputy
Govorov: KGB Intelligence officer
Paul Clary: US Air Force Intelligence officer
Burly: CIA officer
Rafael: Cuban invasion force officer
Jujo: Leader inside prison on Isle of Pines
Sofia Stahl: Secretary at US Interests' Section in Swiss Embassy in Havana
Mike Rogers: Senior Secret Service Agent
Ivan: KGB Officer

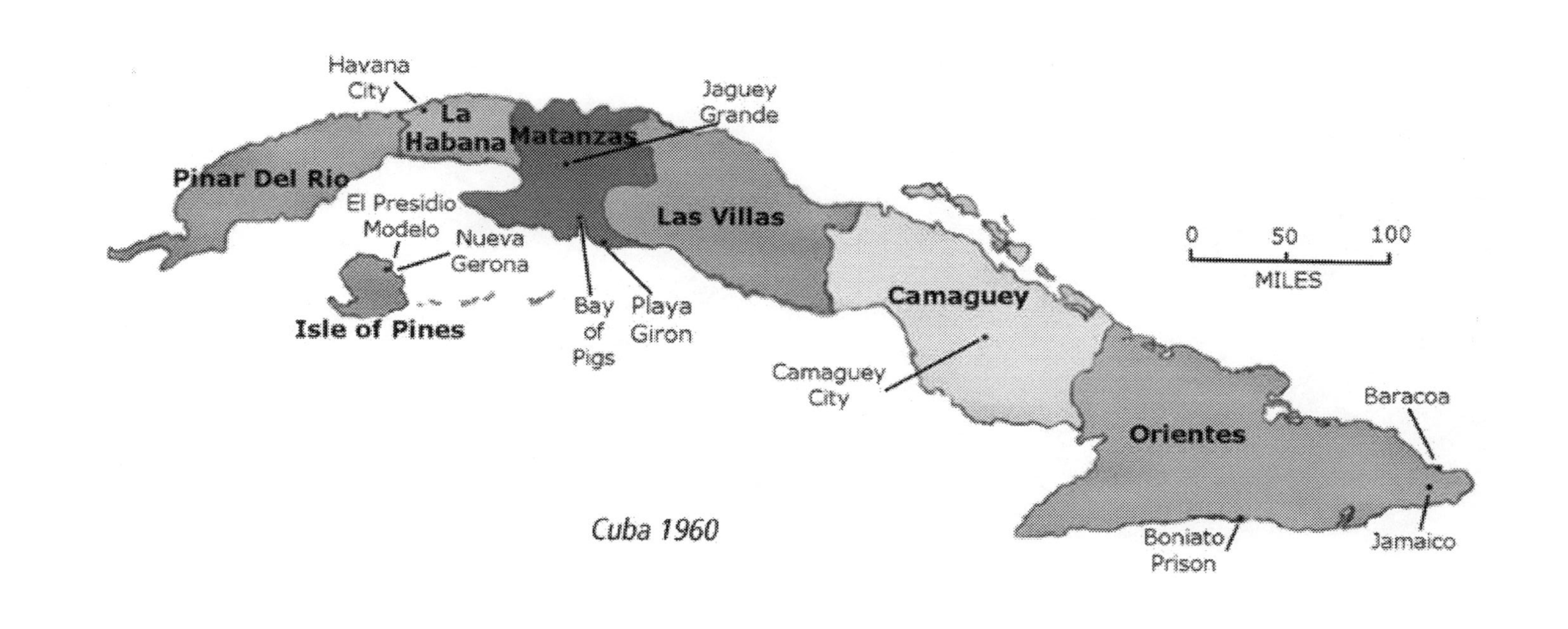
Havana City
La Habana
Matanzas
Jaguey Grande
Pinar Del Rio
El Presidio Modelo
Nueva Gerona
Isle of Pines
Bay of Pigs
Playa Giron
Las Villas
Camaguey
Camaguey City
0
50
100
MILES
Orientes
Baracoa
Boniato Prison
Jamaico
Cuba 1960

PROLOGUE

HAVANA, NEW YEAR'S EVE, 1959

Cuban President Fulgencio Baptista flees the country in the face of an armed insurrection. Five days later, Fidel Castro enters Havana with Ché Guevara, and seizes power. Though he is initially greeted with an outpouring of popular support, Cubans soon learn that they have traded one dictator for another. Hailed as a liberator, Castro demonstrates cruelty and tyranny that eclipses any known before on this island. Within a year, resistance groups spring up around Cuba. They are led by patriots who are largely inexperienced but fearless in the cause of restoring freedom to Cuba.

One of these patriots is a man of unusual qualifications. The few who know him call him Atcho.

1

CUBA, DECEMBER 1960

Atcho slouched against a wall, alone in a small plaza illuminated by the dim yellow light of a single street lamp. His eyes probed the surrounding darkness. His fine, aristocratic features were hidden behind a week's growth of unkempt beard, while his normally well-groomed hair fell in shaggy brown locks below his ears.

Since state security police, the *milicianos*, had never seen Atcho, at least not as himself, they knew him only by reputation. Tonight, they expected his messenger.

Atcho's ears strained for sounds of approach. His powerful frame ached to be released from its tense stance.

In the light of the streetlamp, his silhouette stood out, an easy target. From behind a nearby wall, the first glimmer of the moon tinged the edge of the sky as it began its ascent. Soon, it would cast its ghostly glow about the square.

Screeching tires broke the silence. Atcho shrank further into his loose-fitting clothes. He checked the inside of his left calf for the razor-sharp hunting knife strapped there. His face melted into dull callowness. His eyes became vacuous. He looked like a crude country peasant, nothing more.

His mind raced as two Jeeps drove into view and stopped several yards away, spotting him in their headlights. Muscles tensed. *Keep control.* His heart pounded, and his temples pulsed. He felt adrenaline surge, but his face showed no expression.

The driver of the first Jeep opened his door and stepped out. "Are you José?"

Atcho shuffled away from the wall and moved forward, shoulders drooping. "Yes. I am José." They spoke in Spanish.

"Do you have something to tell me?"

"Do you have a package for me?"

The driver shoved him. "Just tell me the message."

"My boss says I have to get a package first."

The driver delivered a brutal punch directly into Atcho's belly. Atcho rolled with the blow and sank to the ground in pain. "Why did you do that? I'll be happy tell you. But my boss will kill me if I don't get the package."

The driver's boot connected with Atcho's chin, sprawling him across the ground between the Jeeps. He squatted by Atcho's head. "You are going to tell us, or ..." Leaving the threat unspoken, he grabbed Atcho by the hair and jerked his face close.

"I'm dead if I don't bring the boss what I came for."

"What's in the package?"

"He says I'll know it when I see it."

The driver studied him, and then motioned with his hand. Two men stepped from the first Jeep. The driver conferred with one, a lieutenant, while the other stood guard over Atcho. When they parted, the driver squatted next to Atcho's head while the lieutenant moved back toward the second Jeep. "Soften him up a bit while I speak to the captain."

Atcho's guards relished their task. They pistol-whipped him, threw him to the ground, and pounded his head and body with kicks. Then, they stood him up, and while one held him from the rear, the other punched his face over and over. Pain seared as more blows fell, first to his face, then to his stomach. When he dropped to the ground, they continued kicking.

Atcho offered no resistance.

The passenger door opened. The man from the first Jeep leaned inside, talking to the captain.

Through eyes swollen nearly shut, Atcho watched a glow of a cigarette from deep within the dark interior. Lying spread-eagle in the dust, he was unable to make out anything else.

Dogs in the neighborhood, hearing the sounds of violence, barked madly. Nearby doors creaked on their hinges, and then softly thumped as they closed. *The people are afraid.*

The moon had risen high into the sky and bathed the area in cold, white light, sharply contrasting buildings against their own shadows. Atcho craned his pain-racked head to watch the second vehicle. The G-2 *milicianos* spoke quietly by the Jeep.

Apparitions floated before Atcho's eyes. Columns of cadets in gray uniforms marched by. His wife appeared, arms outstretched, eyes longing for the child she would never see. Then, dancing flames in cold moonlight consumed the pale figures of his parents.

He felt himself waning and shook his head, fighting to stay awake. Cruel visions continued, immersing him in waves of grief.

Pain reminded him of his mission. He concentrated his attention on the second Jeep. The glow from inside was again visible. Occasionally, a ghost of a face peered through the windshield, then faded into the black interior.

Voices murmured, low and undulating. The shorter, sharper responses of the man next to the Jeep indicated the authority of the man inside. Believing Atcho incapacitated, the guards ignored him.

Atcho reached alongside his leg. The knife was there, cold and hard, the leather sheath pressing against his skin. He edged the knife from its sheath with his fingertips and inched it up under his body.

A noise halted his movement. The Jeep door swung open. The dark figure of the captain emerged. He was tall and wore a dark civilian overcoat and slouch hat. He strode toward Atcho, grabbed a lock of hair, and yanked Atcho's head into the light, staring into Atcho's beaten eyes. Then, he dropped Atcho's face into the dirt.

Barely conscious, Atcho could not see the captain's features. He watched the officer walk back to the vehicle and swing into the passenger's seat, hissing to the lieutenant too low to make out the words. Then the Jeep door closed, and the engine cranked to life.

Atcho's heart pounded. He fought desperately to sit up.

The lieutenant moved toward him. "You are fortunate." He spoke in menacing tones. "Captain Govorov let you live. For a while. You get to enjoy our company—until you tell us what we want to know."

"I'll tell you." Atcho gasped. "Right now. Please don't hurt me again." He watched the lieutenant, who waved his hand. The Jeep's engine cut off.

Silence settled over the night. The moon looked down, uncaring.

"All right, coward," the lieutenant said. "Tell us."

"Give me the package. Atcho will think I lied if I don't bring it to him. He'll kill me. You'll have nothing."

At the mention of the name, the lieutenant's face became hard. His mocking tone ebbed. "How will you know it's the right package?"

"I'll know."

The lieutenant looked thoughtful, then walked to the captain's Jeep. More conversation took place.

Captain Govorov's tall, lean figure stepped out again. He carried a bundle. His face in shadows, he strode to Atcho and leaned over. When he straightened, a much smaller figure stood beside him—Atcho's four-year-old daughter.

The lieutenant spoke. "Is this what you're looking for?"

Eyes shielded from the light by one hand, Atcho rasped, "I can't see her face."

Govorov shoved the tiny girl forward. The lieutenant shined a flashlight in her face. "Is this what you came for?"

Atcho nodded weakly.

The child began to cry. "I want my *Papá*."

The captain swept her over his shoulder and started toward the Jeep. The lieutenant leaned over Atcho. "Where is Atcho? Give us the message."

Atcho made no move.

The lieutenant prodded with his boot.

Atcho still made no reply.

The lieutenant kicked him.

Atcho let loose a furious cry that burned through the night. He lunged from the ground and buried his knife deep in the lieutenant's chest.

The night exploded with gunfire. The driver and guard of the first vehicle dropped to the pavement, lifeless. The driver of the second Jeep cranked the engine, and then slumped as the windshield shattered in his face.

Govorov held the little girl close. Turning, he stared at the lieutenant's corpse. It lay in a pool of blood.

Atcho crouched next to the body, ready to strike again.

The captain produced a pistol from the folds of his coat. He held it next to Isabel's temple. The firing stopped.

He regarded the ring of men forming around him and gestured with the pistol at Isabel's head. "Atcho," he crooned.

Hatred burned from Atcho's eyes, his muscles tensed to pounce.

"It is you." Govorov spoke fluent Spanish.

Atcho made no reply.

The captain mocked. "It is you." He sighed. "I still don't know what you look like. That was my mission. You're a bloody mess. I should have instructed the lieutenant better."

Atcho circled in a half crouch. His legs wobbled. He shook his head to clear it. If he attacked, Isabel would die. If he did not, he might never see her again. He loosened the grip on his knife.

The captain shrugged. "If I shoot you" he chuckled, "one of your men would put a bullet in my head, your little girl be damned." He peered at Atcho. "You're too valuable to discard. So, you live. And we'll meet again—I have your daughter."

He moved to the Jeep and yanked the dead driver into the dirt. Pulling Isabel onto his lap, he sat behind the wheel. With a grind of gears, he drove into the night.

Atcho watched the Jeep disappear. Then, he slumped to the ground, unconscious.

* * *

Four days earlier

Atcho hacked down sugarcane with a machete. His best memories came from racing on horseback with his father through these rows of sugarcane during harvest, while field hands swung their sharp tools.

Chaos had ruled since Fidel Castro's coup. Weeks ago, the new dictator worried about losing the crop and ordered all citizens into the fields to bring it in.

Atcho looked along the row of laborers to his right, hoping none recognized him. Sweat streamed from his brow. Blisters swelled his hands.

A tall, lean man headed his way, one of his fighters in the counterrevolution. He would take his time making his way to Atcho.

Atcho returned to cutting. Minutes passed. Then the man moved next to him. They did not talk, but when they were close enough, the man handed Atcho an envelope and moved on, continuing to harvest.

Without drawing attention, Atcho went to an area in the scrub brush that laborers used as a latrine. In this pungent, stifling air, he had a little privacy.

The envelope contained two sheets of paper. One was a letter from his sister Raissa, who had been caring for his little daughter. Atcho read it and froze.

Dear Eduardo, Isabel has been taken. Milicianos *came to the house. They know you're alive. And, they know your code name. They said if you want to see her again, to turn yourself in. I didn't tell them anything.*

In a daze, Atcho reread the letter, noting smudge marks where Raissa's tears had landed. He read the second note. The first line startled him.

Eduardo Xiquez (alias Atcho)

It instructed him to surrender to the *milicianos* headquarters in Havana within a week. Failure meant never seeing his daughter again.

Approaching footsteps warned that someone else intended to use the area. Thrusting the papers into his pocket, he assumed the attitude of a peasant comrade and went back to his position in the field. As soon as he could, he left.

Atcho's gut wrenched with fear for his daughter—he had seen little boys led away to face firing squads. *How can they know I'm alive?*

Turning himself in was not an option—that placed others' lives in danger.

That evening, Atcho showed the letters to Juan Ortiz, his best friend. "I don't know how they found out," Juan said, "but you can't be impulsive."

Atcho whirled on him. "We have to get my daughter back."

Juan had helped devise the plan that brought them and four of their best fighters to this empty plaza on this night.

The young guerrilla leader lay motionless in the dust. The cold face of the moon continued its impassive observation.

2

For two weeks, Atcho lay in bed, inhabiting a space between coma and consciousness. In his clouded mind, he cried out for his daughter. She reached for him in his dreams, whimpering in a toddler's voice, "I want my *Papá*." Her dark, matted locks framed a terrified oval face.

In his nightmares, Atcho reached back, only to see a sinister hand snatch Isabel away while he agonized over the flaws in his failed plan. He had endangered her life by exposing her to gunfire. *I should have turned myself in*. Those who would suffer if information was tortured from him could fend for themselves. *But Isabel is helpless*. Faces of people he might betray passed before him, some accusing, some understanding. The ghostly image of his father in US combat gear drifted in and out.

As Atcho's body healed, his mind reached toward consciousness and new questions. How did the *milicianos* connect Atcho to Eduardo? Who else knew he had survived the fire? Where did Govorov fit in? *I never thought about the Soviets.*

He felt sweat, suffocation, oppression. Pain. Pain in his left hand. He looked at it, blurry and wrapped in bandages. He brought it closer to his face, realizing dimly that he was awake.

Turning to one side, sharp pain surged through Atcho's neck and spine. An anesthetic odor met his nostrils. Nausea welled in his throat. Through a narrow window, the moon, now only a sliver, continued its expressionless surveillance.

A chair scraped. A door opened. Men whispered. Someone walked into the room and looked down at Atcho.

"Are you awake?" The voice was soft, familiar.

Atcho forced his eyes open.

"It's me. Juan. Do you understand me?"

Atcho had only one thought. "Isabel?" His voice was scratchy, whispery.

Juan looked grave.

Atcho struggled to ask again. "Isabel?"

Juan continued looking grave and did not speak.

Atcho lay motionless. A slowly rotating ceiling fan cast its shadow across dingy white walls. He moved his lips once more. "Water."

Juan reached for a pitcher on a nearby table, poured water into a glass, and pressed it to Atcho's mouth. The cool liquid brought refreshing life and a respite from his agony.

"You're looking better, my friend."

"Where am I?"

"On the outskirts of Havana. We're safe."

"How long have I been here?"

"Two weeks. We've been worried about you."

Fear wrapped icy fingers around Atcho's stomach. "Where is Isabel?"

Juan sighed and sat heavily in a chair beside the bed. "We haven't found her."

"What about a second meeting? You must have attempted to reopen talks."

"Of course. But there's been no effort to return our inquiries. Not through our informants, not through your sister. No one even retaliated against our attack."

Atcho struggled to grasp the significance of Juan's words. "What about the firefight? Wasn't there an investigation?"

Juan shook his head. "No. You killed the lieutenant. The other three soldiers died from bullet wounds. When we carried you away, no one attempted to pursue. The other Jeep and the bodies were removed by security forces."

"Can you find out anything from our contacts in the *milicianos*?

Juan shook his head again. "It's not that no one will talk. No one knows anything. We've gone to every familiar source, and a few others besides."

"What about the Russian? He shouldn't be hard to find."

"We couldn't him." Juan reminded Atcho that last year, for the first time in three decades, the Cuban government had opened diplomatic relations with the Soviets. The Russians wanted to increase their influence, he said, and had sent in a few advisors. "We checked every Russian on the island through the CIA. So far our informants have located no Captain Govorov."

Atcho closed his eyes and sank into the pillows. Then, he struggled to a sitting position.

Juan had watched his expressions. He placed a supportive arm behind Atcho's shoulders.

"Juan, you're telling me that my daughter and the one man who knows where she is, have completely disappeared."

3

Atcho's own words seemed to echo over and over again: *my daughter has completely disappeared. ... Completely disappeared. ... Disappeared.*

Steel pincers seemed to bite into his stomach. His limbs trembled. He heard his own hopeless voice through the labyrinth of fear. "Is she dead?" Tears streamed from his eyes. He covered his face in the crook of his right elbow.

Juan's gruff attempt at reassurance failed to comfort. No one knew with certainty whether or not she lived, he said. Someone unknown and ruthless held her.

Atcho sank back in bed, powerless. *Keep a clear head.* He struggled back to a sitting position and swung his feet toward the floor.

Juan moved to support him. "What are you doing?"

"I'm going to find Isabel." He legs shook. The room swam before his eyes.

Juan pressed him back into bed. "We all want to find her," he said calmly. "But you're too weak. You won't help her if you kill yourself."

Anger rising, Atcho struggled against his friend. "Let me go."

Juan held him firmly. "You need rest."

"I can't rest. Not while Isabel ..." His voice broke.

"Even if you were strong enough, where would you look?"

Atcho sat on the edge of the bed, head drooping between sagging shoulders. Then, he lunged to his feet and staggered across the floor. "I'll find my daughter," he roared. "Nobody will stop me."

A moment later, he sank to the floor, too feeble to move. He lay with hot, bitter tears streaming from his eyes, his cheeks and neck flushed with humiliation, He saw now that he had planned and executed Isabel's rescue poorly. He had anticipated badly trained Cuban *milicianos* and had encountered an officer of the Soviet Union. He struggled to his feet.

"Please, Juan, help me."

Juan assisted Atcho back to bed.

"What's being done?"

"We're in touch with Raissa. The CIA wants to find the Russian too, for their own reasons. They watched every known Soviet on the island. Our contacts will keep us informed. We have direct communication with the US Embassy, but," he shook his head, "that will end tomorrow."

Startled, Atcho asked, "Why?"

"While you were unconscious, Castro seized American oil refineries. The US countered by boycotting sugar. In retaliation, Castro nationalized American businesses. So, the US cut diplomatic ties." He shook his head. "It was inevitable."

"This is too much, too fast. We might never find Isabel."

"It's a tough situation, but you have to build strength." He paused. "You need to eat."

Reluctantly, Atcho assented. Juan issued instructions to someone in the hall, then returned and sat wearily on the chair. "Lieutenant Paul Clary wants to see you. He's an Air Force liaison officer in the US Embassy."

"What does he want?"

"He won't say. We checked him out. He's on special assignment. My guess is he's planning air support for the invasion—they're calling it Operation Mongoose. I met Clary twice. He seems nice, but if you're going to meet him, you'll have to do it today. The embassy closes tomorrow, and everyone ships out except those needed to maintain the US Interests Section at the Swiss Embassy."

"Does he know where we are?"

"No. We'll use security measures to bring him in and move as soon as he leaves."

A young woman brought in Atcho's meal. As he ate, some of his strength returned. Later that afternoon, he goaded Juan into walking him around the room. A wall mirror revealed his cut and bruised face; he recoiled from his own reflection, appalled at the scars and bruises. After one more circle, dizziness and nausea overcame him. He had to lie down again.

He dozed fitfully, his mind working constantly on the whereabouts of Isabel. Then he lapsed into dreams, his subconscious mind returning to the sugar plantation of an earlier time.

* * *

Four years beforehand

Atcho stood under a giant oak tree in front of his sister Raissa's house. A gentle breeze carried the *woosh* of rustling leaves in early autumn sunlight.

Raissa sat in a chair on the front porch, cooing into soft blankets held in her arms. She was petite, her face refined, a gentler version of Atcho's, and framed by soft, dark locks of hair. Her eyes sparkled when she laughed and glanced up at Atcho, and they clouded over on seeing his expression. She shifted as if to bring him the baby, but Atcho turned away.

His father walked from the family mansion. The patriarch had aged dramatically in recent weeks. He approached quietly and stood next to Atcho as they observed the peaceful scene.

"Have you held the baby yet?"

Atcho shook his head.

"It's been three months."

A lump formed in Atcho's throat as moisture gathered around his eyes. He said nothing.

"I've always been proud of you," his father said. "Not even Isabel's parents blame you. Many women die in childbirth."

Atcho turned away, filled with remorse.

"You can't blame the baby, either," the old man continued urgently.

Atcho still made no response.

Grasping his arm, the old man's voice rose. "Atcho, your daughter is beautiful, a treasure. You have to do everything in your power to make her life happy."

Atcho stared at the ground. He already felt the guilt that would add to his despair. A motto that seemed always to invade compromising thoughts came to mind: *Duty, Honor, Country*. He embraced his father. Then he climbed the steps to the porch and gazed into the bundle in Raissa's lap.

A delicate pink face with wide blue eyes stared back at him. The baby yawned, then smiled fleetingly. Thrusting a tiny hand into the air, she waved it about.

Atcho's heart melted. Through tears of sorrow, he slipped his hand over the baby's. She squeezed her father's thumb. Thrill seized him. He reached down with both arms and lifted the infant. Cradling her, he buried his face in the blankets. "My Isabel," he whispered.

* * *

Lying in bed, watching the fan whir overhead, Atcho tried to block sad memories. He dozed.

In midafternoon, Juan shook him gently. "Lieutenant Clary is here."

Atcho's eyes blinked open. With Juan's help, he sat up and composed himself. Then Juan opened the door to a blue-uniformed officer. The man came to the end of the bed and stood, waiting. He toyed with his service cap.

Atcho regarded him dispassionately. "What can I do for you?"

"I have something for you." He spoke in broken Spanish, with a distinctly American accent.

"What is it?"

The lieutenant reached inside his jacket. Pulling out a long envelope embossed with the seal of the US Embassy, he handed it to Atcho. "My boss said to give this directly to you."

Atcho opened it. A photograph fell into his hand. Isabel. Her wide blue eyes were full of fear under dirty and unkempt hair. A newspaper, dated the day of the firefight, had been set prominently on a table in front of her.

Forgetting pain, Atcho struggled to his feet. "Where did you get this?"

The young officer took a step backward. "From Major Richards. He tried to bring it to you last week but you were too sick. He left for Washington today and told me to bring it."

"Is that true?" Atcho looked at Juan.

Juan nodded. "Major Richards did ask to see you last week." He took the photograph. Wearily, Atcho bent his head. The lieutenant watched in silence.

Juan faced the lieutenant. "Why couldn't you have given this to me?"

"I don't know. The major told me to give it to no one but *Señor* Tomas. He didn't tell me its contents."

"How did he get it?"

"There was a firefight a couple of weeks ago. US personnel scoured the site, which was already picked over by the *milicianos*. Major Richards said the contents of the envelope were found among broken glass and shells from a Russian pistol."

Atcho relaxed. "Tomas" was his alias when communicating directly with the US Embassy or the CIA. No one in either organization knew of Tomas' relationship to Atcho; at least, no one was supposed to.

Atcho scrutinized the man. "Why are you in Cuba?"

"Excuse me?"

"Why are you here? The United States is leaving."

"That's right. Most high-security apparatus and personnel have left. I remained to close out and transfer routine channels to our Interests Section at the Swiss Embassy."

Atcho mulled over the lieutenant's words. "Have you heard of a Russian officer, a Captain Govorov, in Havana?"

Clary looked sheepish. Atcho and Juan watched him closely.

"The answer is yes and no," Clary said at last. "Keeping track of Soviets in Cuba is part of my job. We've had several reports about him, but we've never seen him. He's not on any of our official lists."

Atcho sat deep in thought. Finally, he asked, "Why did Major Richards think it so urgent that I get this?"

The officer shrugged. "Apparently the daughter of someone in your organization was kidnapped. When that photo showed up at the site of the firefight, Major Richards thought there might be a connection."

"Have you seen the photo?"

Clary responded slowly. 'Not until now. Only the major and soldiers inspecting the site saw what was found there, but everyone heard about the picture of a small girl."

Atcho looked up sharply. "You said you were not informed of the contents."

"I wasn't officially informed."

"Why should we care about it?"

Exasperation showed in Clary's face. His obsequious manner disappeared, replaced by cunning. "You'll have to ask Major Richards."

Atcho studied him. "Good idea. Meanwhile, you'll stay with us until your story checks out."

"You can't do that," Clary protested. "My flight leaves tomorrow. My superiors will be looking for me."

"You left us no choice. You learned too much about our organization."

"What do I know?" Clary stormed. "That you're Tomas and he's Juan? And you're both paranoid over a picture of a little girl?"

"You knew enough to contact us," Atcho replied flatly. "And you know this photo caused a strong reaction. If our roles were reversed, you'd do the same thing." He turned to Juan. "See that he's guarded and comfortable. And contact Major Richards."

Juan nodded and motioned the lieutenant to the door. Clary glared at Atcho.

"If everything is as you say, we'll release you into safe hands," Atcho said. "Of course, if it doesn't ..."

Juan ushered the lieutenant out of the room. Pain forgotten, Atcho watched the door close.

Moments later, Juan re-entered. "Clary's under guard, and we've sent a message to the embassy that he's here. We didn't tell them we were keeping him against his will. The wire to Richards is on its way to Washington."

Atcho pondered a thought. "Did you notice the change in Clary's demeanor?"

"It seemed abrupt.," Juan agreed. "I'd be careful with him."

"A Russian captain somehow connected Atcho to Eduardo Xiquez Rodriguez de Arciniega, and the US Embassy connected him to Tomas," Atcho ruminated. "Only you, Raissa, and her husband know that they are the same person. Now an American lieutenant makes a deliberate point of bringing a photograph to me—personally. It could have been delivered through other channels with less risk."

They sat quietly. Juan interrupted the stillness. "If the major instructed Clary to bring the envelope to Tomas, we can't blame him for following orders. That was dangerous for him. Maybe his anger was natural."

"His outburst began before I gave that order. It was such a radical change from the personality we first saw. He's faking something. You met both Clary and Richards before. Can we trust them?"

Juan shrugged. "I don't know Richards well, but I don't have any reason to mistrust him. As for Clary, he can't hurt us, but we'll pay attention to how the CIA and other friendly intelligence agencies react to our holding him."

"I thought of that. He's the last and only link we have to Isabel. If there's the slightest chance he knows more than he's saying, I want him close by."

Juan placed a hand on Atcho's shoulder. "I doubt Clary knows anything. We can't be seeing enemies where they don't exist. We'd better be careful not to alienate our friends. Paranoia could get in the way of finding Isabel and US willingness to help liberate Cuba."

"I don't understand why both the US and the Soviets give me so much attention," Atcho said slowly. "Our group isn't that big." He returned to his current dilemma. "I want confirmation that Clary did Richards' bidding. If his story checks out, we'll let him go."

"What if details get garbled in transmission?" Juan looked anxious. "There is a better way. Let's keep him overnight. We can't hold Clary for days while we wait for Richard's reply.

"We *can* let Richards and the CIA know if there's something wrong with his story. Tomorrow, before he's scheduled to fly out, we'll escort Clary to the embassy and keep him under surveillance until flight time. He won't be able to relay information to anyone about us. We'll close this place and move to a new hideout. He'll have no information to pass along."

Atcho mulled the options. He did not trust Clary, but he agreed with Juan's assessment.

Juan looked at him seriously. "You know you tend to be impulsive."

Atcho jerked as if stung. Then, quietly, he acquiesced. "You're right. Do it your way. Let Clary know."

4

Atcho settled into the back of an old bread truck bumping its way over a narrow country road in the central province of Matanzas. He felt desolate. More than two months had passed since the firefight, and there had been no word of Isabel. He and Juan had paid a surreptitious visit to the plaza but found nothing to suggest the attack even took place.

Through the CIA, Atcho had received confirmation of Lieutenant Clary's story from Major Richards. "He might be overzealous," the note read. "But he's harmless." Atcho remained dubious.

Now, he and Juan were on their way to a meeting of underground leaders in a country house outside Jaguey Grande, a village near the southern coast. They were to help coordinate resistance groups supporting the coming US invasion, led by Miami-based exiles. The CIA had air-dropped armaments that had been stockpiled by the resistance, although coordination was poor, and tons were lost in dense swamp.

Castro already expected the assault.

Atcho had not wanted to attend the meeting. Juan prodded him. "No one else on the island has military education and training like yours. We need you."

Juan was right. Atcho's education at West Point was unequaled in Cuba, and so was his Ranger training. He glanced at Juan's deeply tanned face, lined from strain. He tried to think of the meeting, but his mind traced back to Isabel's plight. All other matters paled to insignificance.

Juan read Atcho's concern. "Other people at the meeting might help find her," he said, and closed his eyes to sleep while the van continued its bumpy ride.

Atcho regarded Juan affectionately. He was twenty years older than Atcho. As a boy, Atcho had revered Juan, the only man whose advice his father had taken without question. After the fire that destroyed Atcho's ancestral home, Juan had become his closest friend. "I owe you my life twice now," he muttered softly.

Juan did not stir. Atcho drifted off to sleep, where memories became nightmares.

* * *

A few months earlier

Smoke billowed, ceilings collapsed, and timbers fell as flames leaped higher, consuming the majestic structure that had been Atcho's family mansion. A serpent of flame streaked across the floor toward his father's and mother's lifeless bodies. He gagged at the smell of their burning flesh.

He tugged desperately against the large cabinet pinning his right leg to the floor. The deadly smoke that had overcome his parents now engulfed him. As flames reached for him, he cried out for Isabel.

Fire streaked closer, lashing within inches of his imprisoned leg. The floor radiated infernal heat. As smoke overcame him, only time stood between him and excruciating death.

A dark figure lumbered over him. Strong arms wrestled with the heavy cabinet until at last, his leg was free. Then the figure seized Atcho under his arms and dragged him through a long hallway, past the kitchen. He felt himself hefted onto broad shoulders and carried down a flight of stairs into the cellar.

A door in one corner stood ajar. The great lock that had secured it lay in its hasp on the floor. Panting with exertion, his rescuer struggled through the door and downward through an earthen tunnel until gradually the air became cooler.

Atcho felt himself lowered to the ground. The light of a lantern shone on him. A steadying hand settled on his shoulder and a thermos of cold water pressed against his parched lips. He drank deeply.

"You're safe for the moment." The light shifted, and Atcho looked into the strong face of the plantation manager, Juan Ortiz.

When he woke up several hours later, Atcho gasped. "How is Isabel? And my sister?"

"Safe," Juan replied. "They were at Raissa's house when the fire started."

"My parents?" Atcho already knew the answer. He had tried to get to them, but the heavy cabinet had crashed down on him. He had seen them fall into the flames.

In the weeks that followed, Atcho struggled with fresh grief. He recovered from the effects of smoke inhalation. Although his leg was sore, there were no broken bones.

During Atcho's convalescence, Juan said he believed the fire had been started by peasants caught up in enthusiasm for Castro's plan to redistribute private lands.

Juan had joined the growing resistance to Castro. "Groups are forming all over the country. We started one here, in Camaguey, but we're leaderless. You could help."

Atcho at first showed no interest. "All I want is to get Isabel back, and maybe go to the US. I'll take Raissa and her husband, if they want to go. You could come too."

Juan reacted angrily. "You owe it to Cuba and our people to fight for freedom. Castro isn't the first dictator here." He paused, and then continued more fervently. "Do you think your father would desert his country?"

Stung, Atcho stood shamefaced.

"If you try to leave, you'll be forced into Castro's army, or you'll go to prison. In this country, you're a rare commodity."

After more heated discussion, Atcho acquiesced.

"Good," Juan said. "Let people keep thinking you're dead. We need to keep your identity secret. You can operate more freely. Your daughter and sister would be better protected. They won't even have to move. We'll use that nickname your father called you, the one you used at West Point."

"You mean 'Atcho'?"

"It's a perfect code name. Only a few people have heard it in Cuba. How did your father get it?"

Atcho thought a moment. "When he went into the US Army for WWII, some of his friends had trouble pronouncing Arturo, his first name. They shortened it to 'Atcho.'"

"It works."

* * *

The little bread truck Atcho and Juan rode in groaned over a rise at dawn. It veered onto a field and halted. They sat up stiffly. Atcho swung the rear door open and stepped into the morning. His spirits buoyed with the sight that greeted him.

The vista dropped gently across lush green fields into wide, thick marshland. Atcho moved away from the van to better see his surroundings.

Thick stands of jungle vegetation ringed the area on three sides. It grew more sparsely to the west. A cacophony of songbirds, screeching parrots, and loud crickets filled the air. Through the mist, a lone dog sounded his morning warning, and was answered by other dogs nearby. The land sparkled with dew, and a breeze carried the rich scent of wildflowers mixed with the dank smell of swamp.

A guide waited for them where a stand of trees led into thicker growth. The sound of the van driving away nearly drowned his greeting. Without ceremony, he led them down a path through dense brush. Minutes later, they arrived at a large bungalow in the center of a clearing.

Inside, a group of twenty men clustered about the single room. Some, known to Atcho and Juan, greeted them. At one end, several guerrillas grouped respectfully around a burly man in swamp fatigues. The man answered their questions in fluent Spanish with an American accent.

"He's the CIA man," Juan whispered.

After several minutes, "Burly" called the meeting to order. He opened his remarks with normal pleasantries and assured the counterrevolutionaries of US government support, recalling the close histories of their two countries. "We helped win your independence from Spain. What happens to you affects the US."

The atmosphere carried a festive air. Atcho's skepticism grew. He reminded himself that Burly's life was at risk for being on the island, and he listened attentively.

For the next two hours, Burly outlined the concept, which called for a force of Cuban exiles to execute amphibious landings. They would be supported by US naval gunfire and air forces. After a beachhead had been established, a government in exile would arrive on shore, declare itself to the citizens of Cuba, and call for popular support to depose Castro. Then, the new government would request military assistance from the United States, which would deploy Marines to reinforce the invasion. From that point, it would be a cakewalk to Havana.

By the time Burly reached this juncture, the gathering had taken on a carnival air, with shouts of "*Cuba Libre*" punctuating his proclamations. Atcho looked around with growing amazement, particularly on seeing Juan swept up in the atmosphere.

"Wait," Burly shouted over the growing buzz of voices. "There's a lot of work to do. We can't succeed without coordinated effort."

He outlined assignments for setting up clandestine radio transmitters, seizing existing communications facilities, and clearing brush from potential landing sites.

"Tons more weapons and ammunition will be air-dropped," he said, "and teams are needed to guide pilots into drop zones using ground signals." Other groups would retrieve, transport, and distribute equipment. Medical squads would organize, train, and assemble to care for casualties in the field. "And everyone should help mobilize the population to join the battle. If we fight hard, Cuba will again be a free country."

Inside the bungalow, the mood reached fever pitch. Men of all ages shouted. Arms pierced the air in wild anticipation of heroic deeds soon to be accomplished.

"Before we close," Burly beamed, "are there any questions?"

Atcho looked around. A few others looked concerned, but they seemed unsure or too nervous to ask. Most already celebrated victory.

Atcho stood. "I have a few questions." He surprised himself at the challenge in his voice. Juan looked up sharply. A hush settled over the room.

Startled, Burly regarded the person behind the voice. He saw a tall young man with broad shoulders, and rippling muscles barely disguised under loose clothing. His face and bearing were proud, eyes serious and street-smart.

Burly composed himself. "What do you want to know?"

"Where and when will the invasion take place?" Atcho asked.

Burly coughed. "For security reasons, we can't yet divulge specifics."

"Then try this," Atcho pursued, his tone rising. "When will the weapons drops take place? Where? What are the signals, and how will you make sure they won't be lost in the swamp one more time?"

Burly coughed again. "That information is only for those who need to know. I'm sure you understand?" Several men in the room voiced nervous agreement.

Juan tugged at Atcho's sleeve. "What are you doing? He's a friend. The Americans want to help."

Ignoring Juan, Atcho pulled away. "Let's see if I understand. The people who will do the fighting don't have a need to know?" He let the question hang. "Let's try another angle. Who makes up this government in exile?"

"You want to know that?" Burly stared at him blankly. "I don't know that I could tell you, even if I knew." He paced the room. He had not expected such an interrogation. Then he relaxed, and a smile returned to his face. "Young man," he began, "we're here to help, but surely you understand that we have to be conscious of security at all times."

"You're here," Atcho cut in, "because America is afraid that Khrushchev will establish a military base in your backyard." Atcho warmed to his argument. "As for security, where is it around here?"

Men exchanged worried glances and whispered comments. Atcho continued. "I wasn't challenged when I arrived. I saw no more than four guards, armed with light weapons, and no one checked my identification. If we're raided while plotting strategy, what is the escape plan?"

Burly peered at him. "What's your name?"

"I am Tomas."

Burly looked closer at him. "I have heard of you, *Señor* Tomas. You must believe in our sincere effort to help your country."

"You're at risk. I get that, but let's don't fool ourselves about US motives."

Burly frowned. "What else bothers you?"

Atcho studied Burly a moment. He was tall, nearing forty, with cropped steel-gray hair wrapped around a balding head. “Mr. ... uh, Burly. Do you mind if I call you Burly?” He grinned. “It fits. You won’t tell me your real name anyway.”

Burly glared at him.

There was no sound in the room. Then Burly relaxed, laughing. “All right, Tomas, but I’m going to stop calling you ‘Señor.’ A snot-nosed kid like you doesn’t deserve respect.” Tension broke. Men breathed easier and even laughed for a moment, but then the room fell silent again.

Atcho drew himself erect. “The way I see things, your government asks us to risk our lives supporting an invasion by people we don’t know, for leaders we didn’t choose. We’re going to do this crazy thing at undesignated places, on a schedule that hasn’t been established. We’ll accomplish this with weapons still to be delivered by unknown procedures at sites not yet chosen.” Noting Burly’s respectful attention and thoughtful expression, he paused for breath. “And I have other major concerns.”

“Let me address those first,” Burly interrupted. “The answers might not be satisfactory, but your points are valid. First, the invasion force includes Cuban exiles of all ages and classes. They mostly come from Miami and live for the day to come back home to Cuba. I can’t give evidence. Time is too short.”

He paced across the room, rubbing his chin. “I won’t deny the US sometimes has selfish motives but give some credit to those of us who go in harm’s way by coming here.” A warm chorus of agreement supported him. “As for the government in exile, representatives were elected in Miami by the exiles themselves.” He raised his eyebrows. “But until my government delivered an ultimatum to choose leaders by a given deadline or lose US support, no representatives were chosen.”

A few men groaned. “You convinced me,” one called. “Foolishness like that sounds like a Cuban government.” Nervous laughter rippled through the room.

Burly went on. “As for operations, training, and logistics, your questions are good, but without good answers. We’ll coordinate as closely as we can. But to be effective,” he paused, and enunciated deliberately, “Cubans have to take initiative. And let me say one more thing to allay fears. We've successfully done this in Guatemala."

As soon as he made the statement, Burly's expression showed he wished he could take it back. Then, bracing himself, he continued. "The exile army is well-trained. They include soldiers who defected from Cuba's national army and are led and staffed by Cuban officers. They call themselves Brigade 2506. I can't tell you where they train. But, if you walked through the swamps in the country I mentioned a moment ago, you might see strange things happening." Laughter rippled again. "Now, Tomas, you have other concerns."

Atcho nodded. "Thank you for being candid." He felt growing respect for the CIA officer. He picked his words carefully. "I appreciate what your agency did in Guatemala, but several factors are different.

"Here you have to do an amphibious landing, and you rely on an uprising by the Cuban people. What will cause that uprising?" He paused. "I lost everything to this regime. I hate Castro and all he stands for. If I had the chance, I would kill him with my bare hands." He lowered his voice. "But I don't see strong opposition from the population. People who had no land now live on what Castro took from others. No one feels the US trade embargo yet, so goods are still plentiful. At this moment, things are better for many Cubans. And when the embargo is in full effect, they won't blame Castro. They'll blame the US," he looked around, "and us."

Men murmured throughout the room. Burly contemplated awhile. When he spoke again, his voice was grave. "If you're right about Cuba's population, we've made one hell of a miscalculation." He paused. "As for the amphibious landing, you know that your guys will be trained and supported by the most successful landing force in history." He noted approving reactions. "You had another question?"

"Just one." Atcho weighed his words. "This situation developed under President Eisenhower. He said he supported the effort, but I doubt his enthusiasm. For two months now, Kennedy has been president. What assurance do we have that he supports this operation?"

"My presence here," Burly answered.

Just then, another voice cut in. "I'd like to answer that." An elderly gentleman in a business suit stood on the opposite side of the room. "My name is Enrique." All heads turned toward him. "I was in Key Biscayne in Florida last October for a fund-raiser at a friend's house for Kennedy's election campaign." The old man reached for the back of a chair. "Mr. Kennedy was there."

All ears strained to hear. "This fund-raiser was sponsored by wealthy Cubans. We were interested in Mr. Kennedy's position regarding Cuba. We asked him the same question about supporting the resistance. Mr. Kennedy replied that he had lost a brother in World War II. He asked how he could do anything else but aid those struggling for liberty." The old man's voice shook. "He said if we are willing to pay the same price, risk our lives, then he would move heaven and earth to help us."

"Enrique," a man called from a far corner. "Is Mr. Kennedy a man of his word, or another clever politician? Can we trust him?"

A hush fell over the room. Enrique regarded the man through aging eyes. "Yes," he said firmly. "We can trust President Kennedy."

Applause erupted, accompanied by loud cheering. Only Atcho and a few others seemed unmoved by the old man's words. When the noise died, Burly called for quiet. "Tomas, you look doubtful. Do you have more questions?"

Atcho spoke slowly. "Meaning no disrespect, I don't believe Mr. Kennedy will risk war with the Soviet Union to save this island." He sighed. "I believe, Burly, that you've done your best to be honest, but the same questions are up in the air, so I see only a small probability of success."

Gloom replaced elation as Atcho's rationale sank in. Finally, Burly spoke. "Then what will you do?"

Atcho thought deeply in silence. He straightened to full height. "I will fight," he said gravely. "It's our only chance to save Cuba."

The room erupted in cheers, with men clapping each other on their backs. Suddenly needing fresh air, Atcho turned and walked out the door. Juan followed, watching his young leader with the light of fresh respect in his eyes. "You were brilliant."

"Juan, that was bullshit in there, and you know it."

Before Juan could speak, Burly appeared before them, having left through another door. He extended his palm to Atcho. "I want to shake your hand."

Atcho gripped it firmly, but stood with feet planted apart, his face expressing respectful skepticism. "I know you want to help. I doubt you can deliver."

"Got it," Burly replied. He started to say something else, but several other men grouped around Atcho. They clapped him on the shoulder; others reached in, trying to shake his hand. One pushed through and handed Atcho an envelope. It was a letter from Raissa.

Atcho took it with forced composure. He excused himself, stepped a few feet away, tore the message open, read the first line, and blanched.

Atcho, Isabel is safe. She's with me now.

In a daze, Atcho headed toward the underbrush to read the entire letter.

Our neighbors found Isabel walking along a road and recognized her. She doesn't know where she's been. A lady took care of her in a house far away, and when they brought her back, they waited until they saw the neighbors and then set her out on the road and drove away.

Apparently, except for one night, she had been treated well during captivity. But her nightmares were of flying bullets and a fierce man, covered with blood, lying in a plaza. Atcho fought almost overwhelming emotion. When Juan came to him, Atcho handed him the letter. Then, feeling relief and elation, he wandered a few more yards into the underbrush.

Abruptly, Burly called to him and tromped through the foliage. "Tomas, we need to talk."

Atcho turned and saw him following hurriedly. "What is it?"

"You're sharp, Tomas." He was either oblivious to Atcho's discomfiture or ignored it. "Your questions aren't being asked anywhere else, and as you said, we are often cavalier with your people."

"Yes, you are. What's the point?"

"Just this, *Atcho*." He emphasized the code name.

Atcho stared, stunned.

"Yes, Tomas, Eduardo, Atcho. We know your identity and background."

Atcho's expression turned to anger.

Burly held up two open-faced palms in a beseeching gesture. "Let me explain.

"Figuring out who you were wasn't difficult once you began using your contacts to find your daughter. We did some backtracking and found her identity. When Tomas was suddenly taken ill for an extended period, then seen by Clary in a battered condition, we were almost certain Tomas was Atcho. Your reaction to a photograph confirmed the relationship between you and the child." He lowered his voice. "You can count on my help anytime, Atcho. Remember that. Anytime."

Atcho rubbed his eyes and forehead. "I guess I couldn't keep the secret forever."

Juan joined them. Atcho took the letter from him and handed it to the CIA man.

Burly scanned the note. "This is great." he said. "Then there's no reason you can't do what I just suggested to Juan."

Atcho regarded him dubiously.

"Look," Burly continued. "There are few men in Cuba with your education and training. The people in this group are brave fighters, but they don't have the skills for this undertaking."

Good choice of words, Atcho thought. *Undertaking.*

"We need someone to organize this group—make them effective—someone who can think, ask the right questions, and lead." Burly's excitement mounted. "I've spoken with the leaders, and we agree. We want you to take charge and lead this local effort."

Atcho stared in disbelief. "Are you crazy?"

Burly drew back at Atcho's unexpected reaction.

"Haven't you paid attention?" Atcho's voice thundered through the thick underbrush. Juan nudged him to soften his outburst. "Nearly three months ago, my daughter was taken. I had no word of her in all that time. Now I receive a message that she's safe at home, and you want me to head up a ragtag outfit on a suicide mission? No, *amigo*. I'm going home."

"But you said ..." Burly stammered.

"I said I'd fight. You tell me when and where, and I'll be there. Personally, I think the effort will fail. I intend to spend as much time as I have left with my daughter." He stopped and glared at Burly. "Does this operation even have a name?'

Burly looked startled, then flustered. "Yes," he said, lowering his voice. "It's Operation Mongoose."

"Operation Mongoose," Atcho repeated slowly. "I had forgotten." His voice took on thick sarcasm. "This time the cobra might eat the mongoose." He turned and left Burly speechless among a small band of men and strode deeper into the marsh.

"Let me talk to him," Juan told Burly. When he caught up with Atcho, the two walked in silence. At last Juan spoke. "Are you going straight to your sister's house?"

Atcho grunted affirmatively.

"Do you think it might be a trap?"

"Of course. I'll be careful." More silence.

"If it's a trap, Isabel might not be there."

Atcho whirled on Juan. "If there's the slightest chance of saving my daughter, that's what I'll do." His face was distorted in fury. "If you have something to say, say it."

"Don't treat me like this, Atcho," Juan said steadily. "I don't deserve it."

Atcho sucked in his breath. "You're right. What's your point?"

"You spoke about security. Now you're running off with no confirmation or support, leaving an organization to flounder when you could help. We can check to see if Isabel is at your sister's house." He paused, and then continued. "We might save Cuba or fail, but one thing is certain. We won't succeed if we don't fight with all we've got." He placed a strong hand on Atcho's shoulder. "Go, if you must, my friend. Of all people, I know what you've suffered. I'll never think less of you, whatever you decide."

A lump formed in Atcho's throat. "I need to be alone."

Juan nodded and walked back down the path toward the bungalow.

Atcho sat under a tree and remained there while shadows lengthened, and the sun slid down the western sky. Though he was outwardly impassive, his mind and emotions wrestled with conflicting desires and responsibilities. *Why was Isabel returned now? If she really is safe ...*

In late afternoon, he walked into the bungalow. Guerrilla leaders seated in a circle eyed him with awe and encouragement. Realization dawned that by now, every man in the room knew his story. Burly stood to one side, watching him uncertainly. Atcho walked over to him and held out his hand. "I apologize," he said. "You didn't deserve that."

The men in the room stirred. Burly stared at him without expression.

Then he stepped close to Atcho, threw his arm around his neck and drew his head down. "You snot-nosed kid. I said you shouldn't get too much respect." He grinned, and as others breathed sighs of relief, he whispered to Atcho, "I told you I would help anytime. Count on it."

Atcho gave him a friendly punch in the ribs, and then turned to the group. "I'm here to fight," he said brusquely. Amid warm greetings and encouraging slaps on the back, he raised his hands for quiet. "I have two stipulations. First, I'll send two scouts to confirm that my daughter is safe. Second, for two weeks, I'll oversee the planning and training. At that point, if I receive word that Isabel is safe, Juan will represent me while I visit my child. If the invasion begins while I'm gone, I'll link up with you on the battlefield. Questions?"

There were none.

Atcho threw himself into his duties with an unaccustomed light heart, anticipating the day he would leave for Camaguey. He imagined hugging Isabel, then playfully holding her in the air. That alone was worth the fight.

Four days later, the scouts returned from Camaguey. For a day and a half, they had sat unobserved on a hill overlooking Raissa's house. They had observed Isabel play in the yard and saw Raissa and her husband moving about. They had seen no evidence that the couple were being guarded or coerced.

"Using extreme caution" they told Atcho, "you should be able to visit your daughter at a time of your choosing."

5

Two weeks later, Atcho sat on the hill overlooking Raissa's house. Five men hid in a nearby stand of trees, armed and ready.

Isabel played outside dressed in a pink dress and pinafore. As she ran through tall grass after a red ball, her dark hair swirled about her shoulders. Seeing again how much she looked like her mother, Atcho's joy mixed with anguish.

A crash of thunder shook him. He restrained the urge to rush down and embrace his daughter. Dusk would be the best time to approach the house.

His mind wandered. For the past two weeks, he had overseen the resistance organization's planning and training, yet he worried over its preparedness. He recalled his last conversation with Juan. "They're not even close to ready."

"We knew that when we started," Juan had replied. "They'll do what they can and fight bravely. They'll be more effective because of your help."

Atcho had bearhugged his friend. "Thank you for everything. I would not have survived without you."

"Take care of yourself and Isabel. I'll see you in a week." They had bid each other farewell.

Now, Atcho scanned the horizon. Dark clouds gathered, gaining size and altitude. A steady breeze blew dust over open fields, and a few scattered showers appeared across the landscape. Moments later, heavy rain hit the ground.

Isabel ran into the house.

In his hiding place, Atcho felt for the pistol in his coat pocket. He stepped out where he could see one of his fighters, waved, and received a return signal. His men were ready.

He looked at the sky again. Lightning shot out of angry clouds. Thunder rumbled as darkness descended.

Atcho stepped onto the road. His heart beat faster as he came within twenty yards of the house. Through a window, he saw Raissa working over the kitchen sink. She looked tired, with dark circles under her eyes. Atcho remembered the sparkle they had once held.

She looked up and saw him. A horrified expression crossed her face.

Alarmed, Atcho increased his speed, but moved into shadows. His men followed.

Raissa disappeared from the window and reappeared momentarily, carrying Isabel. Her husband joined her. She squinted into the gathering dusk. Behind them a fourth, unfamiliar figure loomed. Catching Atcho's movement, Raissa pointed him out. Then they left the window.

Atcho's senses piqued, he heard a Jeep's engine. Pulling the pistol from his jacket, he ran for cover, away from the house.

Moments later, from his vantage point behind low bushes, Atcho watched in dismay as a Jeep sped from around the house and down the road. A cold wind struck him. Ominous, rolling thunder echoed across open fields.

One of Atcho's men crept up beside him. "What happened?"

Atcho shook his head. "I don't know. Raissa saw me, and then someone I don't know appeared. Did you see who was in the Jeep?"

"No, it was too dark. They must have been *milicianos*. I'll take a couple of guys and check out the house. We'll signal when it's safe."

A few minutes later, the man signaled an all-clear. Atcho left his position and walked around the house, up the front steps, and into the sitting room. The place was empty.

An envelope lay on the kitchen table, one single word scrawled on its surface in an unfamiliar hand: "Atcho." He tore it open.

The invasion will fail. Planning and coordination are incredibly poor, and the United States does not have the political will to win. This island belongs to the Soviet Union. And you, Atcho, belong to me.

Captain Govorov

6

With a roar, Atcho splintered a wooden chair across the kitchen table. Watching from the dining room, his men exchanged nervous glances. They had never seen their leader like this. He stood in the middle of the room, head and shoulders drooping, arms and hands limp at his side. Finally, he leaned against the window, motionless.

Outside, claps of thunder echoed across the turbulent sky. Atcho's men kept watchful eyes. The wind moaned against the house, howling through crevices. Still, Atcho made no move. Two hours passed, then he strode across the room, neither looking nor speaking to anyone. Flinging the door open, he walked into the stormy night. Two men started after him but were restrained by another with a shake of his head.

At the other end of the yard, Atcho leaned with his back against a wind-lashed oak. Gusts whipped his hair across his face. Rain fell in driven sheets, pouring cold water down his collar onto his back.

Lightning stabbed through roiling thunderclouds, hurling a shaft of flame, striking the top of the tree and into the depths of Atcho's soul. A large branch fell, landing next to him in a mass of drenched leaves. He took no notice.

His mind turned to cold calculation. *Govorov.* The words of the Russian's note were engraved on his mind. *And you, Atcho, belong to me.*

Atcho's mind kicked into gear and he reviewed the events of the last few hours. His sister and her husband had been threatened, or they would not have acted as they did. Whoever had guarded his family had rushed away, with no attempt to trade Atcho's freedom for Isabel's.

No gunfire had been exchanged. As in the first encounter, there had been no attempt to pursue. *Disrupting my group could be done without a Soviet captain or kidnapping a child.* Something Govorov said the night of the firefight tugged at Atcho's mind. *What you look like is what we wanted to know.*

"Govorov," he cried aloud. "What do you want from me?"

Finally, the storm passed and with it, most of the clouds. Lifting his head, Atcho saw stars glimmering in the rain-washed night. He peered through the darkness. No light glowed from the house, but he knew that his men kept watch over him.

He walked to a high knoll not far from where he had stood under the oak tree. When he reached the top, starlight revealed the blackened ruins of his boyhood home. The mansion lay in desolation, scorched bricks and timber scattered in ghostly piles.

He looked beyond the house to the ruins of a long, low building that had once housed his father's prize horses. Then he gazed over the weed-infested sugarcane fields where laborers had toiled, and he had raced with his father on horseback.

He remembered pride on his parents' faces the day he had left for West Point and the day four years later when he brought his future bride to this very house. Breathtakingly beautiful, Isabel Arteaga had bewitched him and enchanted his family. It was here that she had died giving birth to their daughter, Isabelita. He dropped his head. *Life without my wife, my family, is no life at all.*

Slowly, reluctantly, he walked back down the hill to his sister's house. As he passed the oak tree, a low voice called to him. He recognized Miguel, one of his men. "Atcho, the invasion has begun."

"What?" Foreboding gripped Atcho. "Where are the others?"

"On the hill. They moved away from the house in case the *milicianos* came back. I stayed here to wait for you."

"How do you know about the invasion?"

"We heard it on the radio in your sister's house. The Americans bombed the air base outside Havana, Camp Columbia. Castro ordered the army to set up checkpoints on the major highways. We have to go."

Atcho grimaced. *I don't even believe the invasion will succeed.* "Let's go. They need us in Jaguey Grande."

"Not Jaguey Grande," Miguel interrupted. "Pinar del Rio and Oriente. Reports said Brigade 2506 landed there. I spoke on the phone to our contact in Jaguey Grande before the lines shut down. Juan left a message. He thinks action in Pinar del Rio is a feint and the main landing will occur in Oriente. He wants you there.

"Also, there's activity at the Bay of Pigs, but he doesn't think it's major. Most resistance leaders are shifting to Oriente, others to Pinar del Rio. Juan will stay in Jaguey Grande to handle anything that happens there, unless you say otherwise."

Atcho listened, amazed. Juan's decisions dispersed fighting assets all over the eight-hundred-mile-long island based on "... believing that ... not expecting that ..."

Why weren't we told? He shook his head. *The US didn't trust us.*

Oblivious to Atcho's reticence, Miguel prodded him. "We have to go. In a few days, Cuba will be free. The Russian will be forced to release your daughter."

Atcho nodded somberly. "Let's go. To Oriente."

7

The reported landings had occurred at Baracoa, a village near the northern tip of the southeastern coast of the island. A large flotilla of ships had been spotted off the coast of the same town. Further inland, at a village called Jamaico, the loose confederation of resistance organizations had designated its headquarters.

Atcho and his small contingent hiked for miles to avoid major intersections where checkpoints were most likely. Then, disassembling their weapons and carrying them with loose clothing in bags slung over their shoulders, they split up and hitched rides with members of Cuba's population.

"Ask people how near we are to an uprising," Atcho instructed his men. "Even with US help, unless the people overthrow Castro, we don't have a chance."

While riding with villagers, Atcho learned with sinking spirits that he seemed to be proven correct. "Have you heard about the US invasion?" he would ask.

"Yes," came the typical response. "And our leader, Fidel, will throw the imperial Yankees out."

A day later, Atcho arrived, regrouped with his men in Jamaico. To his dismay, he learned that two landings had been attempted at Baracoa, but for inexplicable reasons, they were abandoned. Meanwhile, a battle raged at the Bay of Pigs, more than halfway up the island on the southern coast, where a brigade of Cuban exiles had seized a beachhead. Castro's forces were moving *en masse* to counterattack in Zapata Swamp, but were bogged down by narrow roads just south of Jaguey Grande. The action at Pinar del Rio had been a feint.

Atcho listened to the news, consumed with anger. After some thought, he instructed Miguel and the others, "Follow as best you can. If we're going to arrive in time to help, we need to move quickly, which means separately." Then, grimly, he set out alone, bound for Cienfuegos, a large town several miles from where Castro's forces massed east of the Bay of Pigs.

8

Two days later, Atcho entered Cienfuegos. Nervous townspeople had heard about the battle raging to their northwest but had only spotty information about its progress. The most useful knowledge he picked up was that the landing force seemed firmly entrenched in Playa Giron, a village seventy miles away on the coast.

At dusk, Atcho set out in a "borrowed" pick-up truck and drove northeast as fast as he dared. Traffic faded as he neared the battle zone. He hoped to get close enough to continue on foot before reaching a checkpoint.

Cresting a small rise, he stopped. Far out on the horizon, tracers streaked the sky. Muffled explosions broke the incessant drone of insects in the surrounding swamps. At an intersection, a squad of soldiers watched the tracers from a barricade. Preoccupied with the sights and sounds of distant battle, the guards did not see Atcho, and he was far enough away that they did not hear him.

Cautiously, he backed the truck down the rise, and hid it in thick foliage. Then he began a stealthy approach to the intersection.

Dusk settled. He lay still, allowing his eyes to grow accustomed to encroaching darkness, and his other senses to acclimate to the screech and stench of surrounding wetlands. Slowly, he crept to the crest of the hill, where he observed the soldiers clustered at the barrier in the middle of the road, oblivious to him.

Someone should be shot for negligence. Thankful that there was no moon and realizing that the invasion had been timed with that in mind, he stole through darkness. Sometimes in a low crouch, sometimes sliding flat on his stomach, he moved in the shadows behind the shrubbery, drawing ever closer. His heart pounded.

The sound of a revving engine halted him. Fifty feet away, the main gun of a tank protruded from a hollow place near the intersection.

Circling wide, Atcho approached it from the rear. Step by careful step, he crept up behind a lone guard standing by the tank.

The guard shifted his feet. Atcho froze. A sound came from the front hatch. The driver was preparing to exit. If he cut the engine, he would eliminate the noise that was Atcho's only protection.

Atcho sprang. Cupping his hand over the guard's mouth, he pulled the man down and yanked his head around until he heard the neck crack.

The engine fell silent.

Atcho ducked behind the tank, mounted it, and crept forward, using the turret for cover. Keeping an eye on the other soldiers, he watched the driver's hatch. It opened, and an arm appeared in the soft light of the tank's interior. Atcho waited until the arm rested on the hull, then slammed his foot down on the heavy steel hatch. An anguished cry and a metallic clang broke the night.

Startled soldiers wheeled, then scattered, some in the direction of the tank, others seeking cover by the side of the road. They were too late.

Atcho whirled and jumped to the cupola, hoping the machine gun was loaded. It was, and he opened fire.

One soldier ran directly at the tank. A burst of bullets caught him in the chest mid-leap. He fell to the ground.

Atcho swung the machine gun in a horizontal arc, firing in short bursts. Two soldiers who had made it to the road fell on their faces, propelled by the force of hot lead. Two more ran for cover in the swamps. They felt stinging impacts, and then watched their own blood oozing into the dank earth.

In moments, all was still. Cautiously, Atcho opened the commander's cupola, and found it empty. Then he checked the driver's compartment. The unfortunate man was alive, but barely conscious and bleeding badly. Atcho dragged him out and propped him by the side of the road where he might be found and rescued.

Returning to the tank, he crawled inside. It was an American-made M41 Sherman. He had driven earlier models during his yearling summer training at Ft. Knox at the end of his first year at West Point, but that had been a World War II M4 model. He had seen pictures of the M41, which had been developed to counter the Soviet T34-85, but Atcho had not been aware that any had been delivered to Cuba. *How did the Cuban army get one?*

Fortunately, the driving mechanisms were not that different. Taking a minute to study controls, Atcho started the engine and barreled through the barricade toward Playa Giron. The war machine groaned over a small rise, then settled into a higher than normal cruising speed as Atcho drove toward the sound of guns.

In the glow of the running lights, he saw a road leading to the right through the swamp. He cut the engine and listened. Explosions and small-arms fire sounded. He re-started the engine and forged in their direction.

He rounded a bend and entered a fierce battle from the south flank. Guns blazed on both sides of the swamp. Bullets pinged off the tank.

Atcho continued his headlong flight through the deadly gauntlet until he came upon a wide clearing. Knowing that the exile forces were to his left, he turned sharply into them. Gunfire from his front increased, concentrated on the tank.

Atcho continued his desperate drive until he was well past the line of men spread out on either side. For fear of hitting their own soldiers, they stopped firing toward him.

Taking advantage of the lull, Atcho cut the engine. He threw the hatch open, waved his hands and shouted, "Don't shoot. I'm a patriot."

Cautious men with camouflaged faces in dark battle dress surrounded him.

"Don't shoot," Atcho yelled again. "I'm a patriot. My name is Atcho. No one else is with me." From behind, he heard men climbing onto the tank. He sat very still in the driver's seat and waited. In the distance, he heard the firefight still raging.

"You're Atcho?" The voice was low, surprised. "Come."

Atcho clambered down. When he reached the ground, the man faced him. "Thanks for getting our tank back. It was captured a day ago. Is there ammunition for the main gun?"

"I didn't have time to check."

The soldier nudged Atcho's arm and led him into the swamp away from the fighting. "I am Rafael. We heard you were on your way but had no idea how or when you'd arrive." He gestured toward the tank. "You lived up to your reputation."

"How's the invasion going?"

"Not good. We're part of the main body of Brigade 2506. We received none of the air support we were promised. The US Navy sits over the horizon doing nothing, and our supply ship was sunk. This is the fourth day, and the invasion is probably over. Most of the leaders are doing their best to execute an orderly retreat." Rafael paused gloomily. "We just learned that news, and it hasn't had time to spread. Only here at the Bay of Pigs is the fighting still fierce. One Cuban-exile commander already took a contingent of soldiers to escape out to sea in small boats."

"Was the underground any help?"

"Hell no. They were disorganized. Contact was sparse, and assets deployed in the wrong places. You'd think they weren't expecting the invasion, or they didn't really support it."

"They did their best," Atcho muttered with an edge of bitterness. "Have you heard from Juan Ortiz? He's one of the resistance leaders in this area."

"I've heard of him, and he's a helluva fighter. He's the main guy who's had any success."

"I need to get in touch with him."

"We were instructed to bring you to headquarters. You can contact Juan there."

They walked far to the rear of the battle area, where a Jeep waited. Atcho shook Rafael's hand.

"I hope we meet again under happier circumstances," Rafael said.

"Any circumstances would be better."

Atcho settled in beside the driver, an old man in his sixties. "Did you come in with the landing force?" Atcho asked incredulously.

The man displayed a toothless grin. "I would do anything to liberate my country." He glanced at Atcho and grinned again. "You think because I'm old I can't fight?"

Atcho looked at him through tired eyes with a wan smile. He grasped the old man's shoulder. "I would never think such a thing."

As they drove, the sounds of battle receded. Soon they left the swamp and turned parallel to the ocean a few hundred yards away. The Jeep gained speed, heading for low buildings silhouetted against the sand. Atcho saw several military vehicles surrounding an antenna-encrusted bungalow.

When they halted by the buildings, he stepped wearily from the Jeep. Waves murmured and broke on the beach. Atcho strained to see the village of Playa Giron. All was quiet. Not even a dog barked. "Toothless" motioned Atcho to follow. They circled to the front door.

Light was dim inside the one-room building. At the far end, an operations area had been set up with maps, radios, and field desks. Several men eyed Atcho silently.

These guys aren't friendly. Tired as he was, he was glad of no need to carry on conversation.

Then he heard a click behind his head. Too late, his exhausted senses sounded an alarm.

"Welcome, Comrade," a steely voice said. "You are a prisoner of Fidel Castro and the Cuban people."

His feet rooted to the floor, Atcho felt the cold nose of a pistol just behind his right ear. "Stay still. You too, old man. Put your hands against the wall."

Atcho's stomach knotted. He complied in silence. Beside him, Toothless did the same. Two Cuban soldiers searched them, took their weapons, and ordered them to join the group Atcho had seen on entering. Those prisoners greeted Toothless and regarded Atcho with dull curiosity.

Atcho said nothing. He settled on the floor in the corner and leaned against the wall, head in his hands. *I walked right into the headquarters Castro most wanted to capture.* "Ah, Isabelita," he breathed, "will I ever see you again?"

He watched for an opportunity to escape, but the guards remained alert. *How would I find Isabel, anyway? My group is destroyed.* He leaned against a wall. *Escape first, then find Isabel. To do that, they can't know who I am.*

Toothless sat next to him. "You're Atcho, aren't you?" he whispered.

Atcho placed his arm around the old man's shoulder. "I'm sorry, but you are mistaken. I am Manuel. I know about Atcho. I saw him killed on the battlefield tonight."

Toothless sat next to Atcho throughout that first night of captivity. The old man never indicated whether he believed the ruse. He seemed to accept "Manuel," but sensed that Atcho's pain went beyond the loss of battle.

Though he did little to encourage Toothless' friendship, Atcho welcomed the caring presence of the old man. Thin and wizened, his empty mouth smiled often, despite the circumstance. *He represents Brigade 2506 and Cuba bravely.*

9

The Cuban army trucked the captives to a holding area north of the swamp. From there they transported them to Havana.

On the second day, Toothless sneaked into Atcho's group. "Manuel," he said quietly. "I have news you should hear."

Atcho returned the old man's worried scrutiny with vague interest. "There was a leader of the resistance," Toothless went on. "His name was Juan Ortiz."

Atcho became alert, but he showed no outward change of expression. "Go on."

"I heard he was killed."

The old man continued speaking, but Atcho heard him as though in a fog. A lifetime of memories with Juan passed through his mind.

Outwardly impassive, Atcho grieved. His body felt heavy and tired. He wanted only to find a dark corner and lie down. "How did he die?"

"I don't know much. I heard he was a close friend of Atcho's. When Juan was captured, they questioned him about Atcho. He wouldn't talk, so they tortured him. When he still wouldn't talk, they shot him." The old man shook his head. "The men who saw his murder say he was very brave."

Atcho held back burning tears. His throat constricted, but he refused to allow even a gasp to escape. He turned to Toothless. "Thank you."

The next day in Havana, the guards segregated Brigade 2506 members from underground resistance fighters. Atcho knew that treatment of those in the second category would be far worse.

He expected public trials. Castro had too much flair to miss an opportunity to show the world his justice. Beatings and torture would be private events, only rumored, and officially denied. Executions would be many, accomplished as official sentence and brutal retaliation.

Atcho's worry over discovery of his alias, Manuel Lezcano, dissipated. Records were poor. He told authorities he was from the province of Oriente.

He stood in a line with other prisoners to have his picture taken. Then, they stood trial, herded into a crowded courtroom with Fidel's disciples screaming for the firing squads.

Prisoners' families watched from the other side of the courtroom. Their misery, etched on their faces, turned into abject grief when, one hour after entering the courtroom, sentences had been meted out and appeals exhausted. On leaving the courtroom, Atcho faced thirty years in prison, to be incarcerated in the most notorious prison in Cuba, the Isle of Pines.

10

MAY 1961

Atcho felt like a walking cadaver when he staggered from a bus with his fellow prisoners at *El Presidio Modelo* on the Isle of Pines. A boat had brought them from the main island of Cuba early that morning. The bus had picked them up at the quay in Nueva Gerona and had taken them to the prison. Five massive towers rose into sight. Four of them were seven stories high and two hundred feet in diameter. The one at the center was only three stories high but had a much larger diameter. The mess hall.

On seeing the towers, Atcho felt a cold chill. He turned to one of his companions. "What do you think?"

The man did not respond but stared vacantly at the ominous round cellblocks. In silence, they trudged under the harsh commands of their guards to one marked *Circular 4*, which would house the newest cargo of "fresh meat." In its cavernous interior, a single watchtower rose five stories from the center, and a mass of humanity moved on the ground floor and on the tiers above.

Access was firmly secured at the base of the interior watchtower. From their perch, four armed guards observed every cell on each floor ringing the outside walls. The building was thirty-seven years old. Having housed generations of prisoners, the stench of effluent, tropical dankness, and decades without cleaning stung Atcho's nostrils. He felt the visceral press of multitudes of dirty male bodies against him.

When the outer doors closed, the guards who had escorted them stayed outside. A tall, muscular inmate wearing a blue prison uniform approached the new group. "I am Javier," he growled. "The prison warden appointed me to govern *Circular 4*." He pointed to several other men in blue prison uniforms. "Those are my assistants. They'll show you how things work here. You've each been assigned a cell and a work group. Don't give me trouble."

He waved his hand to indicate hundreds of prisoners milling about. "Your fellow inmates they think they should not wear these blue uniforms." He indicated his own. "They complained today. They think that because they are political prisoners, that makes them better than us." He leered at them and exchanged grins with his cohorts. "Don't think it," he snapped. "I'm going to divide you into groups. You start work tomorrow morning."

Moments later, Atcho stood with a group of young men roughly his own age, designated for the marble quarries. They awaited further instruction. Then, Atcho heard a commotion to his right.

An old man, skinny and bent over, walked deliberately in front of Javier. Dressed only in his underwear, he carried his blue uniform in his arms. "These towers were built for nine hundred men." he yelled angrily. "There must be twice that many in here." He threw the uniform at Javier's feet. "I will not wear these clothes of criminals." He spat onto the floor. "I'm not a common thief like you. I will not be ruled by convicts."

Javier looked startled, then his face darkened. The cavernous interior had gone quiet, with only a murmur coming from a few who had not sensed the unfolding drama. On the watchtower, the guards moved uneasily, weapons pointed toward Javier and the old man.

Atcho tensed.

Another prisoner walked in front of Javier and threw down his uniform, then a third, and a fourth. Within seconds, twenty prisoners, clad in only their tattered, grimy underwear, stood defiantly in front of Javier, looking alternately between him and the guards in the watchtower.

Atcho saw a guard speak into a telephone. Moments later, the outside door swung open. A band of guards rushed in. They grabbed the old man, beat him, and dragged him outside.

"Silence," Javier yelled above the din. More prisoners quickly drowned him out as they stripped off their uniforms and threw them down. Around the walls, yet more inmates angrily left their cells and descended the narrow concrete stairs, stripping their uniforms off as they came.

Javier's "assistants" drew close to him. On the watchtower, Atcho saw the same guard once again speak into the telephone.

Atcho stepped into shadows and worked his way to one side of Javier. Around them, men yelled and jeered. The assistants' attention remained riveted on the rebellious political prisoners. Javier tried to order calm, but no one paid attention to him.

Suddenly, Atcho delivered two sharp blows, one to Javier's stomach, the other directly into the bridge between his eyes. He heard a crack of bone.

Javier went down. The entire motion took barely a second, and Atcho stepped back into the shadows.

Javier's men grouped around and moved toward the exit, encircled by the furious crowd of political prisoners. At that moment, a shaft of sunlight broke through the doorway, and more guards rushed in. They secured Javier and his men and made a quick exit, closing and locking the heavy iron door behind them.

Inside, the noise died. All eyes turned toward the watchtower. One guard still talked on the phone. The others had spread out so that they had full rifle coverage of the interior. The guard on the telephone replaced the receiver and picked up a bullhorn. "Go back to your cells." His voice was half authoritative and half wavering. "Go back to your cells. Now."

The prisoners began dispersing, each individual headed toward his few square feet of space. Atcho nudged one of the men in his underwear. "Where do I go? I just got here." The man looked at him through sagging eyes. He did not respond, nor did he start walking. He seemed lost in a trance. Then, he faced the tower and called out.

"Listen to me." At first, no one seemed to hear him, so he called again. "Guards. Listen to me."

Movement stopped. One of the guards peered down. "You want more trouble?"

"You tell your boss that we will not be governed by criminals. We are educated men who never broke the law. We will govern ourselves, or you will have to shoot us all." He paused, and yelled again, "We won't wear the uniforms of criminals."

Around him, other prisoners looked at him in awe and fear. "You go too far," one said quietly.

"No," he responded vehemently. "They've taken everything away from us. I will either keep my dignity or die with it." He set his jaw firmly.

Around him, a small group gathered. It grew until every man in *Circular 4*, stood packed together, facing the watchtower defiantly.

The guard spoke into the phone again. A moment later, he lifted the bullhorn and called down, "The warden will meet with your representatives tonight. Go back to your cells." He lowered the bullhorn and picked up his weapon.

A few minutes later, with help from other prisoners, Atcho located his assigned cell, and lay down on the canvas stretched over a steel frame that served as his bed.

The walls were rough-hewn and coated with worn-through, grimy whitewash. The bars had also been painted white at some point in the prison's old history, but that too had been worn through to shiny steel by thousands of sweaty palms that had gripped them over decades. The cells had doors, but they were left unlocked, and inmates were free to move about.

Twice each day, the guards took a head count. Prisoners then had to be in their cells to be seen and counted.

Atcho said little to anyone that night. One of his cellmates, Domingo, had been an engineer prior to the revolution. He had also been captured at the Bay of Pigs.

"What will happen now?" Atcho asked, referring to the commotion.

Domingo was small, in his mid-thirties, and appeared to be a thoughtful man. "I don't know. You can tell by how quiet it is that people are worried. But the guards can't kill us all. Famous people are in here. If they massacre us, the world will know."

The next morning before breakfast, Atcho milled with his work group on the ground floor of the cellblock waiting to go for breakfast. Surprisingly the cadre of criminals was not present. Instead, a fellow prisoner stood at the base of the watchtower and called for quiet.

"The warden brought me and some others to his office last night," he announced. "We govern ourselves."

The crowd roared its approval. He raised a hand for quiet. "We don't celebrate. We are prisoners. But here," he tapped his head, "and here," he put his hand over his heart, "we are freemen—and they will never take that away."

The inmates raised their collective voice again, and again he raised his hand. "To celebrate is to invite retribution," he cautioned. "We will do as we always have done: conduct ourselves with dignity and look out for each other." He smiled softly. "I wish I had something better to say in closing, but," he indicated the outer iron doors opening and guards waiting for them, "have a good day."

With that, the prisoners dispersed to their work groups. Then, a man called out, "What about our clothes?"

The leader laughed. "Oh yes—our clothes. Well, today, we work in our underwear. Tonight, we will receive clothes taken from us on arrival." He laughed again. "You might not get exactly the same clothes, but you'll still look better than in your skivvies. You might have to trade to get something that fits." With that, he left.

Atcho looked across the crowd as he filed out with his work group to meet the guards waiting for them. They would shepherd them to the marble quarries. He felt a nudge on his elbow. Turning, he found the man who had rallied the prisoners the night before. "I saw what you did," the man said quietly. "I told the leaders. We'll be in touch." He started to leave, but Atcho stopped him.

"Wait. What happened to the old man who was beaten?"

The man looked tiredly at Atcho, and his eyes moistened. He said simply, "He was my friend." He shook his head and walked away.

Atcho trudged with his group. His eyes hurt in the sunlight after having been in the half-light of *Circular 4* for the last ten hours. In the center of the compound was the massive mess hall. As he entered, Atcho could not help being awed by the incredible size of the round structure. It was not as tall as the other *Circulars*, but its diameter was much larger, and with all the men from the prison moving in and out at roughly the same time, the loud din made carrying on conversation all but impossible.

"Sometimes we meet family in here," an inmate yelled to him.

"How?"

"The guards make them listen to a speech about how great Castro is and what will happen to them if they don't obey rules. They are searched, and then pushed into here to find their family members."

"I thought that they only get to visit for an hour."

The man shrugged. "True, and it takes at least half an hour to find each other."

Atcho looked down at his plate in silence. His breakfast was watery cornmeal gruel. He noticed lumps in the slop and started poking at them. He looked around. The prisoners who had been there longer picked out their lumps and tossed them on the floor. Atcho gagged as he recognized pieces of cockroaches, soap ...

"What is that?" he asked a man next to him. He pointed at a particularly gruesome-looking morsel.

The man grinned. "Horse penis," he yelled back. "The guards throw this stuff in there. Toss it out, but eat—this is all there is, and you have to take some with you for lunch. If we're lucky, it won't spoil in the hot sun before we get to eat it."

Atcho stared blankly at the man. He looked to be in his early twenties but had a gaunt look of someone who had already suffered debilitating conditions for a long time. Whether he was tall or not was difficult to tell because of a permanent stoop. Long hours in the sun had made his skin dark and leathery. Dirt laced his jet-black hair, which showed signs of gray.

Despite his sarcasm, he carried a wide, friendly smile. "I am Leon." He held out his hand.

Atcho shook it without enthusiasm.

"You just got here?"

Atcho nodded dully.

"Then were you in the fighting?"

Again, Atcho nodded.

"What happened?" Leon asked. "Why did the invasion fail?"

Atcho shook his head. "We'll probably never know."

Leon leaned over and put his mouth close to Atcho's ear. "People know who you are," he said. "Atcho, some of us saw what you did last night, to Javier." Atcho glanced up sharply. "Sorry to tell you so soon. We never know how much time we'll get to talk."

Atcho ate as much as he could stomach. Within minutes, they trooped back outside, assembled with their work groups, and began the trek to the marble quarries.

Leon stayed close to Atcho. As they started out, he said, "Don't worry, no one will give away your identity. We are honored that you are among us."

A guard bellowed, "Hey you, stop talking." He was not a large man, but his rifle was loaded and his bayonet sharp. The prisoners plodded along.

After a while, when it seemed that conversation had started between other prisoners, Atcho asked, "How is the work at the quarries?"

"I won't lie," Leon replied, furtively. "We do everything by hand with picks and sledgehammers. They make young prisoners do it because the work is hard. They try to break us." He looked back at the guard. "They think that if they can kill our spirits, the other prisoners will see, and they will be easier to manage. But always, we resist. The work strengthens resolve. When they push us harder, we slow down—we become *plantandos*, unyielding. They know if they push us too hard, we'll just stop. They can't kill us all."

Atcho recalled that Domingo had told him the same thing last night.

"But you still have to be careful," Leon added. "The guards are not trained. They can be arbitrary."

"I told you to stop talking," the guard yelled. Atcho turned. The was only a few feet away, and he lunged with his bayonet and plunged it into Leon's left buttock. Leon screamed and fell to the ground.

While the other guards circled, the attacker stood over Leon, using his weight to drive the bayonet further in. When he felt bone, he turned the blade.

Leon writhed in pain, and after a moment, the guard pulled the bayonet out, creating a sucking noise. A huge volume of blood spurted, drenching the guard and spraying those nearby, including Atcho.

Stunned, Atcho stared. The action had taken only seconds.

On the ground, Leon writhed, while blood poured into a bright pool. Other prisoners moved around, aghast.

"Get him some help," someone cried. The guards only moved to tighten their perimeter around Leon.

The attacker whirled to face the prisoners. His expression was one of fascination and glee. It mixed with consternation as he confronted the hostility evident on the prisoners' faces.

He grinned at Atcho. "Do you see what you caused?"

Atcho reeled under a wave of guilt.

"We need to stop the bleeding," a prisoner called out.

"We'll get him help," the lead guard said matter-of-factly to no one in particular. "Now get to work." He detailed a guard to stay with Leon and sent another for medical help while he and the remaining guards herded the work group to the marble quarries.

* * *

At the end of the workday, a pall hung over Atcho and his work group when they returned to *Circular 4*. Without inquiry, he knew that word had spread about the atrocity. Given the deliberately slow pace at which the guards had gone for help, Atcho knew Leon's fate—he had bled out among the weeds.

"It's not your fault," someone told him. "Sometimes they let us talk, sometimes not. It's arbitrary. They might prod with the bayonet, but," he shook his head, "that guard is crazy."

Atcho learned later that suicides were rare among the political prisoners despite torture, but that night, as he sat in his fourth-tier cell, he saw a body plunge from above and heard it hit the floor below. The prisoner had been Leon's cellmate and a close friend of the old man beaten to death the night before. Atcho reflected that he had been at *El Presidio Modelo* for less than twenty-four hours, and in that time, he had witnessed the deaths of three men.

Every day in the quarries, prisoners suffered physical torment. The jarring of Atcho's muscles and joints with every blow he delivered with a sledgehammer and pick to hard, raw marble kept him in constant, often excruciating pain. His ears rang with incessant clanging of metal on rock.

The sweltering heat turned his skin into leather and lined his face. But his muscles hardened, and as Leon had told him, the work reinforced determination. Nevertheless, Isabel and his life before the Bay of Pigs seemed distant memories.

From the time of his capture, Atcho had found no chance to escape. Then one evening a few days after his arrival in *Circular 4*, a man paid Atcho a visit in his cell. He was the prisoner who had first stood up to the guards. When he entered, Atcho's cellmates greeted him respectfully, and then left.

"My friends call me Jujo," he said, extending his hand. He was a man of normally medium build, but the ravages of prison had taken their toll. Grizzled like everyone else, he was also balding on top. Gray, feathery strands of hair fell around his neck. He had been a literature professor in Havana. They spoke for a while.

"Some of us know who you are, Atcho."

Startled, Atcho said nothing for a moment. "How do people know me? Leon said the same thing just before he was attacked."

Jujo smiled softly. "You were better known than you might have thought. A West Point graduate from Cuba is rare. You are the only one—well, and your father before you. I am so sorry for your loss."

Atcho acknowledged the sentiment.

"When you graduated," Jujo went on, "the news was on the front page of newspapers with your picture. President Batista called you a national treasure." Noting Atcho's concern, he continued, "Your exploits with that tank at the Bay of Pigs are the stuff of legend, and several people saw you take out Javier that day." He laughed. "I might only know about literature, but I can still add two and two, and I remember the photos I saw of you."

Atcho shook his head. "I need to keep my identity as much a secret as possible." He told Jujo about Captain Govorov and Isabel. "I don't want my family to know I'm alive. If everyone thinks I'm dead, I have a better chance of escaping and finding her."

Jujo listened intently, thought a moment, and then said, "You don't have to worry. We can let the story fade. If it comes up among prisoners, we'll say it was mistaken identity. Even if they don't believe us, they won't ask questions. Men died in here protecting each other, and you're not the only one whose identity needs to be hidden."

He shifted his body. "You mentioned escape. That's what I came to talk about."

"Escape? From here?"

"You brought it up."

"I thought about it in the abstract. Do you think anyone could escape from here?" Excitement stirred.

"Yes, from here. The world does not yet know the tenacity of Cubans." He chuckled. "But some day they might." He reached under his shirt and pulled out a thin metal hacksaw blade.

Atcho stared. "How did you get that?"

"Family members sent it in a package." He smiled again. "Remember, Castro pushed out the educated people. The officials doing the checking are untrained, inexperienced. We use that against them."

Atcho sat back. He felt the beginnings of hope. "So how do we do this? We're on an island, miles from the Cuban mainland."

"It won't be easy. This is the first blade we got in. But the system worked, and others are on their way. Meanwhile, we need to gather clothing, uniforms, identification cards—anything useful that we can get our hands on."

"Why would you include me? What do you need from me?"

"Good question. Everyone would like to escape, but that won't work. We're trying to get a group out, but few in here have combat skills. If I remember correctly, you went to Ranger school." Atcho nodded. "Well, your plan to hide your identity worked. The guards don't know who you are, and neither does the administration. They watch the leaders constantly. We need someone capable of planning and coordinating, training the participants, doing it without drawing attention—and then executing"

"You've done a good job so far."

Jujo nodded. "In working out the concept, yes. We need you to hammer out the details, assign responsibilities—watch for those things that will trip us up if someone with experience isn't looking out for them."

"What's your plan for getting off the island?"

"There's a yacht that ferries guards back and forth. It's different from the one that brings prisoners in. This one is used as a cargo boat, and if we can get uniforms and board as soldiers or stow away with the cargo, we might have time to get to mainland Cuba and disperse."

Atcho mulled a few moments. "Some men will die. That's a certainty," he said. "Even if we make it to the mainland, Castro will do everything he can to find us, and not everyone can evade him indefinitely. Unless we can make it to Key West in Florida, we will always be hunted."

"We know that," Jujo said grimly. He looked around Atcho's cell. "But we won't be here, in this hellhole. Every degree of freedom is worth the sacrifice. Will you do it?"

"Of course. I just hope your confidence isn't misplaced."

Jujo sighed. "Well, now that I've gotten you to say yes, you need to know the worst. If we are captured, we could be shot on the spot, or ..." He looked reluctant to go on. "Has anyone told you about the punishment facility—'the box'?"

Atcho shook his head.

"The inmates in there don't go out on work details. They are there for only one reason: to be tortured." He paused to let his words sink in. "The guards like their work and are inventive." His eyes bored into Atcho. "They leave you in for at least six months." He went on to describe the torture tactics in horrific detail.

Atcho listened, riveted. Despite what he had already witnessed, he could not imagine such depths of cruelty, particularly a Cuban doing those things to another Cuban. *Then again,* he reminded himself, *I've seen savagery I could never have imagined.* He contemplated further while Jujo studied him.

At last Atcho spoke. "My father didn't have to fight in World War II, but he went anyway. He told me that a great American said, 'Those who willingly give up freedom for security don't deserve either freedom or security.' I know what I have to do—and what my father would expect."

Over the next several weeks, Atcho met with participants in the escape plan, and organized. More hacksaw blades came in as expected, and bit by bit, other materials were gathered. From listening to guards' conversations, they learned the schedule of the cargo boat.

* * *

As days passed, Atcho quietly sought out a prisoner named Francisco who had lived in Camaguey. Atcho developed the friendship, saying that he had no living relatives but was interested in various families in the vicinity. At one point, Francisco said that he would ask his wife by mail about people in the general area.

Weeks passed with no news. When not working in the marble quarries, Atcho worked on the escape plan. After several weeks, he sought out Jujo. "I think we're as ready as we are going to be," he said. "We need to go when the moonlight is low and during a rainstorm. Regardless, we should cut the window bars most of the way through. We should do that now. We'll leave a small section of each bar to cut out on the night we escape, to make sure the bars don't fall out." Jujo agreed.

* * *

A few evenings later, Francisco sat next to Atcho in the dining hall. "My wife is coming to see me during visiting privileges this weekend," he said. "Would you like to join us? She might know some of the people you asked about."

"Of course. Thank you for asking."

Dreary days passed slowly. Labor seemed more grueling. The stench of filthy living was onerous, and food seemed even more revolting. Atcho clung to fragments of hope, heightened by working on the escape plan.

Finally, Sunday afternoon arrived, and buses brought loads of waiting relatives to the prison compound. This time, instead of the mess hall, guards herded the inmates into wide fields. They packed the prisoners by groups into large enclosures resembling chicken coops, complete with three strands of chicken wire. A few benches allowed some to sit, but they were overwhelmed by the press of inmates attempting to glimpse relatives among passing visitors. They called out loudly, until at last, family members were able to find each other.

Atcho was with Francisco when he spotted his wife.

"Yolanda. I'm here," he yelled. "Yoli. Over here."

A thin, matronly woman stopped in the mass of passing humanity and looked around. She saw Francisco and headed toward him. Her long face displayed the stress of the trip, and she seemed to have given up on her curly, graying hair. Despite the conditions, her eyes sparkled when she saw Francisco. Then they clouded over when she took in his physical condition.

"Oh my God, Francisco," she cried quietly, and tears formed in her eyes. "This is even worse than the mess hall. I can't hug you and can barely touch your hand." She pounded on the chicken wire angrily with her fists, and then looked around furtively. Then she pushed her fingertips to meet Francisco's between the strands.

With no ability to leave, Atcho watched quietly. Then Francisco introduced him.

People were scared, Yoli said in answer to some of Atcho's questions. "The American embargo is hurting us. There's nothing on the store shelves. And Castro set up neighborhood committees that turn in anyone suspected of anything. Even if they just think we are thinking something, they report us. Children denounce their parents. And in school, they have to sing the Communist 'Internationale.'"

"How are they treating families of political prisoners?"

"They call us *gusanos*," she replied vehemently. "Worms. People wanting to leave Cuba have to quit their jobs, give up their houses, and live with relatives. Then, those relatives are also persecuted." She sobbed. "Food is so scarce. Everything is rationed, and when anyone applies to leave Cuba, their rations are cut off. Their only food comes from relatives, who have to share their rations, and then," she waved her hands in indignation, "and then, the *relatives* are also called *gusanos*—even if the relatives are not trying to leave." She put her hand to her forehead. "It's crazy."

"How are you living?" Atcho asked in concern. "You and your children."

Yolanda waved a hand. "Oh, we get by," she said with poorly concealed despair. "I worry about our children. What kind of lives will they have?"

"But how do you eat? You said there is no food."

"No, but we still have good friends, and they get food to us." She wiped a tear from her eye. "What happened, Francisco? What happened? We were a prosperous country. We could make plans for our lives. How did this ... this demagogue ... this son of a whore convince the country that he would be better for us?" She wiped tears from her face. Francisco looked around, nervous about being overheard. He tried to reach further through the chicken wire to console his wife but could still only touch her fingertips.

They conversed about other things, and then Atcho said, "There was a little girl kidnapped in Camaguey a while back. Whatever became of her? Did they find her?"

"Oh, yes," the woman responded, rolling her eyes. "That was a strange story."

"What happened?"

"Her father was killed in a fire along with his parents. He lived in that great sugar plantation, you know, the one about five miles east of the town of Camaguey?" She paused. "Francisco said you were from Camaguey. Did you know them?"

"I know people there," Atcho replied. "Of course, everyone knew of the family."

"Yes. Anyway, the girl lived with her aunt Raissa. Then, last December, she disappeared. There was a rumor that her father was still alive and that the *milicianos* tried to use her as bait to capture him. But about two months later, some neighbors found her wandering on a road near her house. The story I heard was that a deranged lady wanted a little girl to take care of, and then got tired of her." Yoli shifted her weight. "About four months ago, the weekend of the invasion, she disappeared again, this time with her aunt and uncle."

"What?" Atcho could hardly restrain himself but tried to act casual. "How did she disappear again?"

"No one really knows. They stayed away for three months, then showed up again last month."

"All of them?" Atcho scarcely believed his ears. "The little girl—how was she?"

"Fine, as far as I know. I saw her two weeks ago, in line at the government store with her aunt. They didn't talk to anyone, but they looked okay." While Atcho listened intently, Yoli continued describing Isabel and his sister Raissa in detail. Then she said, "The strange part of the story is that they're gone again."

"What?" Atcho demanded, and then caught himself. "Where?"

"To the United States. They left for Havana last week and boarded an airplane to Miami. They should be in America right now." Other people listened to the story as Yoli continued. "It happened so fast. Most people have to wait months to process papers, wait for Castro to let them go, then reserve space on a plane." She shrugged her shoulders and waved a thin arm. "But they just came and went."

Atcho felt stricken. He leaned against the chicken wire. "That is a strange story. A very sad one. So many families split up. Thank you for telling it."

After a while, he thanked Francisco and Yolanda for sharing their time with him. He struggled through the mass of inmates and made his way to a far corner of the enclosure, to be as alone with his thoughts as he could. Then he sat on the ground and closed his eyes, bitterly recalling his brief intent to leave Cuba after the destruction of the mansion. *Letting Atcho die was a good thing—they let Isabel go.*

11

JULY 1961

"I think we can move tonight," Atcho told Jujo softly. Outside, the wind moaned against the rounded walls of *Circular 4*, and the steady drum of a tropical downpour sounded on the old corrugated steel roof. Streams of water dripped through in various places. The prisoners placed buckets to catch it, as much for the rare joy of sweet, fresh water as to prevent runoff into living areas.

"I was thinking the same thing," Jujo replied. They stood in his cell on the second floor. "Let's go over things one more time."

"The moon is about three-quarters tonight, but the clouds are black and low. The outside lighting is blocked by rain—which keeps the guards from their regular patrols."

As they spoke, thunder rolled, and lightning flashed, lighting up the inside of the massive tower for an instant.

"What about the boat?" Jujo asked.

"It's in the harbor now. One of the men on the orange-picking crew saw it there this afternoon when his group returned from the groves." His voice took on more urgency. "If we wait for a low moon, it'll be another three weeks, and we won't know for sure that there will be rain, or that the boat will be there."

"I was thinking the same things," Jujo said. "I'll tell the men in the escape cell to finish sawing out the bars and spread word to the others that we go tonight. I'll meet you there." He followed Atcho out the door.

They both looked furtively at the watchtower, but the cavernous interior of *Circular 4* was dark, the guards dozing in their chairs, with their arms wrapped over their chests against the unusual chill that came with the rain.

Atcho returned to his cell and changed into a military uniform he had stolen piece by piece.

Domingo watched him. "I wish I could go with you."

Atcho met his look. "I'll let you go in my place."

Domingo shook his head sadly. "No, we all have our parts to play. You are the best chance for this escape to succeed." He stared into the dark tower a moment. "You know, if you're successful, you might save us all."

Atcho looked at him without comprehending.

"Maybe you don't know," Domingo continued. "All these cellblocks were wired to blow up with us in them."

"What?"

Domingo nodded. "It's true. It happened before the invasion. Look."

More thunder and lightning cracked as he crossed to the walkway outside the cell door. He indicated for Atcho to follow and pointed at several depressions in the floor two stories below. "You see those?" Atcho nodded, and they returned to sit on their steel racks. "There was a lot of talk about the coming invasion. There was fear among the guards—and I guess all the way up to Castro, that the island would be attacked, and the prisoners set free to join the invasion.

"One day, the guards drove a truck in here. They made us all get out of the way except for a few that they forced to dig tunnels under the floor. Then they took the stuff off the trucks. The items were covered so we couldn't see what it was. Of course, we speculated, and many thought it might be dynamite. Then one day, a guard came over to mock us. 'You think it's dynamite,' he said. 'Well, you're right. We're going to blow this place up, with all of you in it.'"

Atcho's eyes were wide with disbelief. "What did you do?"

"Well, you know I'm a civil engineer." He saw Atcho nod and continued.

"We dug our own tunnels, came in from the other side, and disarmed the dynamite."

"You did what?" Atcho was dumbfounded.

Domingo laughed. "We've done lots of things in here, Atcho. We built a radio out of scrap. We assembled it and disassembled it every day. Each man involved hid a piece in his room so that if our cells were searched, they would find nothing."

Atcho shook his head, still disbelieving. "Where is the radio now?"

"It wore out, but while we had it, we listened to the stations in Miami. We knew what our countrymen were doing there, and that was a great morale booster."

"What about the tunnels? You had to dig them in front of the guards?"

"That was dangerous. We also had to find the demolitions blindly and disarm them. But we did it." His smile glowed with triumph. "Of course, if the guards had tried to explode them and found them not working, they would just have turned canons on us, and that would have set the dynamite off." He shook his head. "Unbelievable what evil people will do." They sat quietly a moment. "So, you see, when you escape and tell the world what is going on here, you help us all."

Atcho felt a new weight of responsibility. Then Domingo laughed quietly and indicated a makeshift mannequin lying on Atcho's bed. "Your evil twin is ready to do his duty." He pulled a rope, and the mannequin sat up. "He won't fool anyone up close," Domingo added, "but he should get you through the next bed check."

Atcho smiled. The head count was five hours away. The guards in the watchtower would then raise the lights in *Circular 4* to full power, and from their platform, look into every cell and count heads. In at least sixteen cells on this night, they would see the silhouettes of what appeared to be heads and torsos but were the prisoners' best efforts at making puppets to cover their absence. If the ruse worked, their escape would not be discovered until the daily work groups formed, which could be delayed or canceled due to the rain.

Domingo stood and shook hands with Atcho. They clapped their arms about each other's shoulders. "I hope to see you in Miami," Domingo said, "to share a *Cuba Libre—una Mentirita*—a Little Lie." They both laughed, and Atcho headed out the door.

He hung to the shadows, and minutes later entered a cell on the first living tier, just above the ground floor. This cell had been selected because it was farthest from the lights, had the deepest shadows, and was closest to the direction of travel—the escapees would not have to maneuver *around Circular 4*. When Atcho arrived, other men were already assembled, huddled in the shadows against the back wall.

"Are we all set?" he whispered.

Jujo appeared in front of Atcho. "We're ready. It's your show."

Atcho inhaled. "Take the bars out of the window." Two men stepped through the darkness, reached up, and with painstaking care not to make a sound, pulled the four bars from their places. They came away easily.

"I'll go first," Atcho said. "If I think conditions are right, I'll pull on this rope." He indicated a long line of clothes and sheets that had been tied together. It now hung from the window. "I won't call out because you won't be able to hear me anyway in this storm, so be sure someone is paying attention."

He paused. "Stay close together. In this light, we'll need to have no more than an arm's distance between us. As dawn approaches, spread out. By the time that happens, we should be most of the way to Nueva Gerona."

He gave his final instruction. "We've been over this, and we've been lucky up to now. If we're discovered anywhere along the way, scatter. The code word for that is 'Havana.' When you hear that, execute your individual escape plans. That's how we'll protect each other. They might catch some of us, but they might not catch all of us."

When final questions had been asked and answered, Atcho went to the window. Outside, the rain beat a steady rhythm. He pushed his head through, and immediately felt the cold deluge. Twisting his body, he put his feet out, held on to the sill, and shinnied down the makeshift rope.

The ground was about a foot below the end of the rope, and when Atcho felt safe, he dropped the remaining few inches. The wind buffeted him as he settled a moment to acclimate. Then, convinced that no immediate danger lurked, he headed in the direction of the closest guard shack. It was sealed and quiet—not even a sliver of light appeared at the base of the door. He imagined that the guards were happy for the rare opportunity to sleep undisturbed through a whole night. He waited a few more minutes, and then, convinced that no patrols were out in the torrential rain, he moved swiftly back to the window with the rope. He gave it a tug.

Moments later, he felt more than saw someone descend, and heard him drop to the ground. He grabbed the man's shoulder and positioned him a few feet away against the wall. "You are Number One," he said. The man grunted understanding, and Atcho went back to the rope and pulled it. Another man dropped to the ground. Atcho positioned him on the other side of the first. "You are Number Two," he told the man.

Fifteen times, Atcho repeated the action until all the men were on the ground. Then he did a physical check to make sure he had the proper count. As a final precaution, he moved in front of Number One and whispered in the man's ear, "Head count." The man turned to Number Two and repeated the instruction, "Head count." Atcho waited. Very soon, Number One touched him on the shoulder, indicating that the count was complete, and all men were accounted for. He turned to Number One again and touched him on his arm.

"Moving," Atcho whispered. He waited only enough time for Number One to relay back, and then started off in the same direction he had previously gone.

Meanwhile, the wind increased its velocity, and the rain poured in sheets. Atcho glanced anxiously at the sky, hoping that the weather continued its wrath. Behind him, he heard the squish of feet in the mud, and smelled the rank odor of wet ground oozing up its hidden waste.

They had soon passed the guard shack, and as before, it was quiet and dark. They proceeded on toward the center of the compound.

Their exit point had to be the main gate. That meant crossing the breadth of the prison grounds. Once again, they counted on darkness to mask their approach and on the rain to drive the guards into more comfortable shelter. They moved slowly, checking their head count periodically, and stopping to listen.

Atcho kept his eye on the sky. Dawn was still hours away, but behind the clouds a three-quarter moon poised, prepared to radiate light on the sparkling wet ground. The rain still fell in wind-driven sheets, soaking every man to his core.

Then Atcho saw something that stopped him cold. A glimmer of light shone between the clouds, enough for Atcho to see that they flew across the sky rapidly. Just the fact that he had seen moonlight meant the clouds were thinning—the rain cover might end.

He sent word back to step up the pace and altered his course to head more directly toward a key intersection in the middle of the compound, guided by the darker hulks of the circular prison towers. As they progressed, he felt the rain abate. Minutes later, it ceased altogether

Atcho looked at the sky again. Moonlight was visible behind a translucent sky. He looked around. More objects came into view.

As they had trained to do, the escapees increased the distance between them so that the man ahead was still visible, but they were not so closely grouped. With greater visibility, they traveled faster, still conscious of maintaining noise discipline.

Then the moon broke through the clouds, resplendent in its ghostly beauty, deadly in its exposure of desperate men in their flight.

Again, Atcho altered course, heading toward shadows, and still needing to cross the now-dreaded intersection. They came to some low administrative buildings and moved to the dark side, away from the moon. Atcho hoped that the natural inclination of soldiers to like sleep more than patrol would keep the guards in their barracks a while longer.

Several minutes later, they came to the front of the buildings. The wind had diminished, and the rain had stopped altogether. Atcho peered around a corner, and then pulled back in dismay. The moon swathed the streets running to the intersection with illumination. Between their current position and the buildings on the other side, there were no shadows, no cover, and no concealment.

Atcho turned to Number One. "Do as we rehearsed," he whispered. "Stay low, but get straight across that road, fast. If you get caught, yell something out, make noise. If we don't hear you, we'll assume you made it over all right, and then I'll come. Go."

Number One moved swiftly to the narrowest point between shadows, and then ran across the street in a low crouch. As soon as he had disappeared, Atcho turned to Number Two. "You'll be the last one over," he said. "You stay here. Send each man over when you see the previous one disappears into the shadows. After the last one gets across safely, then you come." Number Two whispered his assent.

Atcho turned back to the road. He followed the same route that Number One had, and moments later dashed across. When he reached the safety of the shadows, he encountered Number One. "As the others come over," Atcho told him, "you position them. I'll stay here and look out for anything that might come down the road."

While he spoke, the next escapee ran into the shadows. Number One took him to his position. Seconds later, the next one came over, and then another one. Atcho watched in wonder. All of their training had been indoors, mainly by brief-back, and within sight of the guards on the watchtower.

On a few occasions they had concocted games on the floor of the cell-block for physical practice, but those events had necessarily been few. Atcho marveled that these were farmers, doctors, teachers, engineers—none of them had been professional soldiers. He reflected briefly on the lengths that the human spirit would go to be free. He recalled Jujo's warning about their probable fates if caught.

The last man crossed the road into the safety of the shadows. Atcho took up the lead again. At one point, they thought they heard scuffling feet and froze in place, barely breathing. They were next to a long building that could have been an office or barracks. Several doors stood at regular intervals. The escapees watched warily as they passed.

They were about halfway along the length of one building when one of the doors flew open. A soldier staggered out, still half-asleep, from a dimly lit interior. He stumbled into Number Nine, grunted in surprise, and stood back to take a closer look.

Another soldier walked through the door. On the way out, he flipped a switch, bathing the area in light and exposing every man in the group. Both guards froze as realization spread across their faces.

The escapees flew into motion. Number Nine shoved the guard to the ground and took off running after the others already sprinting down the trail. At the front, Atcho yelled, "Havana. Spread out."

A siren blared, and full lights went on all around the prison compound. "Havana," Atcho yelled again. "Havana. Pass it back." Immediately, the men split off from each other, yelling, "Havana. Havana." Just as quickly, they fell silent again.

Atcho ran as hard as he could, staying in the shadows when he could find them. The moonlight glistened on his wet clothing, and the mud impeded his progress. He turned randomly to his left and then to his right, and saw his fellow escapees running as hard as he was in divergent directions.

He thought he heard screams behind him but pressed on. Ahead in the distance, he saw more lights flick on at the front gate, and then a line of soldiers formed, facing his direction.

They started toward him. At an angle to his right, he saw more buildings with soft shadows and ran for them, unbuttoning his shirt as he ran. Reaching them, he tore off his shirt, then his trousers. He now wore only his underwear and everyday work shoes.

Pausing next to one of the buildings, Atcho wadded up the uniform and stuffed it in a space under the floorboards. Then he continued his flight toward the front of the buildings.

There, he saw the headquarters and main gate clearly. A line of soldiers advanced toward the fleeing prisoners. One of the guards called out and pointed at several men running far to Atcho's left.

Taking a deep breath, Atcho dashed into the light, making himself deliberately visible, running in the opposite direction. He heard a soldier yell and shots fired. Around him, hot lead whizzed by.

Atcho ran until there was nowhere to go—no shadows and no buildings to hide behind. He threw his arms over his head and slowed to a walk. Keeping his hands high and panting deeply, he turned and faced his captors. Visions of "the box" floated in his mind as, very quickly, the line of soldiers formed a circle around him.

12

EIGHT MONTHS LATER, MARCH 1962

The full length of Atcho's legs ached when he arrived back at *Circular 4*. Just standing to full height had been excruciating.

The unforgiving guards had given no quarter. They had pulled him from his "box" that evening, taunting and jabbing him as he lay writhing on the floor. His fouled clothes stank with his own sweat, caked-on feces, and still-damp urine. The sores on his legs were open, full of pus, and they burned painfully.

Two guards yanked him upright, casting one of his arms over each of their shoulders. Despite his emaciated form, they struggled under his dead weight. He was incapable of supporting himself, and they seemed angry at that as they dragged him from the punishment facility back to *Circular 4*.

They opened the door, jostled him inside, and dumped him on the cold dirt floor. He lay there, unable to move even an inch.

Fellow prisoners gathered around. Gently, they picked him up and carried him to a first-tier cell away from the sun. Someone brought him water, while another cut away his clothes. Barely conscious, he sensed more than felt gentle care as they cleaned him and massaged soothing salve into his wounds.

He slept fitfully, nightmares of his most recent ordeal joining the pain that invaded his consciousness—but he slept, which felt like a new experience.

He was not sure how long he had been back in *Circular 4*. He remembered periods of light and darkness, and extended time alone, and then men moving about.

"Manuel, it's me. Domingo." Atcho looked around, realizing that he was awake. He tried to speak but heard only croaking coming from his own mouth.

Domingo put his arm around Atcho's neck, raised him slightly, and poured water down his throat.

Atcho fell back into sleep again. When he awoke, Domingo was there. The room was lighter than it had been before, and the pain in Atcho's legs had subsided. When he tried to move them, they felt stiff and resurrected the pain. His upper body, though emaciated, had had more freedom of movement in the box, and had not incurred the same ravages.

"How long have I been here?" His voice was raspy, barely above a whisper.

"Three days. The guards will let you recover for two more days. Then you'll be back in the marble quarries."

Atcho sank back. "I wouldn't expect less." He coughed. "How long was I in there?"

"The punishment facility?" Domingo exhaled. "Eight months."

Atcho became aware of his long hair and beard, leaving only his eyes and nose exposed. "Eight months," he breathed. "Eight months. How does anyone survive that for eight months?" He grabbed his beard angrily. "Can I please get this off?"

"We would have done it before, but you needed sleep."

Atcho thanked Domingo. "Did anyone escape?"

"Yes. We think three made it."

"Only three?" he said, despair in his tone.

"Three," Domingo said firmly, "but if you hadn't taken off running the way you did, the number would have been zero—or maybe just one—you."

Atcho started to object. "Everyone knows you were the one most likely to make it out," Domingo went on. "You sacrificed yourself to give the others a better chance. No one will forget."

Atcho protested. Domingo shrugged. "Have it your way," he said. "You succeeded. We needed one man to get free to tell our story. You accomplished that."

They were silent a moment. Finally, Atcho asked, "Who were the three?"

"We think there were three. Sixteen went out, including you. Thirteen went into the punishment facility. One made it all the way to Miami. He got word to us from a family member. We never heard from the other two."

Atcho was startled. "One made it to Miami?" he said. "How?"

"You might remember him—Bernardo Martin. He was meticulous about getting his escape clothes together. He stole a full military uniform, including service cap and identification papers, and got away when you created your diversion. Then he walked through the gate like he was going home after his shift, made it to the boat and got off in mainland Cuba. From there, he went north and hid out with friends. He was a mechanical engineer. They had an old pickup truck, so he reworked the drive shaft to make it come out the back at an angle and fitted it with a propeller. Then they tied a bunch of inner tubes around the truck like a raft and drove it to Key West."

Dumbfounded, at first Atcho could only stare. Then he felt a surge of excitement. "Are you kidding?" He struggled onto his elbows. "He did that?" He laughed involuntarily, lay back, and looked up at the dark ceiling. "He should have planned the escape."

"You made good decisions. Without you, no one would have had a chance."

Atcho disregarded the remark. "What about the other two?"

"We don't know. We never heard. They might have been killed, they might have escaped and not reported back—we just don't know."

Atcho was quiet a moment. "What about the ones in the punishment facility? Am I the last one out?" Domingo nodded, but was silent and looked away.

Reading his demeanor, Atcho asked sharply, "Where are the others?"

"Nine came out two months ago," Domingo said. "Three..." His voice trailed off.

Dread seized Atcho. He struggled to a sitting position as realization dawned. "What happened to the others?" He paused, his expression becoming urgent. "Jujo?" he said hoarsely. "What about Jujo?"

Domingo just shook his head and lowered his eyes. "I'm sorry. He didn't make it."

Atcho lay back again, anguished. For a long time, he just staring at the ceiling. Then, as if a switch flipped in his brain, he asked, "Where did you get the medicine?"

"What?"

"The medicine. You treated my legs. Where did you get the medicine?"

Domingo shrugged. "From the clinic. They know we have doctors in here. They let us treat our own when it suits them. It saves them the trouble." They sat in silence a while longer. "Atcho, I have other news. I don't know if it's good or bad. It's just news."

Atcho stiffened against what he might hear next. "What is it?"

"They're bringing the prisoners of Brigade 2506 here."

"What?"

"We heard it through a visiting family member. They still get radio from Miami, and it was announced over there. The Brigade 2506 made fools of Castro."

"How?"

"He tried to divide them, but they stayed united and when they were at trial, they staged public demonstrations, right there with all of Castro's goons around. Fidel thought he was going to show something to the world through those trials, and all he showed was his own ego and foolishness, and the magnificence of our men." He paused. "You know they felt betrayed by the US and President Kennedy."

"We all did," Atcho muttered with a toss of his head.

"They made a pact among themselves to never say anything bad about the US or Kennedy, and they never did."

Atcho thought about what Jujo had said. "Cuban solidarity. We could use more of it." The hint of a smile crossed his lips. "We haven't won our country back yet, but at least they know they haven't beaten us." He sat quietly. "Why are they coming here?"

"Castro has to put them somewhere, and they've become an embarrassment to him in Havana. This is the most secure place. The first ones arrived already. They keep them separate from us. At some point, they'll probably return to the US."

Domingo searched Atcho's face for a reaction, but Atcho looked like he was trying to process with an exhausted mind. "Brigade 2506 already captured world attention," Domingo said. "When they are here, there is no way the atrocities committed in this prison can be kept a secret. That's a good thing. You helped bring it about."

13

FIVE YEARS LATER, APRIL 1966

"How long have we been on the Isle of Pines?" Atcho asked.

"Nearly five years," Domingo replied.

"Five years," Atcho breathed. "Do you believe Castro is really going to close this place?" He looked around as their group of prisoners trudged past the massive mess hall, then between the immense round cellblocks toward the front gate.

"Sometimes world pressure works," Domingo said. "Castro couldn't keep up his façade of a benevolent revolution while this place existed." He nudged Atcho. "You set Bernardo Martin free, he did his job in Miami, and Brigade 2506 brought attention here."

"Brigade 2506," Atcho said. "I tried to see them the whole year they were here, but never got the chance. I kept looking through the windows to see if I recognized anyone. I thought I saw an old man I called Toothless, and a major I met in the swamps on the last night of fighting. I couldn't be sure if they were the ones I saw."

"They went home to Miami—we're going to prisons in our home provinces."

"For me, that means *Presidio Boniato* in Oriente Province," Atcho said quietly.

Domingo swung around to face him. "Isn't it time to let them know your true identity? Boniato is every bit as bad as this place, but no one in the outside world knows about it yet." He spoke with exasperation. "Your daughter is in the US and that Russian officer is long gone. From what I can tell, no one is looking for you anymore."

"I made my own bed," Atcho said sadly. "If I tell them now, they'll think I'm trying to avoid Boniato; or they could retaliate because I evaded them all these years. His voice became even more subdued, "People died protecting my identity, including my closest friend, Juan."

They both fell silent and walked on.

They had reached the main gate and were herded onto buses that would take them the few miles to the boat. No one spoke as they made the trip. On either side of the road, tall sentry pines watched their departure. Soon the bus rolled into Nueva Gerona, the small town on the river harbor providing the only access to the open sea.

The bus headed toward the docks, turned onto a quay, and halted beside a transport boat. Evening settled as they cast off from port, turned downriver, and headed out to sea.

Atcho watched the waters darken as evening fell. The atmosphere became eerily jovial as men settled for a trip that would take most of the night. They talked quietly about hopes and fears.

Atcho found a quiet spot away from the others and stood leaning over the rail. Soviets guarded the prisoners on the boat and took scant notice of them except to prohibit them from sitting on benches. Those were for the guards. Prisoners had to content themselves on the floor.

As the evening turned into night, the guards engaged in their favorite pastime, drinking vodka. But soon, the vodka ran out, so they took shots of rubbing alcohol until they were sick and puking on the deck. The stench rose, vile and thick, and the prisoners scrunched together to try to keep out of it.

Atcho continued to look out to sea, and watched the moon rise, a cold, white orb, gleaming in its majesty, uncaring in its distance. He gazed at it in sad fascination, remembering the occasion long ago when the same full moon had witnessed the theft of his little girl. She was five years older now, a stranger to her father.

"You're always there," Atcho murmured to the gleaming disk. "It seems you are the only benign constant in my life." His mind drifted. "Are you seeing my Isabelita now? How is she? What is she doing this minute?" He lowered his head, knowing the absurdity of his ruminations.

Waves crashing against the bow jolted Atcho back to the present. The moon had drifted across the sky but continued to rule the night. Atcho reflected a while longer. He wanted to sit down next to Domingo, but the fresh sea air kept the smell of bile away. He slid down by the rail. Most of the prisoners were asleep. Soon, in spite of himself, Atcho slept too.

14

FOURTEEN YEARS LATER, APRIL 13, 1980

As the massive prison gate closed behind him, the harsh clang of steel on steel of *Presidio Boniato*'s gates reverberated in Atcho's ears. He took a few tentative steps toward freedom, then turned and looked back at the stark surroundings that had been his abode these past fourteen years.

Fourteen years at Boniato. Five years at the Isle of Pines. Nineteen years taken out of my life—for what?

Encircled by a high, chain-link fence, the dull yellow Boniato Prison was comprised of five massively long two-story rectangular buildings. Low administrative offices and barracks connected them. Razor-sharp barbed wire topped the fence that stretched away in both directions. It only hinted at the brutality within its perimeter.

Atcho shook his head to clear it. He could not believe that he was truly departing the place where he had been incarcerated for so long.

When he had awakened that morning, nothing indicated that anything new or different was in store for him. With other prisoners, he had been called out and shoved at bayonet point into a separate group. The guards herded them into a "shower house," concrete walls with protruding bare pipes, bringing cold water for bathing.

The guards yelled at them to wash and dress in clothing heaped in a corner and cleaner than their own. The clothes had probably belonged to other prisoners. Atcho wondered if they were still alive.

Once showered and dressed, the guards directed them to a separate eating facility where they gulped another, more wholesome breakfast.

The prisoners' eyes glinted with veiled hope. This procedure signaled that they might be returned to their homes for release. Their hopes remained in check by the dread of ending this beguiling dream.

When they finished eating, they trooped outside to sit in the shadow of the iron front gate until well past noon. Then, with guards prodding them, they herded onto a bus that would carry them to the train station.

Still dubious, Atcho boarded with the others, remembering that the last time he had ridden a bus he had been transferred here from the Isle of Pines. He followed the man in front of him to a seat midway to the rear.

"What do you think is happening?" he whispered.

"I don't know," the man responded. "I just hope this goes the way it looks." They exchanged wary glances.

A sullen army captain Atcho had never seen before climbed onto the bus. Glancing at an official-looking document in his hand, he spoke, his voice laced with sarcasm. "It is my duty to inform you that our great leader, Fidel Castro, in the goodness of his forgiving heart, has decided to terminate the sentences of many Cuban enemies and allow free passage to any country willing to receive them."

The prisoners listened in expressionless silence. Atcho heard in disbelief.

"You are the first," the captain continued. "You will be taken to Havana and processed through the Swiss Embassy for travel to the United States. I advise you to watch your conduct."

Atcho's mind raced as the captain droned on, reciting all the bad things that would happen to them, not the least of which would be a return to Boniato, should they offend the government. "President Carter demonstrated an understanding spirit, and willingly accepted US guilt for the difficulties between our two countries. As a result, and in the spirit of compromise, Fidel agreed to free those prisoners who have been the sworn enemies of Cuba. Are there any questions?"

No one spoke. The captain turned to leave. Atcho slowly raised his hand. "*Capitan*," he called. "I have a question." His fellow prisoners glared at him stone-faced.

The officer looked up, surprised. "What is it?" Clearly, release of prisoners was not his idea, nor did it meet with his approval.

Atcho picked his words carefully. "I understood that people sent to the United States must be claimed by family members living there."

"That requirement was waived for this program. But, to demonstrate our goodwill, we selected first those prisoners who were claimed by relatives in America. Anything else?"

"No. Thank you." Atcho hoped the catch in his voice was not obvious.

The captain started to leave again, then looked thoughtful. Turning, he faced Atcho. "Are you supposed to be here?" he asked roughly. "What is your number?"

With a sinking heart, Atcho stared at the officer.

"Well?" the captain demanded.

Atcho cursed himself for stupidity and glared defiantly. "I am number 32558." His words sounded hollow—his family had never been aware of his incarceration. He had never tried to communicate with Raissa.

The captain rummaged through papers, found a list and scanned it. "Well, Manuel Lezcano. Depending on your point of view, you might be lucky, or unlucky. Personally, I love my country. I have no desire to leave."

Resigned to his fate, Atcho sank in his seat. The captain enjoyed his game. Since Atcho already knew the truth, he had no need to play.

Sensing his mood, the captain laughed. "From your point of view, I would consider myself lucky," he said derisively. "Your daughter, Isabel, wants to see her father again. She claimed you three times. She lives in Newburgh, New York. Your sister, Raissa, too."

Atcho felt blood drain from his face. The world seemed to rotate in a slow spin. He sat in stunned silence while the captain, after instructing subordinates to escort the prisoners to the train, exited the vehicle.

The bus lurched into reluctant motion, then wound along the narrow asphalt road that led through the lush bowl situated in low surrounding hills. On the horizon, Atcho saw the Sierra Maestra, the rugged mountain range in this southernmost province of Oriente. There, he knew, was where Castro mounted his insurgency against Batista.

Soon they were at the train station, where they loaded into boxcars for the long trip to Havana. Sitting in the dark interior, illuminated only by light piercing through cracks and slits in the walls, the men had nothing to do but converse and sleep. Knowing that for the first time in years, what waited at the end of this journey might be better than their current circumstances, the inmates relaxed. After a few hours, only their own snoring disturbed their sleep.

* * *

Sounds of a city and the sense of the train slowing awakened the prisoners. Whistles blew, traffic rolled, and the oppressive smell of exhaust fumes roused all the men from their slumber. Soon, the train halted, guards jerked the doors open, and they clambered down a rough wooden ramp. More buses awaited them. Minutes later, they rolled through the streets of Havana.

As the bus drove along the wide, once-stately thoroughfares, its passengers could only stare in silent wonder at the sights. To those who had visited before, changes in the city were stark. Old decrepit cars crept on the streets, which were dirty and in desperate need of repair. Long lines of people stood outside grocery stores, a phenomenon that had just begun when Atcho was first incarcerated.

The men said nothing. They continued to observe the "successes" of the revolution.

Soon, they pulled in front of the Swiss Embassy. The imposing white colonial structure stood in good repair, surrounded by a wrought-iron fence. Large red flags, each centered with a white cross, stood on either side of the enormous gate.

A Cuban army officer boarded the bus. "From this moment, you are on your own," he said simply. "Behave yourselves."

Hardly believing the reality, the ex-prisoners filed off the bus and shuffled into the classical building. They did not look around, lest they be snatched back to the hell they had just escaped.

A Swiss guard met them at the main door and led them through a large foyer into a long hall lined with paintings. They reveled in unaccustomed air-conditioning providing relief from the oppressive heat and the stench of the street outside. Their footsteps, muffled by thick carpet, sounded strange to them.

Halfway down the corridor on the left, a door with an emblem caught their eyes. It depicted an eagle, wings spread wide, holding a quiver of arrows in one talon and an olive branch in the other. A sign under the emblem read: "United States' Interests Section."

Mixed expressions of joy and disbelief glowed on the men's faces as they entered a conference room lined with deep leather chairs surrounding a long oval table. A young woman with a friendly smile ushered them in.

"I am is Sofia Stahl. I'm here to make you comfortable and help any way I can."

Atcho took immediate note of Sofia. She was beautiful even in a business suit, and her shoulder-length dark hair was thick and lustrous. Friendliness danced from her green eyes, and her soft lips were quick to smile.

She left and returned shortly with a serving cart of refreshments the like of which was a distant memory: coffee, assorted soft drinks, and a variety of meats and pastries. Excited voices rose, punctuated with full-throated, happy laughter. Men slapped each other's backs and embraced.

Beginning to relax, Atcho enjoyed the merriment but kept himself apart.

A man in a dark business suit entered the room. His demeanor was pleasant, but he spoke with authority as he introduced himself. "My name is Robert Tilden, Director of the American Interests Section. We're glad you're here, and we'll do everything we can to speed your departure for Miami."

He explained that in this office, his staff would process applications for entry into the United States. "That will take a little time. Meanwhile, relax. We'll help you make phone contact with your families in the US." He left the room amid unbridled cheers. Sofia returned and began escorting men to various locations to place their phone calls.

Atcho paced. A mirror hung at the far end of the room. Curious to see what the years had done, he went to see.

The face staring back startled him. It was the same tanned visage of nineteen years ago, altered by age and elements. His fine, smooth skin had become rough, lending him a craggy countenance. Lines only hinted at around his eyes when he had last seen them were longer and deeper. Gray streaked his hair at the temples.

His eyes traveled over his physique. He was lean, underweight, but his muscles were hard. Broad shoulders were still evident below his loose clothes.

He pulled himself erect. *What do you think my West Point buddies would think of this military bearing?* he wondered in amusement. Then with resignation, he looked at his hands. They were as coarse as any peasant's he had ever seen.

Sofia approached him. "Is there anyone you'd like to call in Miami?"

Atcho shook his head.

"Is there anyone anywhere you'd like to contact?"

Again, Atcho shook his head. This time he turned away, walked to the other side of the room, and sat in a chair. Aware that Sofia watched him, he lowered his head.

Minutes passed. He reminded himself that his life had improved immensely since this morning. Feeling a tug on his sleeve, he looked up.

Sofia sat next to him. "Are you sure no one would like to hear from you?"

Atcho searched the woman's face. A lump formed in his throat. His lips quivered. At last, he whispered in English, "I have a daughter."

"Let's find her." Sofia tugged Atcho to his feet and led him into the hall. "Where is she?"

Composing himself, Atcho was able to rasp out only, "New York." *I wouldn't have known that if that captain hadn't read it from the list.*

"Anyone else?"

"My sister, Raissa," he muttered, "but I don't know how to contact her."

"New York it is." Sofia pulled him into another office. "Where in New York?"

"Newburgh." Atcho's heart pounded. "I don't have any other information."

"Let me worry about that."

They approached a desk that had only a beige telephone on it. To Atcho, the instrument loomed larger than life.

"What's her name?"

"Isabel." He stopped, dumbfounded. "I don't know what last name she used."

"There can't be many Isabels in Newburgh, New York." She searched a directory, then dialed a number and spoke into the phone. After a few moments, she turned to Atcho. "There's a girl's college in Newburgh. Mt. Saint Mary's. Do you know if she's attending school?" Atcho shook his head.

"Let's try it."

While Atcho paced the floor, she dialed another number.

"This should be it," she called out, excited. "There's an Isabel at Mt. Saint Mary's, and she was born in Camaguey, Cuba. Was your daughter born there?"

Atcho nodded numbly.

"I have her dorm number. Her phone's ringing now."

Atcho caught his breath. His heart beat furiously.

"May I speak to Isabel?" Sofia called into the phone. She glanced at Atcho, and then turned back to the receiver. "Not there?"

Atcho's heart skipped a beat.

"Half an hour?"

Relief.

"Please tell her to expect a long-distance call at that time. Thank you."

Sofia turned to Atcho, her green eyes sparkling. "There, you see. In one half hour, you're going to speak with your daughter."

Atcho shook with emotion. Embarrassed to be seen like this, he turned away.

Sofia touched his shoulder. "Stay here to reserve this phone. I'll help some of the other men and be back to place that call."

Atcho nodded gratefully. When he heard the door close, he sat in the chair at the desk and lowered his head into his arms. The room was quiet, the lighting soft.

His nerves, drawn tight only moments before, were numb. His apprehension at talking to Isabel surprised him. He had not expected to speak with her this soon. He thought of leaving the room without making the call but found that the urge to talk to Isabel was irresistible.

A short time later, Sofia came back. Atcho struggled for composure. A clock on the wall indicated that thirty minutes had passed. Sofia appeared unaware of Atcho's discomfiture. "Let's make that call."

Atcho closed his eyes and held his breath while Sofia talked on the phone. "Hello, may I speak to Isabel?" Atcho's hands tightened on the back of the chair. "Is this she? Please hold." She held the receiver out to Atcho. He took it.

Sofia crossed to the door and paused, watching him. He sat down and spoke hoarsely into the phone. "Hello."

"Who is this?" The female voice was rich and musical.

"Is this Isabel?" Taking a deep breath, his mind swimming, he continued. "Isabel, this is your father, Eduardo. I've been released from prison." Suddenly, he was full of things he wanted to say. "They tell me you claimed me three times."

"Who are you?" The voice was low and racked with pain.

"This is your father. Eduardo."

"Is this a joke?" Isabel's voice was flat, almost menacing. "It's not funny."

"No, believe me, Isabel. Listen to me..."

"You listen to me, whoever you are. My aunt Raissa was killed in a car accident two years ago, and my father died in Cuba nearly twenty years ago. This prank is cruel, and I never want to hear from you again."

She paused, as if about to hang up, and then added, "I never claimed anyone. There was no one for me to claim."

Atcho heard a click. The line went dead.

15

Stunned, Atcho stared at the phone. He sat in his chair, limp, unmoving. A whining sound from the receiver caused him to replace it slowly in the cradle. Behind him, the door closed quietly.

Sofia crossed the floor and gently touched his shoulder. "What happened?"

Atcho did not respond. A lump formed in his throat and constricted his breathing.

"Are you all right?"

Atcho nodded, grateful for her presence. He wanted to speak but turned away when his lips trembled, and moisture formed around his eyes. Finally, he murmured, "She thinks I'm dead. She thought someone was playing a joke on her."

Sofia knelt beside him. "I am so sorry. Is there anything I can do?"

Atcho shook his head sadly. "Thanks for trying."

They were silent for several minutes. Sofia stood up. "Stay here as long as you like. I'll keep everyone else out. If you need anything, come and get me." Atcho nodded and Sofia left the room.

Placing his arms on the desk, Atcho rested his head on them. Pain and disappointment were such a part of his adult life that they no longer generated the ferocity of his youth. He felt abandoned, uncared for, forgotten.

New concerns formed, and he thought through the events that had occurred as the bus had prepared to leave Boniato. Atcho had never before seen the captain, and when asked, he gave only his prisoner serial number. Nevertheless, the officer had connected the number to the correct name on a list. He had read Isabel's name from the same document, associated with Manuel Lezcano. *How? Who knew I was alive? Raissa?* A new round of grief engulfed him as he contemplated her death.

Through his anguish, Atcho admitted that the potential for his discovery had been good. His presence was known among prisoners. Like Atcho, they had been captured during the invasion, and had received the same rough treatment.

He had masked inquiries about his own family by asking about many in the area. In all that time he had never used his real name, and never in conjunction with his code name. Over the years, some of Castro's worst enemies had been allowed to leave Cuba, usually after prolonged efforts by family members and friends in other countries. Apparently, without Atcho's knowledge, someone was doing the same for him as Manuel Lezcano.

Without more information, Atcho knew that further thought on the matter was useless. *I should leave Isabel alone. She's established a life of her own and doesn't need my interference.* He wondered how she lived, what her major was in college, and how she had afforded tuition. *Might as well be happy that at least one aspect of my life is a success.*

He knew of Mt. Saint Mary's, a Catholic college situated on the Hudson River fourteen miles upstream from West Point. He had dated girls there. Knowing that Isabel was safe and doing well was comforting.

He glanced at the clock and was surprised to see that three hours had passed since arriving at the embassy. *I'm in the Swiss Embassy, on the way to Miami.* Despite himself, he felt a slight thrill.

A stray thought entered his mind: *Mt. Saint Mary's isn't far from West Point—maybe I can get classmates to help.* The prospect of seeing old friends improved his spirits. *I'm not ready to dismiss Isabel from my life.* He stood up, strode to the door with a renewed sense of determination, and went back to the conference room.

When he entered, the room buzzed with excitement. More ex-political prisoners had arrived. Many found comrades they had thought long dead.

Someone grabbed Atcho by the elbow. "Señor Tomas," he exclaimed.

Atcho whirled. No one had called him that since his capture. A man stood in front of him, smiling enthusiastically. "You don't remember me. Many of us remember you, though." He gestured, indicating a group of men forming a circle around him. "We were at Jaguey Grande with you." He laughed. "We were in the meeting with that CIA guy you called 'Burly.'" He laughed again, and his companions joined in. "I don't think he liked that much."

Atcho was at first speechless, but then warmed to the men. "I'm happy to see you here safe and well."

"And we're glad to see you," another said. "You might remember my father, Enrique. He was the man in Jaguey Grande who said he had met John Kennedy at a meeting in Miami when he was a candidate."

Atcho looked at the man. He must have been a mere boy during the invasion—and then Atcho reflected that he had not been much more than that himself. *Nineteen years is a long time.* "I do remember Enrique. He was a class act."

"Yes, he was," the man said, "and much too old to have been in that swamp. Our family is very proud of him. I am Pedro." He extended his hand and shook Atcho's. Then he became serious. "You were right."

Atcho looked at him inquiringly.

"In the meeting that day, you were right about how things would go with the invasion. We didn't want to see it, but you called it just like it turned out."

Atcho shook his head and waved his hand in a dismissive gesture. "Maybe if I had been more thorough—"

"No," Pedro said firmly, "you were right. If you had not been there to train us, every one of us here would be dead." The others nodded their agreement.

"Well, it's past history. How is your father now?"

"He passed away. Old age. He couldn't get back to Miami and died in his home a few weeks after you met him. Maybe of heartbreak, but he was old. He really hoped for a free Cuba." The other men muttered their agreement.

A few moments later, Pedro's face brightened. "We heard about what you did with that tank. That was amazing."

Atcho shrugged it off. "Things are easy to do when the enemy is not paying attention. Anyway, they took it back. I heard that it's in the war museum here in Havana. If I'd been really good, Cuba would be free, and we would be telling these war stories over beer in the Club Tropicana."

The men laughed. One called out, "We'd be drinking real *Cuba Libres* instead of *mentiritas*."

In late afternoon, Director Tilden entered the conference room, his face bleak as he called for quiet. "Our staff is working hard to expedite processing," he said gravely.

His demeanor caused a pall to settle in the room as looks of hope left the former prisoners' faces, replaced by anxiety and a tinge of fear. Atcho felt his stomach tighten.

"There's been an incident at the Peruvian Embassy," Tilden went on. "Castro suspended all travel for political dissidents." Deathly silence descended on the room. Tilden continued, "We have fresh clothes for those who need them, and we'll issue passes supplied by the Cuban government, so you can come and go from here freely."

A slow murmur started and broke into questions and exclamations. "How long will this last?"

"Will we still get to leave?"

"Fidel is insane."

"Madre de Dios."

The director raised his palms for quiet. "Please. That's all I am at liberty to say. If you decide to go into town, exercise caution. We're here to help, but as you know, we are constrained." Regret showed in his expression as he left the room.

Heartbreak was evident on many faces. The room acquired an unearthly stillness. Some men wept bitter tears. Others cursed Castro.

Pedro appeared at Atcho's elbow. "Things will be OK," he said optimistically. "We're better off today than we were yesterday. This is temporary. Castro has already announced publicly his intent to let us leave. He won't back down from that entirely."

Atcho was less optimistic.

A new group of former prisoners entered. They wore the same looks of confusion, wonder, and hope that Atcho imagined had been on his face and those of his companions only hours before. Then he saw someone who looked familiar. He walked over quickly and grasped the man's shoulder.

"My God, Domingo." Atcho was overjoyed. "Is it really you?"

Domingo looked up into his face and was overcome by emotion. He threw his arms around Atcho and buried his face in his chest. "I thought I would never see you again," he said after a moment. "We didn't even get to say goodbye." They moved to a table laid out with food, and Domingo eyed it hungrily. "I can't believe it," he said. "Eggs. Bacon. Ham. Bread." He turned to Atcho, wide-eyed. "Are we still in Cuba?"

"Technically no, my friend. We are on Swiss soil. But the reality is that we are still in Havana."

As they ate, Atcho filled Domingo in on what the director had told them.

"I refuse to be pessimistic," Domingo exclaimed. "I left prison this morning on the other side of Havana. Even this morning when I woke up, I had almost no hope of ever being free again." He looked at his sandwich and held it up. "But here I am."

Pedro sauntered over next to Atcho, who introduced him to Domingo. "Some of us are going to walk by the Peruvian Embassy to see what's going on. Would you like to go with us?"

Atcho looked at Domingo. "Would you come, too?"

"Let me put on some of those fresh clothes," Domingo responded. Minutes later, they left through the front door.

16

Walking through the city, Atcho was again struck by the disintegration. Streets were filthy. Trash lay in heaps. Crumbling faces of once-magnificent white buildings with classical architecture were turning black. People in the streets showed listlessness and despair. Cuba's new heroes, Marx, Lenin, Ché, Camilo, and Castro himself, stared somberly from huge, weathered posters peeling from walls and billboards.

The atmosphere felt stifling, and not just because of the heat. Everyone he saw looked poorly dressed, dirty, and they moved past each other either without saying a word, or with a surliness that he had not known in the Havana of his youth. Rickety bicycles rambled past, looking like they were serving their last tortured mile.

The cars captivated Atcho. The cars! He had heard about them while in prison, but thought the stories to be improbable, if not impossible. The Havana that he remembered thrived, proud of its industry and commerce. It had been filled with glamorous and merchandise-laden glass-fronted stores, with multitudes of gleaming late-model American cars gliding by.

Now, the same stores were vacant, the glass either dirty and yellowed or boarded over. The same cars creaked by—literally, the very same cars. Some limped, spewing dirty exhaust and missing bumpers, and rusted areas where paint had scraped off. But some were clean, ran quietly, and sported bright paint jobs and gleaming chrome.

Atcho had to smile. *Nothing speaks to the Cuban spirit more than the way they keep their cars going against all odds.* Ahead on the wide avenue, the warm aroma of his favorite pastry, *churros,* ascended through the dirty-street smell.

He looked around. Tall palm trees still lined streets. Tropical plants and greenery grew out of every crack in sidewalks and piece of ground not covered with concrete.

From somewhere down a side street, he heard the soft, undulating beat of Cuban music. When he found the source, he saw middle-aged men and women sitting on scattered boxes and in doorways, watching youngsters dancing and laughing on the cobblestone surface. *Ah, salsa.* An image of his late wife flashed before his eyes, smiling and whirling as they had danced. He blocked out the vision.

The group neared the Peruvian Embassy. The crowd around it thickened. People left buildings and crossed streets in throngs, headed to the same place.

Reaching Avenida Quinta, Atcho and his companions turned the corner and stopped. The sight was ghastly.

The embassy's imposing structure was readily identifiable. But a swarm of humanity clutched to every visible resting place on the twenty-acre compound. People sat in trees, clinging to even the smallest branches that could hold their weight. They bunched against the fence, struggling for slightly more room. The crush of writhing bodies spilled onto the porch of the elegant building, transforming its appearance to that of a slum tenement.

As Atcho's group neared the gate, more people appeared, cursing, shoving, and pressing in desperate attempts to gain entrance. Some, pushing small children ahead of them, scaled the fence. Several tossed infants across the barrier into the waiting arms of a friend or relative. Cars, used to force entry, sat in gaping holes along the fence, as did the broad backs of buses used for the same purpose.

Adding to the tumult, another crowd formed on the opposite side of the street. This second group screamed at the swarming crowds, "*Gusanos.*

Gusanos. Worms. Traitors. Sons of whores." As a chorus they taunted their victims, pummeling them with stones and garbage.

Atcho looked for the Cuban security guards normally posted around embassies. They were present in large numbers but remained uninvolved at the opposite end of the street. Incredulous, Atcho and his friends joined the press of bodies struggling to gain entrance at the front gate.

The sun had begun its descent, but the heat was still oppressive, exacerbated by ten thousand sweat-drenched bodies pressed tightly together. A stench arose from the crowd and invaded Atcho's nostrils. He gagged and glanced at his comrades. They were similarly affected. They pushed farther into the compound, where space was slightly more available.

Atcho caught the eye of an old man sitting on the ground and crouched next to him. "What's going on here?"

The old man eyed him dubiously and turned away.

Atcho grasped his shoulder. "Please. My companions and I were released from prison this morning. We were political prisoners. We're going to Miami through the Swiss Embassy, but whatever is happening here is slowing the process."

The old man regarded him distantly, and then spoke hesitantly. "You have to be careful, even here," he said. "I hope you are not one of Castro's bullies." He studied Atcho's face and then went on. "Yesterday, six men forced their way onto this compound, seeking asylum. They killed a Cuban guard. Castro demanded their return. Peru refused. In retaliation, Castro pulled security from the gate and said that anyone not satisfied with socialism was welcome to enter the embassy and leave Cuba."

Atcho looked around, amazed. "Who are these people? Are things so bad they would suffer like this for that chance?"

"Who are we?" The old man repeated the question. "Castro would like you to believe we're criminals, thugs, and social deviants. But look." He swept his arm to indicate the crowd. "There are peasants and professionals here. I am a doctor." He indicated a man close by. "My friend is a truck driver. Look over there." He pointed in another direction. "There are white, black, all races here. And women and children. A baby was born here today." He smiled fleetingly and added proudly, "I delivered her. The mother named her Peru as a way of thanking that country for giving us a chance."

His expression dropped again. "You asked if things are so bad. Why else would we suffer heat, filth, hunger, thirst, abuse?" He shook his head. "Ask around," he said sadly. "Our people are starving on government rations. They send our children to Communist schools. Our national produce is shipped to Russia in exchange for military equipment. We can afford to buy nothing, and there is nothing to buy. If we speak out against the government, we are thrown in jail."

He sat dejectedly while Atcho reflected on what he had heard. Then the doctor spoke again. "Leave this place and keep working with the Swiss Embassy. Castro has been letting political prisoners go that way. He'll keep doing it because you are a bother to him, and he can't kill you all."

He sighed. "We really don't know what will happen to us in here. We risked everything because this was our only chance for freedom." He fell silent and looked away.

Atcho sat quietly absorbing the scene around him. Babies cried. Children sat where they had just relieved themselves. Faces were transfixed in strange expressions of incredible hope and dreadful fear.

Gloom possessed Atcho. He shook the old doctor's hand and stood. Then, with his companions, he made his slow way toward the entrance gates. When his group reached the street, the nature of the crowds outside the compound had subtly changed. Refugees pushed harder to enter the estate, while their tormentors across the way stood in a sullen, menacing mood. A platoon of security guards had strung themselves in a line between the two groups.

Atcho gazed around warily. Dusk approached. He wanted to be away from this place as fast as possible but dared not draw attention.

Anguished cries caught his ear. Down the street, ruffians beat people attempting to reach the gate. Refugees still outside the portal became more urgent. They jostled each other, trying to squeeze through whatever openings were available in the fence. Guards made no move to intervene or interfere.

From the corner of his eye, Atcho saw a sentry gesture in his direction.

He inhaled sharply but pretended not to see. The guard walked toward him.

Atcho's companions had also seen the soldier. Trying not to appear obvious, they stepped up their pace. Another guard turned in their direction. A string of guards spread out, cutting off their progress.

A shot rang out. A woman screamed. Refugees ran in all directions. More shots were fired. A man fell, his chest blown open, his eyes glazed in death. More people fell. Blood spilled onto the hard surface of the street. Someone tossed a baby into the air, intended for the sanctuary of the foreign embassy. It fell to the ground, its tiny form riddled with bullets.

Atcho dove onto the asphalt, as did his companions. They lay stunned, not comprehending the savagery they had just witnessed. The agonized cries of the wounded and the wailing of those who had lost loved ones cut through the ominous quiet. A chant of approval rose from the loyalists, "*Gusanos. Gusanos. Gusanos.*"

A soldier jabbed Atcho roughly with his rifle. "Get up."

Atcho complied and saw his companions being taken prisoner. Behind them, loyalists roared their approval, while in the embassy compound, refugees pressed against the fence to see what had happened. Others wailed over loved ones lost in the carnage. They hurled invectives at the soldiers.

The soldiers herded Atcho and his companions into the back of a van and drove away. Eyes dull, and prisoners once more, they sat in silent shock on the hard benches.

The sun's waning rays shone feebly through the small van window. Minutes later, the shadow of a great building blocked the remaining light. Atcho stared at the part he could see. Recognizing its outline, his every nerve stretched taut. They were at *La Cabaña*, Castro's private house of horrors, the prison that hid Cuban intelligence's most brutal interrogations and tortures.

In the portal of the ancient fortress, the driver honked the horn. When the iron gate swung open, they drove into a medieval courtyard. Sentries emerged and butted them from the vehicle, down a winding corridor into the bowels of the notorious prison. Long halls led away into darkness in multiple directions. Atcho and his companions followed down one passageway lined with heavy wooden doors. The first, on the left, was open, leading into a single cell. A guard grabbed Atcho and shoved him roughly into the interior of the dimly lit, smelly chamber. Then he closed and locked the door.

Emotionless, Atcho leaned against a wall, his mind taxed almost to its limit. For several minutes, he was impervious to any feeling beyond physical fatigue. He lowered himself onto a cot, numbed by the atrocity of the afternoon.

Footsteps sounded in the corridor. A key turned in the lock. The door swung open and in the dim light, a sentry motioned Atcho into the hall, ordering him to stand facing into a corner.

Too tired to speculate on what was happening, Atcho complied. More footsteps sounded, and someone groaned, as if in pain. He heard the cell door close and lock.

Arms seized Atcho from both sides. Two guards led him back along the corridor, up the winding passageway into another room, and left him there alone. They were barely beyond earshot when two new guards entered.

"Good evening, sir."

Surprised at the courteous greeting, Atcho looked sharply at the two young soldiers. Then he noticed their uniforms. They were Soviets.

"Please come with us, sir." They led him back into the old courtyard to another van and motioned him into the vehicle. Inside was a man in a business suit and two Soviet soldiers armed with submachine guns. All three returned Atcho's stare but said nothing as the van's engine turned over.

"Who are you?" Atcho asked the man in the business suit.

"Sir, my orders are to answer no questions and deliver you to Camp Columbia as quickly as possible. Also, I am to shoot you if you attempt to escape."

As the van wound through the streets heading toward the city's outskirts, Atcho was too tired to think or speak. He wondered why three people had treated him respectfully and called him "sir."

Through thin metal walls, he heard the high-pitched whine of aircraft. The distinct odor of fuel and exhaust permeated the vehicle's interior. The van made several turns, and then halted again. A soldier opened the door, and Atcho and the men accompanying him stepped outside.

Though weapons were pointed at him, this time, no one took his arms. The man in the business suit led him toward a brick field house. On the other side, an asphalt road led to a runway. A single large plane faced away with its rear ramp down, exposing its cavernous interior. Crewmen loaded cargo onto it.

Atcho followed his escort into a terminal. Men lounged, awaiting flights. Some wore uniforms, some dressed in civilian clothes. No one paid him attention.

"We'll wait here," Atcho's escort said with a heavy Russian accent.

"Where are we going?"

"That will become clear."

"Do you have a name?"

"No, but you can call me Gregor. Come on. We're ready to board."

Speechless, Atcho saw that the other passengers, about fifteen of them, had left their seats and started toward a door leading to the runway. He followed Gregor. The two soldiers who had accompanied them stood at the corner of the building watching them, but apparently would not travel with them.

Gregor turned to him. "I will tell you now that I don't know who you are," he yelled over the roar of jet engines. "I know nothing about you, not even your name, or why you're traveling. I can only tell you that my orders are to treat you with all courtesy and respect unless you try to escape, in which case I will not hesitate to kill you. We will make a refueling stop in the Azores. Our final destination is Moscow."

Atcho had no opportunity to react or even think about this startling revelation. A crewman signaled. Passengers boarded, jostling for position. They treated Gregor with deference, and Atcho benefitted by association. As a result, they sat in two of the most desirable seats, although they could hardly be considered comfortable.

Generators whirred, the cargo ramp raised, the interior lights dimmed, and the huge aircraft rolled ponderously down the runway. It ascended to thirty thousand feet and settled into its cruising velocity.

Atcho looked over at Gregor. He seemed to have relaxed, perhaps relieved to have had no incident during boarding, but he studied Atcho steadily.

An abrupt thought flashed through Atcho's mind. *The way we were arrested at the Peruvian Embassy was planned.* Security police had surrounded them. No one else had been taken away. While Cuban soldiers escorted the captives to their cells at *La Cabaña*, Russian soldiers had retrieved Atcho, leaving someone else in his place. *And Gregor is KGB.*

They pulled a switch. They want someone to believe I'm still there. What do they want with me?

17

The cargo plane landed at an airbase near Moscow in the middle of the night. Unknown men in a long black car waited for Atcho and drove him through the dimly lit streets of the capital city. He strained to see through the windows but came away with only vague impressions of massive buildings and wide streets that trailed into narrow, empty roads leading into the country. He felt more than saw the twists and turns and had no idea of where he was.

As predawn light brightened, they arrived at a large chain-link gate topped with concertina wire. The driver rolled down the window and showed documents to a guard, who waved them through. Fifty feet further on, they encountered a second gate. The space between them was bereft of vegetation and was very well illuminated. The guard at the second gate waved them through.

The road turned into a gravel surface and rose at a slight incline. On either side, tall fir trees rose like sentries, reminding Atcho of his departure from the Isle of Pines.

The road soon broke into a clearing and wended through a garden of sorts. Ahead of them, a house came into view—seemingly pleasant, and not at all what Atcho expected. "What is this place?"

"A *dacha,*" came the response.

"What is a dacha?"

"A country house where people go for holiday," the escort chuckled. "This one was built before the socialist revolution. I don't think anyone comes here now for holiday."

The dacha was a large frame house, painted deep green, the roof metallic and steepled. When Atcho stepped out of the car, the chill of dawn caused him to suck in his breath, reminding him that he was very far north where cold weather extends well into spring, and nights become short very quickly. Above him, a strong wind swayed the firs.

His escorts led him up some stairs, across a wide porch, through the main door, and into a foyer. The house was heated and reasonably well maintained.

A thin middle-aged man with sparse hair came through a door to the left. He wore a uniform and projected a reserved manner, but not unfriendly. He held out his hand, but the move was perfunctory, almost an afterthought.

"I am Major Karlov," he said in heavily accented English. "I am the commandant of this camp. Please follow me." He dismissed the escorts, led Atcho into his office, and indicated a wooden chair.

Atcho sat and looked around while the major went to the other side of the desk. The room was utilitarian, but not uncomfortable—the furniture appearing to be quality holdovers from better days. The walls evoked a feeling of an era past. The desk was large and ornately carved oak.

The major seemed comfortable enough in this environment, yet out of place. Atcho guessed that he descended from the proletariat, not the bourgeoisie.

"I know virtually nothing about you," Karlov said. "I understand you spent many years in deep cover, and you served the Motherland well."

Atcho gazed steadily, refraining from any reaction.

"My job is to provide you with an opportunity to rest, and to prepare you for your next mission. However, ..." He removed his glasses and his stare bored into Atcho. "Your preparation is only general, as provided to all agents. You'll be trained in weapons, combat, espionage, and counterespionage methods. I know nothing of future missions, nor should you ask me about them. Is that understood?"

Atcho nodded, hearing as if through a void. *They're training me to be a spy? What makes them think I'll cooperate?* He had no choice but to listen.

"You're a mid-level guest of the Soviet Union. As such, you'll be afforded every courtesy and comfort. But you are expected to train hard."

He stood and leaned across the desk. "You must understand what I tell you now. I'm an officer of the Spetsnaz. That's a special division of the Soviet army to disrupt enemy operations before a war begins. During peacetime, we train." He took off his glasses again and cleaned them with a handkerchief.

"We cooperate with KGB Section S, which trains and manages 'illegals'—those operators who will be active in other countries. You'll also train with Section V, which is responsible for wet operations."

Atcho winced. *I'm training to be an assassin?*

Karlov pointed to a map of the facility on the wall behind him. "You are free to go anywhere on this compound. We have a library. It's robust; we don't restrict anything you read. In this location, the current material focuses on the United States."

Atcho shifted his feet. His shoulders ached with fatigue, but his mind registered the significance of what he had just heard. *I'm to be a spy in the US.*

"You are free to use all of the facilities at your own leisure. However, and this is the key point," his face became set, "our security measures are severe. This compound is surrounded by two rings of razor-sharp electrified fences. Motion-sensitive shotguns are stationed at their corners, aimed along the sides. German Shepherd dogs are kept deliberately hungry and roam between the fences at night."

Atcho returned the expressionless look.

"There's more. There are minefields on both sides of the outer fence. And finally, our guards are Spetsnaz. There are other precautions too. Questions?"

Atcho thought he should respond. "Did you say that I am a guest?'

The major smiled quietly. "Of sorts. Let me take you to your room."

* * *

Over the next weeks, Atcho trained for missions not yet known. When not in training, he read in the library, catching up on events that occurred while he was in prison.

The library was housed in a large comfortable room, which also gave a sense of being from another time. Atcho was surprised to find various American classical books, as well as some by contemporary authors. More surprising were current periodicals, including copies of *Time* and *Newsweek*. He found uncensored copies of the *New York Times* and the *Herald Tribune* and sat down to read.

One late afternoon at the library, Karlov entered. “I see you enjoy your reading.”

“Keeping up. So much is happening.” Atcho had read old articles about the American lunar landing with intense interest. Rather than being inspired, he felt angry at the resources denied his countrymen while so much was poured into the space race. Not wanting to reveal his ignorance of world affairs, he did not mention that to the major.

“I’m intrigued with the US response to the Soviet entry into Afghanistan,” he said instead. “Boycotting the Olympics?”

The major chuckled. “We don’t know what to make of that either. It’s a weak response, and irritating. It’s more insult than injury. We would have enjoyed hosting the US in Moscow. President Carter seems to know a lot about the technicalities of submarines and peanut farming, but not much about governing.” He chuckled again. “There are still two months until the Olympics. Maybe he’ll change his mind.”

“Do you think the grain embargo will hurt your country?”

Karlov gave his quiet smile again. “Carter seems not to know Russian history. Russians are nothing if not long-suffering. We do without things. Worse, we are stubborn. He is only punishing his own farmers, but if he wants to do that ...” He shrugged, leaving his sentence unfinished, and then said, “Can you believe he gave away the Panama Canal?”

Atcho was dumbfounded, but kept his expression neutral, only shaking his head as if in agreement—he had not yet run across that gem.

He had spent much of the morning reading about the takeover of the US Embassy in Tehran a few months earlier. “What do you think about that?" he asked, indicating a headline showing that one hundred and sixty-one days had passed since the event occurred.

"Unbelievable," Karlov exclaimed. "Can you imagine the Soviet Union allowing any nation to occupy one of its embassies and hold its diplomats hostage?"

Without comment, Atcho agreed that he could not.

"I'm glad you are doing well in your training," Karlov said, "and that you're taking time to keep up with the news." He left.

Atcho returned to the article he had been studying when Karlov had entered. He had avoided discussing the subject. It pertained to more retaliation by Castro against the government of Peru for the events at their embassy in Havana.

The dictator was also angry with the Cubans who had thronged the embassy seeking political asylum. He had announced that anyone wanting to leave Cuba was free to do so by whatever means, including boats from the US. The article showed aerial and close-up views of thousands of small boats docking at the small port of Mariel. They departed with thousands of his countrymen for Miami.

Atcho read and re-read the article in silent dismay. *I should have been on one of those boats.*

18

Atcho felt like every moment he was not asleep was a moment spent in training. Even the movies made available at night were American slices of life. He realized they were used to familiarize agents-in-training with American lifestyles.

One night, Karlov stepped into the small viewing room just off the library, where Atcho watched *The Graduate* with two other people. "Do you suppose life is really like that in the US?" he said. "Or is that CIA-developed propaganda?"

Atcho answered cautiously, not knowing whether the question was a sincere inquiry or a test. "I don't know. When I find out, I'll drop you a postcard."

Karlov said nothing. He watched the movie for a few minutes and left.

One morning in hand-to-hand combat training, Atcho found himself paired with a bull of a man with close-cropped hair, an instructor he had dubbed Boris. The instructor had taught him techniques for close fighting that he had not learned at West Point. There, Atcho had boxed, as all cadets had done. He had even won a regimental intramural championship.

Here at this nonexistent outpost deep in Russia, the emphasis was on martial arts, street-fighting techniques, and using every advantage to take down an opponent. "Fair fighting will get you killed," Boris told him.

Atcho had been amazed at the perfect Midwestern American accent when Boris spoke in English. "If death is the only option, your job is to make the other guy lose."

"Go easy on me," Atcho said as they squared off on this morning. Suddenly, the heel of Boris' hand slammed upward against Atcho's jaw. Boris spun low on the ball of his right foot, and his outstretched left foot kicked both legs out from under Atcho.

Atcho rolled over quickly and came to a crouch.

"You don't have time to be funny in a fight," Boris yelled. His eyes bulged. "You think your enemy is going to take time to appreciate your joke? Think. Watch the eyes. Distract." He jabbed a finger at Atcho. "If you joke, you'd better do it only to distract the other guy and know exactly what your next move will be."

In surveillance and countersurveillance training, Atcho learned to follow undetected, and to spot and lose a tail. His trainers took him into a nearby town for a practical exercise. He felt refreshed to be among ordinary citizens going about their business freely. *What I wouldn't give right now for even a Soviet's level of freedom.*

He went through classes on covert communications, including the use of blind drops, and was familiarized on all sorts of weaponry. The AK-47 was new to him, but most of the firearms were American, and many well-known to him. He had little trouble regaining competence and confidence in shooting.

He spent many hours in the gym and running. Hardened by forced labor, and now with far better food and more rest than he had had in decades, the strenuous exercise brought Atcho to a superb level of physical fitness.

He had expected ideological classes, but after several weeks, he concluded that there would be none—no attempt to indoctrinate him. *Whether or not I'm a good Communist must be irrelevant.*

Isabel stayed constantly on his mind. *She's better off without me.*

One evening, while Atcho read in the library, Karlov entered. He took a seat in an overstuffed chair near Atcho. "You've done well here."

Atcho felt uneasiness forming in his stomach. Despite antipathy toward his captors, he had grown accustomed to the predictability and security of the training facility. He had enjoyed the camp's creature comforts and the physical and intellectual opportunities, even as he felt pangs of guilt over the continued suffering or deaths of his comrades left behind at *La Cabaña* in Havana.

The major's choice of tense seemed to signal an impending change. "Is my training coming to an end?"

"You've been here five months, Comrade. Tomorrow you leave for Moscow." He stood. "I will not see you again."

19

SEPTEMBER 1980

Why Moscow? The former guerrilla leader, political exile, and apparent new KGB operative slept poorly that night, tossing in apprehension of what might lie ahead.

Nightmares that had been dormant returned in full detail. With them, his fear, pain and feelings of failure resurfaced. He saw clearly Isabel's terror-stricken face in the moonlight. The scene morphed into a baby thrown into the air, and he felt revulsion on seeing its tiny body struck with bullets. He rode again in a battle tank riddled with bullets as it bumped through a dark swamp.

He sat up in a cold sweat. Rubbing his temples, he got out of bed and paced, and then tried to sleep again. It came in fits and spurts.

* * *

Two men sat in the foyer the next morning when Atcho finished breakfast. "This way," one said roughly. They showed no courtesy as they led him to a sedan parked in the driveway.

Atcho sat between them in the back of the car, while a third man drove. They wound their way back along the tree-lined gravel road, and after passing through the two sets of electric gates, turned onto a hard-surfaced motorway. Through the darkened windows, he saw wide, flat fields dotted with villages and isolated houses. Occasionally, large stands of trees interrupted the bare horizon.

After two hours on the M4 highway leading into the capital, they crossed the great Moscow River. The road widened, and the sedan joined traffic heading into the throbbing heart of the Communist world.

Atcho tried to glimpse landmarks he had seen in pictures, taking in the vast scale of Red Square, and the multicolored beauty of St. Basil's Cathedral.

One of the escorts rolled down a window as they passed Lenin's tomb. Foreboding gripped Atcho as his eyes followed the guard's pointing finger. The resting place of the Father of the Socialist Revolution was plainly visible in the wall of a long building. Nearby were the sculpted images of Marx, Lenin, and Stalin. Atcho stared coldly at them. *Butchers. Stalin sent eighteen million Ukrainians to slaughter. How could he be a national hero?*

Pedestrians passed by their vehicle as it made its way along the river opposite the unmistakable red walls that seemed to stretch endlessly. On the other side, polished gold domes of Russian Orthodox churches gleamed in the sunlight. They challenged his previous perceptions of a cold, gray capital.

At a bridge, the car turned and proceeded along the front wall. Atcho stared in stony silence. This, he knew, was the Kremlin.

The colossal compound seemed to pulse with an unholy life of its own. He remembered pictures of terror-stricken people ground under Red Army tanks in Czechoslovakia. The orders, including those to dominate his beloved Cuba, had come from this very building. An almost irresistible urge to retaliate coursed through him. He set his jaw and prepared for whatever was to follow.

They continued past the Kremlin and down another avenue. The number of buildings of classical architecture surprised Atcho. He had not been prepared for that, in spite of the elegant cathedrals. They belied notions of a perpetually austere Russian history. *What happened in Russia's past that we don't know much about in the West?*

A few blocks further along, another imposing building appeared. This one was yellow and set off from other buildings by wide streets. At its front was a garden, in the center of which was an enormous statue.

One of the escorts saw Atcho studying it. "Felix Dzerzhinsky," he grunted, "the father of the KGB, the sword of the state."

The pit in Atcho's stomach jolted at the mention of the KGB and its motto—the Sword and Shield of the Party—and its notorious founder, a murderer and torturer of millions.

They turned along the side of the building. It continued far down the street. Before reaching the corner, they turned into an alley cut into the building that led to an underground tunnel.

In spite of himself, Atcho grimaced. One of the escorts saw his expression. "Welcome to the Lubyanka," he said with a sarcastic laugh. "KGB headquarters."

When they exited the vehicle, one man grasped Atcho's arm, ushering him inside. They moved quickly down a short flight of stairs and followed a long hall. A bank of elevators stood halfway down the corridor, one waiting with its door open. The escorts steered Atcho inside. One of them pressed a button, and they descended into the bowels of the huge building, from which so many never again ascended. They maneuvered through more halls and took Atcho inside a room, leaving him there alone with the door closed.

The room had no windows or furnishings except a table and a steel chair, facing a wall made entirely of smoked glass. The room was well lit, but a drape was drawn on the other side of the glass. He wondered what lurked there.

He looked around for some indication of what to expect and found none. After a few minutes he sat in the chair facing the glass wall. A tray on the table contained fruit and a pitcher of water. Absently, he picked up an apple and began to nibble.

Minutes turned into an hour, then two hours. He stood, walked around the room and tried the door, to no avail. Returning, he sat down and rested his head in his arms on the table.

The purr of a small electric motor caught his ear. He looked up. The drapes opened. Atcho's attention focused on the formidable presence in the dark room on the other side of the glass. Someone breathed out his code name.

"Atcho."

The voice, low, sonorous, and unmistakably familiar, echoed through Atcho's brain. Fury gripped him. He leaped to his feet, and advanced menacingly.

"Captain Govorov," he snarled, his features twisted with twenty years of hatred.

"I'm glad you remember me after all this time. I'm General Govorov now." He laughed, the same mirthless sound Atcho had heard all those years ago. "You look better than the last time we met."

"What do you want with me?"

"Aren't you going to ask how I am?" Govorov crooned. His Spanish was better than it had been that night in Havana so many years ago.

"How did you find me?"

The general laughed again with genuine amusement. "We never lost you."

Atcho froze at the implication. "You knew where I was?"

"You weren't exactly subtle," Govorov's voice acquired a matter-of-fact tone. "I tried to keep you out of battle, so you wouldn't be killed. That's why I returned your daughter to Camaguey. But you had to get back into action. You stole a truck in Cienfuegos, demolished a squad of soldiers, and stole a tank they had captured. Then, you entered a firefight from the flank, delivered your prize to the invasion force, and died. Meanwhile, a man, whom no one had ever heard of, appeared on the scene calling himself Manuel Lezcano."

Atcho reeled at the knowledge of how completely he had fooled himself.

"We routinely took your picture with other prisoners. When we saw Manuel's photo, *voila*."

Visions of lost friends and rumors of torture seared Atcho's memory. "Why did you kill Juan, and torture others?"

"I wasn't there, but my good friend Fidel must have felt he had a justifiable reason for shooting Juan. After all, he was a significant figure in the resistance." Govorov chuckled. "The episode lent reality to our search for you. As for the others, well, we had to put on a good show."

Seized by fresh grief, Atcho lowered his head into his hands. "Why?" He dropped his hands from his face and glared into the dark interior beyond the glass. "Why did you keep me all those years? Why not just kill me?"

"I'm surprised you haven't already figured that out," Govorov exclaimed in mock amazement. "I left a note for you. Didn't you read it? You are too valuable to discard. Your career has been carefully managed."

Atcho's muscles tightened. He pulled his head erect. "Career? Managed?"

"Let me tell you plainly." Govorov's voice took on a paternal tone. "Your father graduated from West Point. You did, too. Then you rose to leadership in a counterrevolution against a Communist regime. Don't you see? You are among the most powerful alumni in the world. They occupy sensitive posts. Your personal history makes you acceptable anywhere."

Atcho was speechless, struggling to comprehend. He stood in silence, a few moments. "Why hold me all that time, and bring me out now?"

"Good question." Govorov spoke as though to a briefing session. "Timing. Timing is everything. Your credibility was increased with imprisonment. Like aging fine wine. Keeping you in prison was a convenient way to warehouse you until, at a strategic juncture, we could bring you out. We made other preparations."

"Other preparations?"

"We gambled a bit, but things worked out better than we hoped." He was obviously pleased with himself. "We wanted your entry into an assignment to come about naturally. So, we used Isabel to help us with that."

Atcho's heart skipped a beat. He tried to speak but found himself almost voiceless. "Isabel?" he managed at last. "Have you done something to Isabel?"

"No. Relax." The general's mocking voice changed to sarcastic, soothing. "You should be grateful. We went to great lengths to ensure her good care. You'll be happy to know that she grew up in the Western ethic. She's a fine girl. You'll be pleased."

"Will I ever see her? She thinks I'm dead."

"Of course, you'll see her. She no longer thinks you're dead. You took care of that. But back to what I was saying." Govorov seemed mildly impatient. "We arranged for Isabel and your sister to emigrate with your brother-in-law to Miami. We found good work for them, with good pay, and set up a trust fund for Isabel. We insisted that she attend the best schools, and when she reached college age, we set up a scholarship fund at one of the girls' schools near West Point, through anonymous donors. Then, we quietly politicked to make sure that she received one of the scholarships."

Understanding edged across Atcho's mind. His feet felt heavy as he trudged back to the center of the room. Sinking into the chair, he cupped his chin in his hands. "You wanted her to marry a West Point graduate," he said, remembering that this was the dream of many parents of girls he had dated.

"Exactly." Govorov seemed genuinely pleased. "We could not guarantee the outcome. But, as you know, the odds are good for a girl attending one of those nearby schools." He became enthusiastic. "I'm happy to announce success."

Atcho raised his head sharply. "Isabel?" he asked incredulously. "Married?"

"Isn't that wonderful? You'll be so proud. Her husband was a sterling cadet, graduating near the top of his class. He was on the football team, and ..."

You'd think we were long-lost friends catching up on old times. "When?"

"Late spring. Isabel graduated in May, and her husband in early June. They married the following week. His name is Robert Bernier."

Atcho sat in silence, trying to interpret the revelations of the past few minutes. Recall of all he had lost swept over him again, but he forced it aside.

He poured some water and sipped it, feeling the presence of Govorov studying him from beyond the window. "Did you have anything to do with the death of my sister and her husband?"

"No, we really didn't."

For a moment, Atcho thought he detected a note of regret in the general's voice. Then he decided that he had either imagined it, or it had been affected for his benefit.

"It was an auto accident," Govorov went on. "They were hit straight on by a drunk driver. You know, the US really should do something about that problem. But," his tone became lighter, "I have to admit that the incident helped us. You see, Isabel was left alone, with no living relative that she knew of. Her loneliness and vulnerability ultimately increased the probability that she would meet a cadet and marry him after graduation."

Fresh sadness overcame Atcho, imagining his grown daughter struggling with grief over the loss of her aunt and uncle. He knew the despair she must have experienced on finding that she faced the world alone. "It was you who claimed me," Atcho said disconsolately.

"Yes. That was to increase the credibility of your cover. The process was easy. The US was loose in checking to see who was claiming whom. We convinced your sister to do it, without Isabel's knowledge."

"What about the atrocity at the Peruvian Embassy. Was that your doing?"

"That was Castro. When the incident began, and all those people entered the compound, he decided to allow political prisoners to leave the country. We knew this was the perfect time to bring you out. We followed your movements through Havana and were happy when you walked into the Peruvian Embassy. If you had stayed in the Swiss Embassy, we would have picked you up after you arrived in Miami. This way turned out better. We alerted the Cuban security police and told them to arrest you and your companions if you came back out of the compound. I'm not sure what triggered the shooting. Probably a young officer got carried away. You have to admit, it added reality."

Sickened at Govorov's callousness, Atcho took a quick breath. "Where are my companions?"

"They are still in solitary confinement at *La Cabaña*, waiting for you."

"Waiting for me?" Atcho gasped. "You brought me all the way here and put me through training to take me back to that hellhole?"

Govorov laughed. "You're not going to stay there," he said patronizingly. "We have to get you back, so we can insert you into your assignment as unobtrusively as possible. You'll be kept in isolation for a few weeks and then be released to the US with the others. They don't know you've been gone." He chuckled. "We had someone fill in for you. Don't worry." The general was almost jocular. "You'll be fed enough to stay alive, and you won't be abused. Think, Atcho. The last time you were beaten was the night we met in Havana. I didn't mean for them to almost kill you. But I gave strict instructions that you were not to be harmed again."

"What about the box on the Isle of Pines?"

"Didn't they give you enough food to sustain you? Were you beaten? Give me some credit. I looked out for you. You might recall that not all of your companions in the attempted escape survived."

Atcho sat numb, mouth set firmly, remembering Jujo and the others who tried to get away with him. Dread of being incarcerated again dulled his incredulity at the easy way that Govorov spoke of protecting him these last twenty years.

"What do you want me to do?"

"I don't know."

Atcho's head jerked up. "You don't know?"

"We haven't decided yet."

Deathly silence filled the room.

Atcho sat in the chair. His muscles flexed as rage coursed through him. Relentlessly, the feeling snaked, distorting his features and turning his eyes into burning coals. In a frenzy, he leaped to his feet, determined to break the barrier separating him from Govorov. He grabbed the steel chair and rushed the window.

"I'll kill you," he shouted and thrashed the chair against the unyielding glass. "You destroyed my life for a reason you haven't even figured out yet?" The glass fractured. Atcho swung, panting heavily, sweat streaming from his face and arms.

"Stop that," Govorov commanded, his tone threatening.

Atcho ignored the general and the piercing pain in his arms. "Stop, Atcho. I'll shoot." He enunciated his words as the gleam of a pistol appeared.

Atcho bashed the window again. A shot fractured the glass. Splinters flew, and a small round hole appeared in the glass. Heedless, Atcho beat the window harder.

"Stop, or your daughter will die."

Atcho halted in mid-swing, straining to stop the momentum of the chair.

For several moments he stood, sweat running over his face, head bowed in defeat. He raised haunted eyes to peer through the smoked window. There, just beyond his reach, was the dark figure of General Govorov.

"It's good to see you in such good physical shape," Govorov sneered. "I own you. That's the way it is. You serve the KGB for the Soviet state."

He paused for impact. When he spoke again, there was a deliberate softening of his tone. "Life won't be so bad. You'll be in Havana less than a month. You and your friends will return to the Swiss Embassy. A short time later, Castro will experience another touch of humanity and allow you to emigrate. Then you'll lead a normal life in the United States until we need you."

Atcho sat quietly, comprehending Govorov's words, too numb to react. "This could be good for you." The general had regained his enthusiasm. "You'll be with your daughter and meet your son-in-law. We'll make sure you're able to maintain a comfortable lifestyle.

"Arrangements are being made to welcome you as a hero. We'll let the press know of your release. Friends and fellow counterrevolutionaries will learn of your arrival in Miami. The West Point homecoming is next month, and I'm sure you'll receive a special invitation. You'll be loved and respected." He paused, peering through the window at his quarry.

On the other side, Atcho faced him in a half crouch, panting heavily, his contorted features dripping with perspiration.

Govorov chuckled. "You're down, but not beaten. That's good. We need that spirit. Look at it this way. All you have to do is enjoy life and be ready when we call."

Atcho heard the general as though through an echoing void. "And if I complete your mission?"

"Atcho, for someone with your talents and background, the assignment will be special, so I wouldn't expect it to happen anytime soon. Years could pass before we need you. And we want you to spend that time developing and expanding contacts. But, if you do a good job, we'll want to use you again."

"You have no intention of ever letting me live my own life."

"Remember that note I left in Camaguey. It established our relationship. You belong to me." He paused a moment. "It's not personal. I'm an intelligence officer. You're an asset."

Atcho raised his head, peering morosely through the dark glass. "And if I just end my own life?"

General Govorov's tone became grave. "We have too much invested in you to let that happen. If you so much as scratch yourself shaving, if we think it was deliberate, you, whatever family you have, and whatever extended family there is, will be obliterated." He paused and then said, "I have to go. I'm glad to see you in such superb condition. Enjoy."

20

Atcho stared through the dark glass into an abyss. His heart beat furiously, his mind churned. He trudged to the table, dragging the chair. Sinking into the seat, he draped his upper body across the table, and remained there until his escorts arrived.

Scarcely noticing those who accompanied him, Atcho retraced his journey in reverse order. From the Lubyanka, his minders drove him to the air base where another agent, less amiable than Gregor, took charge of him and warned him again against escape. Atcho barely took note of anything on either leg of the flight to the Azores or back to Cuba. He ate nothing and drank very little. His body felt heavy and old.

In Havana, Soviet drove him back to the gloom of *La Cabaña*. They jostled him through the same long halls and left him in the same room he had been in before. Two Cuban sentries then jostled him down the winding passageway to the cell he had occupied five months ago. No trace of the man who had taken his place existed.

Atcho lay down on the rough cot. For days, he took no sustenance, drinking only enough to moisten his parched mouth. His mind mulled the merits of life versus death.

Every hope he clung to came with a price so high it seemed impossible to pay. Death, he thought, had the greater advantage. It became his morbid fascination. He longed to welcome it and imagined various ways he could achieve his own demise, but Govorov had been clear about what his suicide would mean.

There was no escape. In his torment, his daughter came often to mind. He obsessed over her well-being.

By the end of the first week, he was gaunt, his clothes hanging loosely about him. His body began to devour itself. For three more weeks, he lay in the dank cell while cockroaches and mice consumed his untouched food. Occasionally the pests ventured close to him, but a slight movement sent them scurrying.

His mind wandered while his body wasted away. One night he awakened, suddenly aware that he was not alone. Two figures stood at the end of his bed. A third, in a dark shroud, loomed in the corner, his features hidden under a cowl. Pinned by the piercing gaze of this evil, terror seized Atcho. The figure moved toward him. Atcho struggled onto his elbows and leaned away from the inexorable, advancing entity.

"Leave him," a familiar voice commanded. "You have no business here." The apparition disappeared. Atcho stared at the two figures still standing at the end of his cot. The voice was his father's. The old man looked at his son through gentle eyes. "I'm proud of you, Atcho. Isabel still needs you."

The other figure glided to the side of his cot, and in the dim prison chamber, Atcho recognized his old companion, Juan. "You're doing fine, my friend," Juan said. "Keep going." He reached down to touch Atcho's arm. Instinctively, Atcho reached for him. A mouse scampered from a place on Atcho's sleeve where it had begun to nibble.

Atcho peered around the cell. He was alone. A sound caught his attention. Squinting through the dim light, he saw the usual pests competing for his food. Suddenly ravenous, he crossed the floor and consumed the remaining scraps.

21

Another week passed. Then, bright sunlight pierced Atcho's eyes as he and his companions staggered through the courtyard of the old fortress to a waiting van. He was pleased to see Domingo and Pedro and the others but appalled at their skeletal appearance, shadows of even their emaciated states of six months ago. They greeted each other with weak smiles. *I am so sorry,* he wanted to tell them.

The prisoners had been awakened early in the morning. They repeated the process they had gone through during their previous release to the Swiss Embassy. After breakfast, the guards provided them with showers and a change of clothing. As on the earlier occasion, they wore expressions of mixed hope and fear. Mindful of how easily freedom could be withdrawn, they regarded each other in silence.

After loading into the van, their guards drove them to the Swiss Embassy. Administrative personnel led them through the same doors and corridors they had seen six months before. This time, even while waiting to be processed, they maintained their guard. The conference room again filled with political prisoners anxious to leave Cuba.

Atcho looked for Sofia, the secretary who had helped him contact Isabel. She was nowhere to be seen. Disappointed, he inspected himself in the mirror he had used previously and was dismayed to see the toll exacted by his self-imposed starvation.

As before, Director Tilden entered the room. “I understand that you are part of the group whose departure was delayed,” he said to Atcho’s group. The gravity of his face expressed knowledge of their re-incarceration. “I’m sorry that happened to you.”

A strained voice called out, “How long will we wait this time?”

“Let’s get you to Miami,” the director responded. “Now. The bus is waiting.”

Still not trusting their good fortune, the former prisoners filed silently out of the United States’ Interests Section to a yard at the rear of the embassy. There, watchful for signs that this dream would end, they clambered aboard another bus.

Atcho and Domingo sat next to each other. No one spoke.

The bus started up and drove through the decrepit streets. Each blackened hulk of classical architecture seemed an emblem of a proud history long gone.

They arrived at José Martí Airport and found a chartered passenger jet waiting on a secluded runway. The bus drove alongside the aircraft and stopped next to a portable stairway. The refugees climbed out and almost ran to the plane. They took seats aboard the jet and waited quietly for takeoff.

Within minutes, the aircraft taxied down the runway and climbed into the sky. The pilot’s voice came over the intercom. “Gentlemen, we have cleared Cuban airspace. We will land at Miami International Airport in twenty minutes.”

Silence.

The men looked at each other, afraid to believe. Then, a joyous roar thundered through the aircraft as they leaped from their seats in exuberant celebration. They laughed, jumped, hugged each other, cursed Castro, blessed the United States, kissed the floor, and danced in the aisle.

Atcho remained in his seat. Govorov had said that Isabel no longer believed him dead. *Has someone let her know I’m alive? Will she meet me?*

Govorov also said that the press, former members of the resistance, and West Point classmates would hear of his release. *I don’t know how to meet any those people. All that matters is Isabel—and she probably doesn't want to meet me.*

Domingo noticed Atcho sitting quietly. "Aren't you excited?" He clapped Atcho on the shoulder.

Atcho shrugged. "It's my daughter."

Concern crossed Domingo's face. "Won't she be waiting for you?"

"I don't know." Atcho appreciated his friend's sympathy. "Until six months ago, she thought I was dead."

Domingo nodded his understanding.

So begins a life of half-truths and subterfuge with my own people.

The captain's voice came over the intercom again. "Please take your seats and buckle up. We're on final approach into Miami airport."

A hush fell over the cabin as the former prisoners looked at each other. Atcho leaned back and closed his eyes. His heart beat rapidly. His palms sweated. He breathed deeply several times and glanced through the window as the plane circled and began its final descent.

Moments later, the jet touched down, screamed to a standstill, then taxied slowly to the terminal. Atcho watched as an exit ramp unfolded and extended from the terminal to the aircraft. *What else is new in this modern world?*

Heedless of the pilot's instructions, refugees sprang to their feet, jockeying to be first out of the aircraft. Then the door opened, and they poured through, eager to reunite with loved ones.

They found themselves in an empty part of the terminal except for a line of police officers that stood at each door. For an instant, anxiety clenched their stomachs and throats. Then, from far down the terminal, they heard cheering and saw a crowd of people waving from behind a police barricade.

A welcoming committee of three men wearing traditional Cuban *guayabera* shirts came forward and shook their hands. They spoke in Spanish.

"We are so happy to welcome you to freedom," the leader said. "We have a bus to take you to a convention center. Your families and friends are waiting there."

Atcho and his companions were unprepared for the scene that greeted them as the bus turned out of the security section of Miami International Airport onto Lejeune Road. Ahead of them, a police escort led with flashing lights and wailing sirens. On both sides of the street, cars parked along their path.

People honked and waved, jumping in the air and hugging each other. They held up signs welcoming their countrymen to a new life.

The former prisoners now felt free to join in the revelry. They waved through the windows, their smiles exuberant and hopeful.

Atcho observed quietly. When the buses arrived at their destination, he let his euphoric companions push past him.

Soon, he exited the bus. Crowds on either side resounded their welcome, and while his companions laughed and waved energetically, Atcho smiled perfunctorily as they made their way into the convention center.

On entering the building, the refugees pressed against a crowd of relatives seeking family members. People laughed, cried, and embraced, exclaiming in surprise at changes or lack of changes in relatives and friends. Shouting with exhilaration, some refugees knelt and kissed the floor.

Badges easily identified members of the press, along with notepads, microphones, and electronic cameras. They were on the flanks of the crowd, eagerly insistent on meeting and talking with refugees.

Looking for a familiar face, Atcho edged along the side of the throng. A dark-haired girl, face bright with anticipation, rushed toward him. He stopped and stared into her eyes, but she passed into the arms of a man behind him.

Feeling foolish, Atcho continued moving along the outside of the crowd. He looked for officials to direct him through the immigration process. Then he would be free to go about his own business. *Whatever that is.*

"There he is." A rush of press representatives pushed in Atcho's direction. Feeling a tug on his arm, he turned, and found a microphone thrust close to his mouth.

"Mr. Xiquez, how does it feel to be free after all these years?"

"Is it true that your daughter thought you were dead until just a few months ago?"

"What part did you play in the resistance against Castro at the Bay of Pigs?"

"Why did Castro decide to let you go now?"

"What was the significance of the code name, 'Atcho'?"

"What was a West Point graduate doing in Cuba, anyway?"

Atcho found himself surrounded by reporters, pushing and jostling to get closer. He sought escape in another direction but encountered TV cameramen shining bright lights at him and shouting requests for exclusive interviews. Anger rising, he pushed against the swarm, looking for an opening. "Please," he shouted, finding no way out, "let me through. Thank you for your interest, but I played a very small part."

Reporters continued to press and Atcho struggled against them. Then he had a thought. *If they know so much about me, maybe they know something about Isabel.*

Seizing a newsman by the shoulder, he thrust his face next to the man's ear. "Do you know my daughter?" he yelled above the noise of the crowd.

The man nodded. Atcho's heart leaped. "Do you know where she is?"

The reporter looked at him, a calculating expression on his face. "Will you give me an interview?"

Disgusted at rank opportunism, Atcho breathed deeply and nodded. The man grabbed his arm, turned to the right, and pointed.

Atcho's heart stopped.

Across the reception center, apart from the crowd, a young woman leaned against a column. Her hair was dark, her blue eyes large, with full lips firmly set beneath a delicate nose.

Atcho gasped. She was the image of his beloved late wife. As in a dream, he made his way slowly through the crowd of reporters.

Sensing another story, they parted to let him through.

The woman's gaze met his and she froze. Her eyes widened in apprehension and she glanced around, as though seeking a place to hide. Then she composed herself and walked toward Atcho.

He was deaf to the tumult. His heart beat furiously. Perspiration broke out on his forehead. At last he stood in front of her. Meeting her gaze, he remembered the same expression in the eyes of his dear wife.

"Isabel?" he whispered, tears running freely down his face.

She nodded. Then, throwing her arms around her father's neck, she wept softly.

Atcho drew his arms tightly about his daughter. "I can't believe it's you."

The two remained embraced, surrounded by reporters still hammering questions at them.

"I didn't know you were alive," Isabel said, in a broken voice. "I'm sorry I treated you so badly on the phone."

Atcho mumbled something unintelligible, hugged his daughter once more, and leaned back to look at her. "You look so much like your mother. How did you know I would be here today?"

"Someone from the state department contacted me. Aunt Raissa had claimed you in my name." Tears flowed again. "I didn't know."

A man touched Isabel on the shoulder. "Let's get through immigration and get out of here."

Isabel wiped tears from her cheeks and nodded. "Papá. This is my husband, Bob Bernier."

Thrilled at being called "Papá," Atcho surveyed the young man. Bob was tall, blond, and blue-eyed, with a rugged look indicating the willingness and ability to handle any situation. His smile was friendly, but his manner warned that he would be difficult to deal with if he discovered he had been misled.

He thrust out his hand. "Pleased to meet you, Atcho. I've heard so much about you, and I want to hear a lot more."

Atcho's spirits rose as he shook Bob's hand. He liked his son-in-law immediately.

Bob turned and barreled through the crowd, pulling Isabel and Atcho with him.

22

"Atcho! Atcho! Atcho!" The crowd outside the convention hall called his name over and over, huge grins on their faces as they thrust their arms overhead in celebration.

Sitting next to Isabel in the back of a sedan, Atcho could only gaze in wonder. He opened a window and waved, hoping that his smile did not expose him for the impostor he felt himself to be.

Isabel squeezed his hand and laid her head on his shoulder. Emotion such as Atcho had never experienced gripped him. He sat almost numb, not knowing how to react in such a public setting.

The crowd parted to make way for the sedan, and soon, they headed for a hotel in Coconut Grove. "Some friends own this hotel," Bob called from the driver's seat. "It'll be quiet, and you can rest. Unfortunately, not much, because tomorrow we fly to New York." He turned his full attention to the road as he steered across lanes to enter the freeway. "Your West Point classmates are anxious to see you," he continued. "They insisted that we bring you to West Point. Your class reunion starts in two days."

Dread seized Atcho. His face took on a stony expression. *Govorov predicted this scenario.* "That's great." He hoped his tone matched the expected reaction.

Next to him, Isabel pulled away slightly. He glanced at her and saw that she studied him with a quizzical expression. He smiled and patted her hand, and then gestured his fatigue. "That will be really great," he said again, this time with more genuine feeling—seeing old classmates would be a wonderful event.

They spent most of the afternoon near the hotel. It was a beautiful representation of Floridian art deco of the early 1920s and had been updated to modern standards.

Atcho took in the lush foliage in the courtyard. It bloomed with broad green ferns, purple wisteria, red bougainvillea, and other flowers of all colors. He enjoyed them, startled at the new dimension they suddenly added to his life. "Colors," he murmured to Sofia. "It's good to see colors. Everything in prison was gray or brown."

His room, furnished in heavy oak, was fresh with the scent of lilacs. "Cleanliness." he said to Isabel. "A new experience for me."

"Oh, Papá," she cried, her eyes moistening. She buried her head in his arm.

"Now, now," he said, embracing her. "The bad things in life have to be put in the past. Almost everything will be a new experience for me. Don't be sad as I enjoy it." They held each other while Bob hovered by the window.

Atcho did not feel like sleeping. Only seven hours ago, he had left *La Cabaña*. He found himself too excited to rest. "Sleeping means darkness," he told Isabel. "I want to stay out where there is light, color, good smells, and happy music. I want to be with people I love." A glimmer crossed his eyes. "Where can I get good Cuban espresso?"

Isabel objected, but with Bob's support, she relented. They strolled across the street to a walking mall.

Cuban influence was unmistakable. Soft, undulating tones of Latin music surrounded them, and Atcho had a weird sense of being transported back to Camaguey in the days before Castro.

They found a small café with outdoor seating and sat at a table. "Espresso," Isabel told the smiling waiter, "and six meat pastries with *guayaba*."

Atcho noticed that as the waiter went to fill his order, he kept his eyes on Atcho and smiled wider than normal. He soon returned with a small plastic container and five tiny plastic cups and set them down. Bob lifted the lid, and the aroma of rich Cuban coffee wafted into the air.

Atcho listened to passersby and turned to Isabel. "Does everyone speak Spanish here?"

Isabel laughed and pointed to the window of a clothing store on the opposite side of the walkway. "Look."

A sign prominently displayed in the window proclaimed, "English Spoken Here."

Atcho's eyes expressed his wonder. "Cubans have done well in Miami."

"We'll shop around here and buy you some new clothes," Isabel laughed. "We can't have a prominent Cuban walking around out of style." Her mood changed to melancholy. "There is so much I want to ask," she said, "so much I want to tell you."

Atcho grasped her hand. "Me too," he said warmly, even as warnings rang in the back of his mind. He withdrew his hand. "Let me have one of these," he said gruffly. He picked up one of the meat pastries and took a bite.

He sat back relishing the taste, and then took a sip of espresso. He savored the sweet bitterness as the liquid rolled over his tongue, and he relaxed into his new surroundings.

A group walking by turned to look at him. Their eyes expressed friendliness and curiosity, and they smiled and waved, but otherwise did not intrude into his family's privacy. He glanced around and saw other people noticing him, stopping momentarily, and nudging companions to point him out.

"Bob," Atcho said. "These people, and the waiter—they act like they know who I am. How can that be?"

Bob laughed. "I'll show you." He stood up and walked into the café. A moment later he sat back down and handed Atcho a newspaper.

It was that morning's edition of the *Miami Herald*. Prominently displayed was a photograph of Atcho. Next to it was one of Isabel. The headline read: "Bay of Pigs hero released to Miami." In smaller text, a subhead read: "Political prisoner reunited with daughter after 19 years."

"These are your people, Atcho," Bob said. "Welcome home."

23

The next morning, they flew to New York and rented a car for the fifty-mile drive through the Palisades to West Point. During the trip, Atcho told Isabel everything he could about his experiences in Cuba. The result was a glossed-over explanation of how he became a resistance leader, and why he chose to hide his identity. Though Atcho noted troubled expressions cross her face, Isabel seemed to accept his story. When he had finished telling it, she sat in quiet contemplation, and then her muted mood passed.

Bob said that Atcho was to be an honored guest at the homecoming celebration. Recognizing that his value to his Soviet controllers was already rising, he was apprehensive about attending the three-day event. But he also wanted to go.

Bob drove through a set of stately gates that Atcho remembered well, into West Point. They admired the steep, tree-covered hills around the small valley that hosted a golf course. Then they passed officers' housing and the commissary complex and reached a section of road that passed by the cemetery where many famous graduates were buried, including General George Custer.

A little further on, Atcho strained to look over a low wall on his left where the Hudson River was visible. Far below were the old fieldhouse and athletic grounds where he had practiced soccer as a young cadet. To the right, around the bend, was the Catholic chapel. As a cadet, Atcho had marched to this place for Sunday services.

Now he shrugged, refusing to contemplate the existence of God. They passed another row of stately houses and rounded a bend. He gasped at the view spread before him. "It's changed."

"Yes, it has," Bob agreed. "During the early seventies, they tore down most of the old barracks and built bigger ones. There are several new structures, including the library and a huge mess hall." He pointed to an elegant, tree-shaded mansion set off by itself. "You'll recognize the superintendent's house. It's the same as always."

Bob pointed in another direction. "See that statue of General MacArthur? There's also one of General Patton by the library. I'll point him out when we pass. Look there." He indicated a massive brick building down the hill to the left. "That's Eisenhower Hall, an activity center for cadets."

The sedan wound around a wide parade field bounded by monuments. Then, turning onto Thayer Road, it rolled between barracks and academic buildings. Cadets in class uniform, faces clean-shaven and serious, scurried in all directions on both sides of the car. Recalling his own days of studious activity, Atcho smiled.

As promised, Bob pointed out the bronze statue of "Blood-'n'-Guts" Patton directly across from the library. The car continued beyond the buildings, past more residences overlooking another segment of the Hudson, toward the gate leading into Highland Falls. Just inside the portal was their destination, the Thayer Hotel.

Bob parked the car across from the entrance of the old Gothic structure, and the trio walked into the lobby. Atcho observed the ornate furnishings and fine block paneling in the lobby. Then, he checked in at the desk. "Your luggage is already on its way up to your room," Bob told him. "If you don't mind, we're going to settle in at my friend's house. We'll come back for you in an hour."

Atcho kissed Isabel's cheek. Welling with pride, he watched the couple exit through the front door. An hour later, showered and smartly outfitted in dark slacks and a tweed jacket, he met Bob and Isabel in the hotel lobby.

The elegant restaurant at the far end was subdued. Soothing piano music played in the background and Atcho remembered how much he had enjoyed sparkling crystal, polished silver, and luxurious dining.

He noted that Isabel seemed fidgety but decided he was being overly sensitive. The day had been active, and she was probably tired. After dinner, they sat back to wait for coffee. Atcho enjoyed the soft music, and his doting gaze took in his lovely daughter.

Isabel dropped her eyes and glanced at Bob, who gave a slight nod.

Isabel began. "We have something to tell you. We didn't mention it before, because we didn't want to spoil things."

Atcho's heart sank. *I knew this couldn't last.* "What can be so bad?"

"We're being transferred," Isabel said. "I'm sorry. When Bob chose his first assignment, we didn't know you existed. So, he picked Germany. We're leaving right after New Year's." Isabel eyes brimmed with tears.

Atcho's reflexes jerked as though he had been shot. His face went white.

"I'm sorry," Isabel persisted. "Please don't be upset. We would love for you to come with us, but regulations controlling refugees won't allow that."

Atcho felt hot. He reached for a glass of water. As he did, he caught a glimpse of his son-in-law's face. Bob studied him with a curious expression.

"We'll be in Germany three years," Isabel went on. "You can't come because you have to stay in the United States or lose your refugee status. Please understand." She wiped her mouth with a napkin. "We'll come home every chance we get."

Feeling Bob's intense scrutiny, Atcho spoke brusquely. "I understand. You caught me by surprise. I'll be fine. Let's enjoy the evening. There's so much I want to know about you."

"Me too. I don't want to lose you again."

"You won't. New Year's is a ways off. Lots of time to get to know each other."

They lingered over dinner, listened to the music, and engaged in light banter. Bob was interested to know details about the Bay of Pigs but had enough sense not to make that a major topic of this conversation. "But, you're gonna tell me sometime." He laughed with a broad grin.

Atcho arrived in his room just past nine o'clock. He stood at the window looking over the Hudson River. Despite the news about Bob and Isabel, he enjoyed the sound of the passing water, and slowly, the taste of yet another disappointment left his mouth.

Nevertheless, he slept fitfully. He dreamed he was back in Russia trying to smash through the dark, invincible glass to confront the faceless, menacing general.

"Govorov," he shouted. His own voice awakened him. Bathed in sweat, he slowly realized that he was at the Thayer Hotel at West Point, in New York, in the United States of America.

Once more, he was astonished that, after nearly twenty years in prison, he was free. *Not free,* he corrected himself. *Only the bars are gone.*

The phone rang early the next morning. Isabel greeted him. "We let you sleep late, but we want you to have lunch with us on the other side of the river, upstream from Poughkeepsie. It's one of our favorite places. Bob proposed to me there."

"What time is it?" Atcho's voice was gruff, both from sleep, and because a lump still formed in his throat whenever he spoke with daughter. He still could not believe that she was nearby, talking to him, and wanting to be with him.

"Just past nine."

Sunlight streamed through his sixth-floor window overlooking cliffs above the Hudson. "I want to jog through West Point. Is noon a good time?"

"Great," she enthused. "We'll pick you up at twelve thirty in the hotel lobby."

A few more words passed between them, then Atcho hung up. The phone rang again. Thinking Isabel might have called back, he softened his tone when he answered.

The desk clerk had called. "Sir, we have a special delivery letter requiring your signature. The courier is on his way up."

"Special delivery?" Atcho was surprised. "Very well. Thank you."

A few minutes later, Atcho closed the door behind the courier and slit the envelope open. He froze when he read the black words in bold relief against pale ivory parchment:

Atcho, don't forget why you are here.
Your friend, General Govorov.

"You son of a bitch," Atcho bellowed. "Couldn't you leave me alone long enough to enjoy my daughter before she leaves for Germany?"

He threw the note onto the antique desk and crossed to the matching dresser, pulled open several drawers, and rummaged until he found a wool warm-up suit Isabel had bought for him. Then he looked in the closet for the new pair of running shoes. He changed quickly.

On his way out the door, he flashed by a mirror and stopped to consider his appearance. His hair was still jet-black but with streaks of gray, trimmed to its former refinement. Age and deprivation had sharpened the lines of his features. His frame was thin from the four weeks in *La Cabaña*, but his muscles were hard, and his chest conditioned from training at the dacha outside Moscow. Still, he looked like what he was—a man recently released from dungeons.

He grimaced, resolving to rebuild and stay in good physical shape.

Five minutes later, he left the hotel and began his run. He had become accustomed to exercise in Russia, but the lack of it while imprisoned this past month had made him lethargic.

Though sunshine had streamed through his hotel window, ground fog hung in pockets in the hills and valleys. Trees blazed with gold, yellow, and the russet colors of autumn. The cool October air felt enlivened, taking off the edge of Govorov's note.

Pushing thoughts of Govorov from his mind, he expanded his lungs, appreciating exertion in a way he had not known in twenty years. He headed along Thayer Road, stretching his legs and exulting in his body's response to strenuous demands.

The sound of the river caught his ear. At the first intersection, he turned onto a road that angled downhill to his right and jogged toward the river. Pockets of mist hovered over the surging Hudson.

The ground leveled out, and Atcho ran parallel to the waterway, now coursing on the other side of a wide field. Ahead was a long, low building he recognized as the old train depot. He sprinted the last yards to reach it.

It was a typical station from times long past. Before the advent of automobiles and buses, it had been West Point's main transportation terminal. A canopy hung over the long, narrow platform. A glass-paneled door led into the main lobby. Trains had long since ceased to stop here, but the depot, now obsolete, evoked reverence.

Atcho imagined thousands of cadets who had passed through this quaint place during the academy's long history. He remembered newsreels of young graduates, commissioned early to fill manpower requirements for World War II. The film clips had been taken at this very spot as young officers loaded onto trains amidst a celebratory send-off by the remaining Corps of Cadets. Similar scenes had taken place during the First World War, and probably the Civil War.

He peered through the windows at tables and chairs spaced around the interior. From the looks of it, the old station was now used for cadet parties and other functions.

Recalling the revelry of his youth, he sighed. Sitting on a bench on the platform, he pictured great generals and presidents—Grant, Lee, Eisenhower, Patton, MacArthur—arriving here as young men. They too, must have been full of energy, high ideals and matching ambitions. Atcho wondered how often, during their illustrious careers, they had been compelled to compromise principles, and how they had reconciled such departures with their consciences.

A passing runner called to him. Aware that several joggers had gone by while he explored the depot, Atcho returned the greeting. *How great it feels to be able to move around freely and be alone.*

Startled at his own sentiment, he realized that the last time he had been alone was during the hours before his capture at the Bay of Pigs. He contemplated his own definition of "alone." Certainly, he had spent time alone in the box on the Isle of Pines and in isolation at *La Cabaña*. However, sitting in front of the old station, he felt a sense of solitude that, despite the frequent passing of joggers, was both liberating and comforting. *The difference is that I want to be here.*

Remembering that West Point had also been the site of Benedict Arnold's treachery, Atcho wondered how his classmates, the alumni association, and Isabel would react if they knew about his own double life.

Suddenly melancholy, he rose to his feet and jogged toward a set of tennis courts. He veered right and walked until he found a bench on the bank of the flowing Hudson River. For several moments, he stared into the dark water while mists dissipated. They seemed like ghosts, dancing in slow rhythm with images of what could have been. This was the place where he had proposed to Isabel's mother.

Slowly, Atcho stood, turned away from the river and jogged to the road. It climbed steeply toward the academic complex. Expanding his lungs for more oxygen, he pushed to a harder pace.

He reached the level of the parade field and found himself near the library. Crossing the street, he approached the tall statue of General Patton standing silent vigil over West Point and all the precepts that made it a venerated place.

He touched the base of the statue. Strong chords of an old West Point song sounded through his mind:

The long gray line of us stretches,
Through the years of a century told,
And the last man feels to his marrow,
The grip of your far-off hold.

Imagining a file of proud figures in gray uniforms, with faces offering hope and encouragement, he glanced again at General Patton's bronzed, battle-hardened visage.

"I'll do my best," he muttered. Then he walked across the street and entered the library. A glass case hung near the checkout desk. Atcho studied the collection of class rings displayed inside, recalling that the tradition of wearing them had begun at West Point. Then he ambled to a corner where yearbooks and graduate directories were kept.

Selecting the most up-to-date volume, Atcho flipped through it until he located his father's name. Turning to the page indicated, he found a biographical sketch. With fond memory, he read the four-line description of his father's service record in Europe. Then he looked up his own name and read that Eduardo Xiquez had died in a fire in 1960.

He sighed and replaced the directory, then rummaged until he found the yearbook for his graduating class. He searched its pages for photos of his former company, smiled to see his own young face grinning out of the page, and continued perusing the book.

He turned to the section on sports. West Point had been a football powerhouse in those days, and the undefeated season, captured on film, reflected the dominance of the team. He turned another page, noting with amusement a photograph of himself in soccer uniform. He was in midair, right leg extended, the blur of a ball being driven off his foot between two goalposts. The caption made him laugh. "ATCHO SCORES!"

That was the Princeton game. In his mind, Atcho heard again the call of spectators chanting his name to urge him on. He scrutinized their faces, trying to match them with fading memories

Only one face looked familiar, but he could not place a name to it. Then he realized that the photo showed only the attendees from the Princeton side.

Glancing at his watch, he decided he should start back to the hotel.

The letter from Govorov rose in his mind again. *He spent years setting me up for this. He won't let me feel independent now.*

24

Atcho spent the next few days with Isabel and Bob attending homecoming festivities. There, he became reacquainted with former classmates and friends.

He found his old Texas roommate, Mike Rogers, and learned that he had left the Army and occupied a senior position in the Secret Service. "Somehow I'm not surprised," Atcho told him, alert to the prospect of enlisting Mike's help. "You always were circumspect about everyone."

A number of graduates had read or seen news accounts of Atcho's plight in Cuba and made a point to seek him out to welcome him home, genuinely pleased to see him. They offered whatever help might be useful to settle into his new life.

The levels of distinction his classmates had attained amazed Atcho. Among them were a few generals, many colonels, and more lieutenant colonels. A number had resigned earlier in their careers or had recently retired. Some had transferred into other military branches or government agencies.

Among civilian members were congressmen, presidents and senior executives of major companies, entrepreneurs, attorneys, doctors, engineers, and various other professions. They worked in industries as diverse as paper manufacturing and defense contracting.

Several classmates expressed a desire to help him find work and asked to be contacted when he was settled. Although grateful for the concern, Atcho felt growing unease as he sensed Govorov's plan beginning to work.

Relishing the camaraderie he had missed for so many years, he was determined to enjoy the festivities. He marched in the parade honoring the oldest living West Point graduate and attended the football game with the same thrill he had known as a cadet.

On Saturday evening, Bob and Isabel drove him to Washington Hall for the homecoming ball. Atcho was excited. He had seen the new mess hall flanked by granite barracks only from a distance and was eager to view the interior.

Bob escorted him to various points of interest before they located their seats. Then, since they had arrived early, they walked about and mingled with old friends, classmates, and members of Bob's class. "There's someone you'd probably like to see," Bob said, leading the way. Atcho followed absently, caught up in his surroundings. People called to him and he greeted them cordially.

Soon, they rounded a corner and stopped at one of the tables. Bob stood talking to a tall Air Force colonel. The officer looked familiar, but so did most people by this time, so Atcho paid little attention.

A voice behind him greeted, "Atcho, it's good to see you."

Atcho turned.

The colonel stood before him, hand extended. "You might not remember me. I'm Paul Clary. You knew me as Lieutenant Clary."

Momentarily bewildered, Atcho studied the man's face. "Colonel Clary," he said at last, shaking the proffered hand. "I didn't know you were an academy graduate."

Clary laughed easily. "I'm not. I'm on the faculty here, so I'm invited to some of these events."

"He's being modest," Bob cut in. "He teaches national security affairs, and the powers that be in Washington keep him on tap to advise on arms control."

Trying to remember why he had so mistrusted Clary in Havana, Atcho regarded him with increased respect. *I must have been paranoid.*

Clary was still stoop-shouldered, his face lined with middle age, but the intelligence that Juan had observed was there in his amiable eyes. "I owe you an apology for the way I treated you."

"Forget it. That was a long time ago. We were both in difficult situations. As you said then, under similar circumstances, I might have done the same thing."

They shook hands again. "How do you know my son-in-law?" Atcho asked.

Clary clapped an arm around Bob's shoulder. "He was one of my star students last year. Isabel told him that you tried calling her from Havana last April. At the time, we studied the effectiveness of freedom-fighter movements in third world countries. Bob mentioned you in class. We saw news reports about your release, and I figured you were the guy who kept me overnight in Cuba. When I heard you were coming here, I asked Bob to get us together."

He turned to Isabel. "Your father was determined to find you." He chuckled. "He was ready to take on Castro, the United States, and the Soviet Union to get you back." He looked somberly at Atcho. "I'm glad you two are finally together."

Isabel stepped closer to her father and slipped an arm around his waist. Atcho felt a lump in his throat.

Just then, the commandant of cadets addressed the guests over the PA system, requesting them to take their seats.

"I'm pleased to see you again under better circumstances," Clary told Atcho.

"My pleasure," Atcho said, grasping his extended hand. *I wonder what you'd think if you knew the rest of the story.* He returned to his table with Bob and Isabel.

Throughout the banquet, Mike Rogers sat next to Atcho, while Isabel sat on his opposite side, next to Bob. Other dinner companions were men Atcho had known, and their wives. The wine was excellent, the food satisfying, and the music relaxing.

During announcements, the commandant introduced Atcho. "We've read stories in the news, and we don't want to embarrass him or upstage our speaker, so we'll just wish Eduardo—now better known as Atcho—a warm welcome."

The guests clapped, and Atcho stood to acknowledge them. The people at his table rose, and the same occurred at the next table, and then the surrounding tables. Soon, everyone in Washington Hall gave him a thunderous standing ovation.

Atcho felt humbled. He only hoped that his smile looked like that of a man thrilled at being released from abysmal conditions after two decades. He waved, turned to acknowledge in all directions, and sat down. Isabel squeezed his arm.

"We're all proud of you," Mike Rogers said. The other guests at the table smiled at him. He did his best to return a suitable expression. *If they only knew.*

The keynote speaker was the commanding general of the 82ND Airborne Division. He was a contemporary of Atcho's, though not a classmate. He also lauded Atcho and then launched into a speech about future force structure.

When he had finished, music played again, and Atcho danced with Isabel and the wives of his classmates. They lingered late into the night, enjoying the atmosphere of elegance and charm permeating the grand dining hall.

All through the evening, classmates and well-wishers sought out Atcho. "If you're looking for work, I have no doubt we can use you," one told him. "We're a defense contractor, one of the largest."

Another said, "Hey, have you decided where you'll settle yet? We could sure benefit from your knowledge of Latin America."

Yet a third said, "I own one of the largest real estate management companies in Washington, DC. If you don't mind living in that chaotic mess, we could make it both challenging and rewarding."

Atcho lost count of the offers. He accepted the business cards and expressed genuine gratitude to the people for their consideration.

Long after midnight, he went to his room at the Thayer Hotel, showered, and crawled into bed. With memories of two satisfying days drifting through his mind, he fell asleep.

An hour later, the harsh ringing of the phone awakened him. Half-asleep, he reached for the receiver and cradled it against his ear. "Hello."

"Atcho." The raspy voice crooned.

"Govorov." Atcho jerked awake, his nerves tensed like steel fibers. "What do you want?"

"I'm calling to make sure you're comfortable. Are you settling in all right?"

Atcho swung his legs to the floor, glaring viciously through darkness at the telephone. "Didn't you think your note was enough?"

Govorov chuckled. "It arrived. You know, with the mail system the way it is, I was afraid it might not reach you."

"Have you decided what I'm supposed to do?"

"No, no, no. This is much too soon." Govorov assumed his jocular tone. "First I want to say how pleased I am that you are having such a good time. Truly, I am. I understand that the run by the train station is one of the more pleasant routes."

In stunned silence, Atcho recalled his celebration of being alone.

Govorov continued. "I hear that various employment opportunities came your way. I want to discuss them with you before too much time passes. Atcho, are you there?"

"I'm here." His mind spun.

"I think you should take the real estate opportunity in Washington. The company owned by your classmate has an excellent reputation."

In an instant, Atcho decided that he would object to everything Govorov said and acquiesce only when he had no choice. "I don't know anything about real estate."

"You've been out of the mainstream a long time," the general said in his mocking voice. "What do you know about anything?"

"I don't want to live in Washington."

"As I was saying," Govorov interrupted. "The company is a good one. The contacts are superb. You'd be at the center of influence and power, meeting people you'll need to know."

"Wouldn't you rather have me with one of the defense contractors?"

"That's too technical, and too obvious," the general snapped impatiently. "We have most of the defense establishment covered already. We want you in a position that has flexibility, and where you can rise. For the time being, I think the real estate job suits our requirements ideally. We can move you later if we need to."

"You don't leave me much room, do you?"

"What are you saying? You're out of prison, in a free country, preparing to enter a career that will be financially rewarding. With Isabel leaving for Europe—"

"Did you do that?" Atcho growled.

"We knew about it, of course," Govorov said, without answering the question. "But we didn't want to spoil your reception.

"I don't have time for chitchat. You'll return home with Isabel and Bob and stay there until they leave in January. Meanwhile, you'll accept your classmate's real estate offer. For the sake of appearances, wait a few weeks, and bargain with him over salary. But be ready to move to Washington after Isabel leaves. I'll talk to you when you're settled." Govorov paused. "One more thing." His tone became menacing. "You've already made good contacts. Be careful how you develop them. I'll be keenly interested in your activities."

Atcho heard a *click* and a dial tone. Strangely, he felt no emotion. Walking to the window, he stared into the night. Stars shone bright in a cloudless sky, and a new moon made its appearance low on the horizon. Occasionally, headlights followed the river road and disappeared around a bend.

West Point, tucked in the hills Atcho knew so well, seemed peacefully asleep. But somewhere beyond his window, a watcher knew his every move. That had been inevitable. There was no other way to keep him trapped in this hellish web.

He stared into the street below, recalling the face of each person he had spoken with during the past two days. Several stood out in his mind, including Mike Rogers, Paul Clary, and the man who offered the real estate job. But, how could they have known about his jogging trip past the train station? How could Mike Rogers or Paul Clary know about the job offer?

He walked slowly to the bed and sat down. He was alone. His first urge was to expose all that had been done to him these past twenty years. He could tell authorities of Govorov's tentacles, reaching to the highest places in American government. Mike Rogers would be a good place to start. Atcho could tell him of his own KGB recruitment, and the threat to Isabel. Surely the US government could stop Govorov's activities.

Atcho knew better. He had no proof, and given his long periods of confinement, his own mental stability would fall into question. At the extreme, he could be deported. Worse yet, Govorov could carry out his threat to kill Isabel and Bob's family. Until he devised a viable plan, identified a source of allies, or found a way to guarantee Isabel's safety, he would have to bend to Govorov's will.

In darkness, Atcho raised his fist and stared at the moon. "I'll bide my time," he muttered, "but I'll push back at every step, and somehow, someday, Govorov, I'll put you away."

25

SEVEN YEARS LATER, WASHINGTON, DC, JANUARY 1987

"No," Atcho said adamantly. "I've been in this country seven years. Why the sudden popularity?" While his classmate, an aide to the president's national security advisor, spoke rapidly over the phone, Atcho looked through his window at trees bending before a blustery wind. Then he spoke again. "I'm privileged that President Reagan would consider honoring me in his State of the Union address, but I could not accept. I don't deserve it, but thanks for thinking of me." He hung up, shaken.

In the predawn hours of the following morning, Atcho's telephone rang, its harsh sound jarring him from deep sleep. His nerves tightened even before he heard the steely voice at the other end of the line. This was the normal hour for Govorov's calls. The general had telephoned periodically over the years to "develop and maintain their relationship."

"Atcho."

"What do you want? Are you finally going to make a traitor of me?"

"Why do you describe things in such dramatic terms? You know I always have your best interest at heart. You've prospered as a result of our association."

"Get to the point, Govorov."

"It's General Govorov to you. I hear you declined an opportunity that could provide a quantum leap in your development. I want you to change your mind."

"I don't know what you're talking about."

"Don't play games. We both know about your classmate's suggestion. The potential benefits are great for both of us."

"I don't want to do it, and the president will never pick me."

"There are no guarantees," the general said reasonably. "Your classmate is going to ask you again to allow your nomination. I want you to accept."

"No."

"That's not a request. I don't tolerate disobedience." His laugh taunted. "I've become fond of you and Isabel." His tone turned steely. "But I will not hesitate to carry out my promises should you fail to follow instructions. Do you have any questions?"

Atcho sat in stony silence for a moment. "Why do we never speak face-to-face? And how did you connect Atcho and Eduardo in the first place?"

The general chuckled. "You always ask the same things. Goodbye."

26

"Ladies and gentlemen, the President of the United States."

At the sonorous announcement, Atcho rose to his feet with the crowd. From his position on the chamber balcony in the House of Representatives, he could not see the president shaking hands with members of the House and Senate and other dignitaries clustered about the door but knew he would make his way down the carpeted aisle, stopping to greet loyal followers and distinguished members of the opposition until he reached the imposing dais at the front of the room.

A stir in the crowd below caught Atcho's attention. Ronald Reagan had come into view and moved down the aisle toward the rostrum. He waved to the crowd, beaming with the smile that had won adulation from his countrymen.

Atcho regarded the president with affection. He had met him earlier that evening at a White House reception, and was amazed at how his warmth, so apparent in person, could pervade a crowd as large as this.

The "Gipper" took his seat. The speaker of the House rose to quell the applause and allow everyone to be seated. To Atcho's left, Isabel took her seat next to Bob. The elegantly dressed First Lady, looking much younger than her years, sat on Atcho's right.

She smiled at him. "Are you nervous?"

"I just don't think I deserve this recognition."

"Don't fight it. A lot of people think you do, including my husband."

The speaker finished his comments. Amid applause, the president took the podium. After appropriate greetings, he looked directly into the cameras. Then, with the twinkling eyes and familiar voice that made him famous, he addressed his audience.

"In a few minutes, I'm going to talk about the federal budget, expound on concerns regarding defense, and explain a plan for social programs.

"First, we've come to my favorite part of the evening." He smiled as if enjoying his own private joke before sharing it with his listeners. The technique had endeared him to millions. "I always like to recognize ordinary citizens who, through acts of courage, or by extraordinary dedication, achieve a level of accomplishment distinguishing them as true American heroes."

He reviewed names he had introduced in previous years, and then continued. "Most people might not know of our exchange program bringing foreign cadets to study at our military service academies. The program has existed for decades and created many long-lasting friendships for our country.

"Tonight, we are fortunate to have with us a man who first visited the United States as a participant in that program. His father attended West Point during the mid-thirties and distinguished himself as a member of our armed forces in the war against the Nazis. Years later, the son followed him to West Point.

"After graduating from the academy, the son returned home to Cuba, and within five years found himself leading freedom fighters against Fidel Castro's Communist regime. His daughter was kidnapped before the Bay of Pigs invasion and returned to her aunt after he was reported killed in action."

For the next few minutes, the president extolled Atcho's heroism. He spoke of his efforts to organize the resistance, related the episode with the tank, and reviewed the dark days of prison.

This makes a good story. If they only knew the truth.

"Since his release from Castro's dungeons," the president continued, "he's lived in Washington and built a real estate management company that enjoys one of the best reputations in the area. And, last year, before the vice president, he took the oath to become an American citizen."

The room erupted in applause. The president waited it out and went on. "His friends and family call him simply Atcho. Ladies and gentlemen, I present to you a real American hero, Mr. Eduardo Xiquez Rodriguez de Arciniega." The president gestured in Atcho's direction, and the assembly jumped to a thundering standing ovation.

Atcho rose to his feet and bowed. Television cameras zoomed in, beaming his picture to the nation. *Govorov, you had your way.*

The First Lady kissed his cheek and the roar of applause grew louder. Atcho turned to embrace Isabel. She tolerated his embrace and kissed him dutifully but remained rigid.

He was not surprised at his daughter's lack of warmth. For reasons he could not fathom, she had been distant since her return from Germany four years ago.

The audience sat back down, and the president launched into his speech. When he had finished and while the crowd applauded, the First Lady's Secret Service detail escorted her away.

Minutes later, Atcho stood below the great dome of the capitol rotunda. The size of the structure and the elegant artwork on its massive, arched sides awed him.

A friendly crowd jostled him, stopping to shake his hand. Bob and Isabel stood near one of the columns conversing with well-wishers.

A stout man in his sixties spoke animatedly to Bob and Isabel, but before Atcho reached the trio he hurried away. Atcho was sure they had met before but could not place where.

Bob tugged his arm. "C'mon. I told friends we'd meet for drinks."

"Who was that man talking to you?" Atcho asked.

"Some guy who wanted to say how much he admired you. He would have told you himself, but there were too many people around you."

Atcho accepted the answer dubiously and followed Bob and Isabel through the crowd. They reached the car parked in a nearby lot, and negotiated through traffic Thirty minutes later, they left the sedan with a valet in front of a fashionable hotel.

As they walked through the lobby, Atcho was startled to see the man he had seen speaking with Bob rise from a chair and move quickly out of sight. Atcho was more surprised when Bob led through a door into a dark room. He heard rustling and felt the presence of unseen people. Suddenly, the lights flicked on, party horns blew, and a ring of faces beamed at Atcho, while a chorus of voices yelled, "Surprise!"

He looked around in amazement. Most of the faces seemed familiar, but many he did not recognize. Then, his gaze rested on someone he could not forget: Francisco, the fellow former prisoner he had befriended on the Isle of Pines, the man who had helped him keep track of Isabel while she was still in Camaguey.

He bearhugged his old friend. Then a voice caused him to turn around. "Remember me?"

Atcho recognized the man who had hurried out of the hotel lobby. "Burly?" Atcho gasped in disbelief.

Burly stepped forward, grinning. "That's right, you snot-nosed kid."

Remembering the meeting at Jaguey Grande, Atcho chuckled. "What is all this?" He glanced about.

"A reception in your honor. Look around. A lot of people came to see you. These are former Brigade 2506 members, leaders of the resistance group that met with us in Jaguey Grande, and people you knew in prison. We even tracked down the secretary who helped you call Isabel from Havana."

Atcho's heart skipped as he caught sight of Sofia Stahl standing nearby. She blushed but maintained composure. As on the first day they met, her soft smile radiated friendliness. He walked over to her. "I never thanked you properly," he stammered.

"You did." Sofia held out her hand.

Atcho grasped it, absorbed in her brilliant green eyes. A tingling sensation swept through him. Embarrassed, he turned to regard the rest of the group.

A jocular man of above medium height approached. "You won't recognize my face," he said. "We were together for a short time in the middle of the night, but you might remember me anyway. I am Rafael Poncé. We met in the swamp when you delivered the tank to me."

Atcho regarded him enthusiastically and pumped his hand. "Of course. I remember you and your Jeep driver. Whatever became of him?"

"Toothless?" Rafael laughed. "He said you called him that. He's here, and he remembers you."

Atcho looked where Rafael pointed. A very old man sat in a wheelchair. His deep wrinkles could not mask the eyes shining from behind their folds, nor a smile that broke across his face.

Atcho went to kneel beside the wheelchair and placed an arm around Toothless' shoulder. The old man clasped Atcho's hand. "I knew it was you," he rasped with glee. "I knew you were Atcho." His face became serious. "I never told anyone." He grinned again, and pointed at his mouth, "Look," he beamed, "I have teeth."

Recalling the man's compassion when relating Juan's death, a lump formed in Atcho's throat. His eyes misted. As emotion overtook him, he hugged Toothless.

Mercifully, Burly broke the tension. "Bar's open," he announced. A band broke into lively rhythms of Latin music.

Atcho stood up. "It's good to see you," he said. The old man nodded contentedly.

"We're proud of you," Burly said. "The way you handled yourself in the fight, how you bore up in prison, and what you've made of yourself since your release. We figured if the president of the United States could honor you publicly, we could do it privately."

"Thank you," Atcho whispered. That was all he could manage.

Bob approached and embraced him. "I'm glad you're my father-in-law. You're a wonderful example of how to live life."

A rare wave of pride caught Atcho's throat. He acknowledged Bob and looked around for Isabel. She stood by the bar, drink in hand, watching with a strange expression. Other well-wishers closed around Atcho, clapping him on the back and shaking his hand. He accepted their compliments, and then watched as people moved onto the dance floor.

Burly stood next to him. "You were right, you know."

"What about?"

"President Kennedy's support for the Bay of Pigs. Privately, he never liked the idea because of the probable impact on world peace. He made clear that he would not support the invasion."

"I know. I studied the record. Khrushchev threatened retaliation in Berlin if the United States participated in the action. Mr. Kennedy issued instructions that American personnel were not to land in Cuba."

Burly nodded sadly. "I'm sorry, Atcho. I feel like I personally helped mislead your people."

Atcho grasped Burly's shoulder. "If others in the CIA had cared as much as you, resources and planning might have been better, or the whole thing might have been called off earlier. I understand that one top man decided to go through with the it, lawful authority be damned. He had instructions issued to Brigade 2506 leaders in Guatemala to arrest their American trainers if a presidential order cancelled the invasion."

"That's true," Burly agreed. "But in the field, we didn't know the controversy existed. So far as we knew, the operation was a go as planned."

"The planning wasn't good, and the related tragedy was Kennedy's agreement with Khrushchev a year later. After the Cuban missile crisis, Khrushchev pledged to pull missiles out of Cuba if the US promised to stop supporting anti-Castro rebels. That made the United States the *de facto* guarantor of Castro's power." He sighed. "Between you and me, Kennedy blinked."

They let the statement ride.

They observed the guests on the dance floor, and then Atcho continued. "Burly, I thought about you a lot over the years. I have only respect for you. Thanks for trying." They shook hands and chatted a while longer. After exchanging business cards, they parted to mingle.

Rafael introduced his wife to Atcho. "I wish I had known you were interested in real estate," he said. "I would have asked you to join my business in Miami."

"I didn't actually go into real estate," Atcho answered. "The business found me. A classmate offered a job here in Washington. Then I was able to buy another company."

"Well, your reputation is tremendous. From what I hear, you own or manage some prime pieces of property around the city."

"I've been lucky." Atcho put on his most sincere smile and hoped the irony in his voice was not obvious. *What would you think if you knew who financed my business?*

"Maybe we can joint venture a project sometime," Rafael said. "I feel as though we are destined to do something together."

"I'd enjoy that. Stay in touch. If I hear of something, I'll let you know. You do the same." They exchanged business cards.

Atcho looked around for Isabel. She danced with Bob. Their affection cast a magical aura. *What a beautiful picture.* The thought brought nostalgia for romantic evenings he had spent with Isabel's mother.

"Mr. Xiquez, it's so nice to see you again." Atcho's heart skipped a beat as he recognized Sofia's voice.

"Thank you for coming," he replied, unable to think of anything else to say. He stared, taking in her lustrous hair and smooth skin. Then, he caught himself. "Would you like to dance?"

"I thought you'd never ask."

As they moved onto the floor, Atcho was entranced. Sofia wore an elegant black gown that shimmered in the soft light, silhouetting her lovely figure. When they danced Atcho felt lighthearted in a way he had not known in many years. He wished the evening could go on and on.

Feeling someone staring at him, he turned in time to meet Isabel's eyes. She stood by the bar holding a fresh drink and looked away quickly. Bob was out of sight. "Sofia, have you ever met my daughter, Isabel?"

"No, but I'd love to. She must be very special to have such a dedicated father." They moved through the crowd.

Isabel saw them coming and set her glass down. Her mouth formed a perfunctory smile.

"Isabel. I'd like you to meet Sofia. She found you while I was at the Swiss Embassy in Havana."

Sofia smiled warmly. "Your father was very anxious to locate you." She extended her hand.

Isabel took it dutifully. "Thank you for your help." She leaned on the bar and grasped her drink. "What do you think of our hero?" Sarcasm tinged her voice.

Sofia glanced uneasily from Isabel to Atcho. "I think he's someone to be very proud of," she said gently.

Isabel snickered. "Maybe you're right. Would you excuse me? I need fresh air."

Startled, Atcho watched her go. Then he faced Sofia. "I'm sorry."

She looked at him questioningly. "Is there a problem?"

Atcho sighed. "She's angry with me, but I don't know why. She's been aloof since she returned from Germany four years ago, but she's never been deliberately rude before. Would you mind if I went to talk with her?"

"Of course not. I know how you love your daughter."

Atcho pushed after Isabel, slowed by people who wished to speak to him. When he reached the edge of the crowd, Isabel was nowhere to be seen.

Along a wall lined with full-length windows, a door stood open and a breeze ruffled the drapes. Atcho walked over and looked outside. Isabel stood on the other end of a terrace, her back to the door. The full moon looked down, expressionless.

Atcho crossed the terrace quietly. He heard her crying softly. "Isabel, what is it?" He embraced her.

"Don't." Isabel gasped through sobs. She pulled away brusquely.

Stung, Atcho stood rooted to the terrace floor. "Did I do something to upset you?"

Isabel made no reply. "Please, Isabel. If I have done something, tell me. I love you. There is no one in this world who means so much to me."

"Oh, really." Isabel whirled on him, her eyes squinted in rage. "Is that why you stayed in Cuba while I was sent over here?"

In shock, Atcho took a step backward. "I had to—"

"I know. You had to stay and fight for the country." Isabel was sarcastic. "Well, you lost. Meanwhile, all those who didn't stay brought their families out and lived normal lives. Their children had fathers to love and care for them." She paused to catch her breath. "Even Brigade 2506 members came out after fighting for their country." She spoke in uncontrolled gasps. "Do you know what I had?"

Fury broke across her face. "An aunt who loved me but an uncle who loathed me. He never let me forget that I was not his daughter and blamed me for every difficulty they had." Agony laced her voice. "I used to cry myself to sleep thinking that if I had a daddy, he would love me and hug me and make all bad things go away."

Atcho moved close to Isabel. "I'm sorry. I didn't know."

"I used to have nightmares about a man lying in the dirt with blood all over him. He stared at me, and he had a knife in his hand. I always thought he was going to kill me. Years later, my aunt told me that was you. That was my first and only memory of you until I saw you in the Miami airport."

She pulled a handkerchief from her purse while Atcho stood in silence. "Neighbors referred to me as 'poor Isabel.' Kids called me an orphan. My uncle always told me I was lucky to be with him and Aunt Raissa."

Her voice was steadier, but still marked by fierce anger. "I knew that a good education was my only hope for a better life, so I worked hard in school. But kids who didn't like Cuban refugees taunted me. Somehow, I earned a partial scholarship to Mt. Saint Mary's. Even then, I had to take out student loans and work to pay tuition. Someone had set up a trust fund for me, but it wasn't enough." She wiped more tears away.

"My aunt Raissa was the one person in this world who loved me. I wanted to die when she was killed." She sobbed softly. "I met Bob about six months later. He made life worthwhile again, and even helped pay tuition in my senior year. There was just nowhere else to turn for money." She calmed down and stared into the darkness.

"Why didn't you tell me any of this before?"

"Why didn't you ever ask? I inquired all about what happened in Cuba." Her tone was laced with bitterness. "You gave me elusive answers. You're hiding something." She faced him. "Either that, or you're a coward, worried about saving your own skin."

Atcho reeled under the onslaught.

Isabel whirled angrily. "I still don't understand why you kept your identity hidden all those years." Fresh tears ran down her cheeks as her voice took on new fury. "Why were you fighting at the Bay of Pigs while I was still in the hands of kidnappers?" Eyes aflame with accusation, she faced her father. "I accepted your explanations all these years. I even refrained from telling you about the baby we lost in Germany because I didn't want to add to your pain."

Atcho's head jerked up. "You lost a baby?" he whispered.

"Yes. And I might never be able to have another one. I had a late miscarriage. We didn't tell you because you couldn't come to Germany anyway." She paused again, breathing hard, and wiped the tears from her face.

"Tonight," she continued, her voice acquiring a hard edge, "I listened to the president and all those people talk about what a great hero you are. Well, Hero, when are you ever going to be around for your family?"

Numbly, Atcho stared into the night. Behind them, Bob called through the door, "I found you two. Is everything all right?" He advanced across the terrace.

Eyes furious, Isabel glared at Atcho. "I was happier thinking you were dead," she whispered and ran past Bob into the ballroom

Atcho watched her go and turned back toward the railing, feeling broken.

Behind him, Bob approached. "I'm sorry, Atcho. I saw this coming. I should have warned you." He grasped Atcho's shoulder. "We've had lots of discussion on this subject, and our opinions differ. I hope she doesn't resent my combat in Grenada. Doesn't seem to. And if you'd won in Cuba, she might see things differently." He waited, but receiving no reply, he continued. "She's a wonderful woman, but she hurts. I hope her pain passes with time. Meanwhile, you're always welcome in our home."

"Thanks," Atcho managed through trembling lips.

"Are you ready to leave?" Bob asked.

Atcho shook his head. "I'll find my own way home."

Bob nodded. "I'd better find Isabel. I'm sorry your evening was spoiled."

Atcho heard Bob's footsteps trail away. Every emotion he had ever experienced churned within. Rage, hatred, sorrow, and all their mutations moved in counterpoint against an overwhelming sense of failure.

Standing alone in the ring of cold moonlight, his shadow cast a dark specter across the white marble floor. As strains of music floated through the crisp night air, he stared into blackness.

For the last four years, Isabel's aloofness had separated them. Although saddened by the situation, Atcho accepted it as necessary in order to protect her life. *I never saw this coming.* He ached to think of her as a child, crying herself to sleep. He felt the loneliness and despair she must have known when Raissa died. Thinking of his sister, he cursed his dead brother-in-law for adding to Isabel's misery.

Recognizing the worth Bob had added back into Isabel's life, his affection and regard for his son-in-law grew.

And he grieved for the loss of his grandchild. Isabel's words rang through his mind: *When are you ever going to be around to do something for your family?*

He felt very old, staring at the bright, impassive moon. "You've been there for every scene of this tragedy. Could I have done things differently? Does it matter now?" He shrugged. "I'll finish the fight, and then see if life is still worth living."

27

Atcho heard a light footstep behind him, and then felt a warm hand touch his arm. His chest constricted, but he remained outwardly impassive.

"Are you all right?" Sofia regarded him with the same compassion he had seen in Havana.

"I'm fine," he snapped. Immediately, he felt embarrassed for his rudeness. "I'm sorry."

Sofia moved to the rail and looked up at the stars. "I didn't intrude deliberately. I came out for fresh air. I heard you arguing and went to find your son-in-law."

Atcho hung his head. "Some hero, huh?"

Sofia did not immediately reply. She searched his eyes as if trying to see behind a veil. "Were you more disappointed when Isabel hung up on you in Havana?"

As the rush of tragic memories collided, Atcho turned away. "Please, I'd rather not talk about it.

"I don't mean to meddle." Sofia's tone was gentle. "I've seen you suffer twice now. You could use a friend."

His emotions churned. Several minutes passed before Sofia spoke again. "I didn't intend to add to your discomfort. I'll go back inside."

As her footsteps receded, Atcho called after her. "Wait."

Sofia halted and faced him.

"Thank you. Again. Please excuse my rudeness."

She nodded and turned toward the ballroom.

"Sofia." His heart pounded at the realization that she grew more beautiful each time he saw her. Moonlight shimmered on her hair and softened her finely sculpted features. Her eyes sparkled.

"You've been kind," Atcho said at last. "Give me a minute, then please dance with me."

Sofia nodded graciously and disappeared into the ballroom.

Soft music greeted him when he re-entered. Most of the guests were still present, including Burly and Rafael. Bob must have told them that something personal had occupied Atcho, because no one remarked about his absence. Everyone seemed deliberately jovial. As he strolled through the room they relaxed into more natural behavior. Their affection moved him. He spotted Sofia standing near the door leading into the lobby and crossed the floor to dance with her.

28

Two days later, Bob called. "Atcho, can we get together for drinks?"

"You're worried about that argument with Isabel the other night at the reception. Don't be. I'm fine."

"Can't a guy have a beer with his father-in-law?" Bob's voice boomed over the telephone. "I was gonna take you to my favorite Irish pub."

Atcho was reluctant. "Where and when?" He hoped he sounded suitably enthusiastic.

They met at Cowan's Irish Pub in Alexandria, a fixture of local nightlife a block off of Washington Avenue near the town center. It occupied most of the first floor of an ivy-covered redbrick building in a recently restored colonial area.

Bob lounged on a barstool when Atcho arrived in midafternoon the next day. He had already struck up banter with the bartender. "Come over here and meet my buddy, Aengus," he called. "I promised to introduce you if I could ever get you in here."

Aengus extended a massive hand. He towered above Atcho and was even a few inches taller than Bob. "Pleased to meet you, sir," he enthused. "Your son-in-law told me so much about you. The first pitcher is on the house."

Atcho felt embarrassed but took the praise in stride. He said simply,

"Thank you." They chatted a few minutes, and then Bob asked for a table in the corner.

"Not a problem," Aengus said. "I'll keep the other customers away." He grinned and winked at Atcho. "I know the two o' you must be ginnin' up somethin'."

Atcho followed Bob to the table. "Why do I feel like I'm being taken to the woodshed?" he asked with a wry smile as he took his seat.

Bob laughed. "So I asked you here because of what happened the other night. I don't think that's going to bring down the Berlin Wall."

Atcho smiled sheepishly. "You're right. What do we hope to accomplish?"

Aengus brought their order and left quietly.

Atcho poured ale into the two mugs and took a long swallow. He held the mug in both hands at eye level while he leaned on his elbows and appeared to contemplate the dark liquid. Then he looked at Bob. "What are we going to discuss?"

"Don't look so serious," Bob said. "This isn't an inquisition. I have far too much respect for you." He grinned broadly. "I'm not gonna say I like you, and if anybody ever tells you I do, you'll know it's a flat-out lie." He reached across the table and clapped Atcho's shoulder. "Seriously, you know how proud I am to be your son-in-law."

"You've done fine till now," Atcho grunted. "Don't get sappy on me."

"Fair enough." Bob took a deep gulp of his drink. "We have a strong mutual interest."

Atcho nodded.

"I'm going to get sappy for one moment," Bob continued. "Only for a moment." He shifted in his seat, and Atcho perceived that he was uncomfortable expressing whatever he was about to say.

"I love your daughter very much, and I have the highest regard for you." He grinned slightly. "I'll even admit to a little affection."

Atcho smiled. "That's good but go on about my daughter."

"Yeah, your daughter. Isabel." He looked like he was searching for words. "Help me out. I want to understand you, so I can help her. It hurts to see my wife and her father estranged, and they're both wonderful people."

Atcho felt the blood drain from his face. "What do you want to know?"

Bob contemplated him a few moments. “I understand why you fought for Cuba. I’m fine with that. I’m a soldier.”

“You’re a captain, soon to make major.”

Bob waved away the comment. “What I don’t understand is, why did you assume another identity and stay hidden all that time? You could have left Cuba years ago. Your classmates would have helped. They thought you were dead.”

Atcho sat in silence and sipped his ale.

“I’m not here to make your life more difficult,” Bob went on. “I really want Isabel to be happy. She had a rough time too. I’m not saying her resentment is justified—but these are the same questions she’s asking. If I could understand, maybe I could help her understand.”

Atcho continued his silence, his emotional warnings blaring. Bob looked frustrated. “Is there anything you can tell me?”

Atcho tried to deflect. “I hardly know where to start. So much happened to so many good people.”

“Let me ask some questions then. I’ve spoken with former political prisoners, many who remember you. You really are a legend.” He paused, and Atcho looked away. “I’ve read reports that included mention of ‘Atcho’ and ‘Eduardo Xiquez’ ...” He stopped as he saw Atcho react.

“You checked me out?” Atcho asked with a tinge of anger.

Bob drew back. “I’m an Army officer. I have access to information. I read reports about what took place in Cuba during the invasion. I was a cadet when I met Isabel. She thought you were dead, and I had no reason to think otherwise. I was curious about a West Point graduate in action during the Cuban revolution. Don’t you think that’s a normal curiosity for an Army officer?”

Atcho nodded tiredly. “I suppose so. Go on.”

“Those reports mentioned you as both Atcho and Eduardo, but the two were not linked as the same person, and only Atcho was in action. Then, at the Bay of Pigs, you disappeared.”

Atcho’s mind headed toward darkness, but he steered it away.

“Then, nineteen years later,” Bob went on, “you resurfaced. I know you were in prison, because your fellow inmates remember you, and some knew you were Atcho. The question is, why didn't you let anyone else know that you, Eduardo Xiquez, were there?"

Atcho felt anger rising again. "Why is that important to you? Apparently, you asked other refugees about me. Were you checking on me? What do you think? That I'm a spy?"

Bob drew back. He scrutinized Atcho and leaned forward. "I'm your friend, not your enemy. Because my wife is Cuban, we mix with a lot of Cubans. Some of them are refugees. They tell their stories, and generally they love life. They party. They dance to *salsa* and *merengue*. You don't."

Atcho looked at him morosely. He had the strange feeling of being a cornered animal. "I don't know what to say. I lost my family, our farm—"

Bob shook his head. "Don't go there. You're deflecting. You're well-known for bravery. Lots of refugees lost as much. They've moved on. Your financial success in the US is beyond most of theirs, and they've done very well. But you still carry a sense of being anchored in the past. Until we can get beyond whatever it is, I don't think things will change with Isabel."

Atcho shifted in his chair to stand up. "Maybe you're right," he whispered. "Maybe I should leave."

"Please don't," Bob said quickly but firmly. He reached across to put a restraining hand on Atcho's arm.

Atcho stared at it.

Bob removed it. "Sorry. Please don't leave." He leaned forward and looked Atcho in the eye. "I love my wife. I love her father. I want to see them both happy." He lowered his voice and enunciated his words. "I will do anything to protect Isabel, and I'll take apart limb by limb anybody who makes her unhappy."

"Meaning what?" Atcho snapped.

"Meaning that something is going on that you won't talk about, and it's affecting the lives of two people I care about deeply." His voice had risen, and he stopped as if just realizing that, and looked around. Then he looked back at Atcho. "If you won't tell me anything, I can't help you. But let me tell you this. If anything comes around that could harm Isabel, I won't leave anything lying around but blood 'n' guts."

Atcho had to smile. "I know," he whispered. "That's why I love you and am so proud and happy that Isabel married you." His spontaneity surprised himself. He felt embarrassed by the emotion that threatened to dump moisture from his eyes. His throat constricted, and his mouth twitched involuntarily. He hoped Bob did not notice.

Aengus came over. "How's the ale?"

"The best," Atcho quipped awkwardly, welcoming the release of tension.

Aengus beamed, and then eyed a plate of untouched pub grub.

Atcho looked around. More patrons had entered, and the place was filling up. True to his word, Aengus had left vacant the seating in their immediate vicinity.

Atcho leaned back in his chair and stretched his legs. Bob followed suit. They sat in silence a few minutes. Aengus refilled the pitcher and traded out the pub grub for a fresh plate. "You'd better eat this one," he jibed.

When he had gone, Bob asked, "Do you mind if I ask about your time in prison?" He saw Atcho tense up, and held up both hands, palms forward. "No pressure here, just curious. So many stories float around about you. It's hard to separate fact from fiction." He saw Atcho's hesitance. "You're my father-in-law," Bob went on, "I'd just like to know about you from you." He shrugged. "Maybe it'll help."

"What would you like to know?"

"The tank hijacking in the swamp, did that really happen?" Atcho nodded, and Bob shook his head in amazement. "Wow. And did you really punch out a guard your first night on the Isle of Pines?" Atcho nodded again. "Criminy. You were a regular hell on wheels." He leaned his chair back and sprawled his legs in front of him. "And the thing about the escape attempt. Did that happen?"

Atcho nodded again. "You saw how successful that was."

"Are you kidding me?" Bob's eyes widened, and his normal broad grin crossed his face. "I know the guy who made it out of there. He says there is no way he could have done it without you."

"You know him?"

"Well, I met him. Bernardo Martin, right?" Atcho nodded. "We met him in Miami while we waited for you to arrive. He wanted to see you, but in the rush of things, it slipped. He was meeting family members, too, so ..." He shrugged. “I guess it just didn’t happen. We tried to get him here for the reception, but he had another engagement.

“I spoke with him for a while before your plane arrived. He was emphatic that without your experience and training, none of the prisoners would have had a chance. People don’t widely know this, but his reports of conditions on the Isle of Pines played a huge part in raising awareness and brought pressure to close that dungeon.” He leaned forward and allowed the front of his chair to fall to the floor with a slam. “You see, Atcho, you succeeded.”

Atcho looked startled. “A friend of mine in prison said the same thing. His name is Domingo.” Atcho felt bewildered. He looked around. Other customers were looking at them, apparently reacting to Bob’s enthusiasm.

“Yes, Domingo,” Bob interjected. “I met him at the reception. He told me the same thing.” Bob reflected a moment. “Is that it? Have you been beating yourself up all these years because you thought you’d failed?”

Startled, Atcho stared at Bob. *I won’t get a better alibi.* He nodded without saying a word.

29

Bob looked genuinely relieved. “Aw, geez, guy. That’s what you’ve been carrying around all these years. You think it’s your fault because the others didn’t make it out.”

“And some died,” Atcho said quietly. He thought of Jujo.

“You can’t put that all on yourself.”

Atcho was silent. He kept his head down and sipped his ale.

Bob watched him. “I think I can make things better with Isabel. There’s so much I’d like to ask, but I guess that can come with time.” He took a large gulp of his drink. “Do you mind if I ask you about your time in prison?”

“Which prison? I was in three of them. What do you want to know?”

“Anything you feel free to tell me.”

Atcho remained silent, sipping his ale.

Finally, Bob said, “Tell me about the box.”

“The box,” Atcho said softly. He felt his muscles tighten and heard his own voice as though from far away.

“I’ve heard of the box, but I’ve never heard a firsthand account.”

“Why do you want to know? You were in Grenada. Do you like talking about your combat engagements?”

Bob thought a moment. "Fair enough, but I'm not just your son-in-law. I'm also a military officer trying to understand things."

Atcho looked up at him sharply.

Bob grinned facetiously. "Okay, you caught me on both sides of an argument. I won't lie to you. I think talking about it might help, and I'm curious."

Atcho sipped his drink. "All right. I'll tell you about the box. You probably know I was in one for an extended time after the attempted escape."

Bob nodded. "I've heard. Domingo told me a little bit at the reception."

"It was dark. Always dark. Have you heard how they were constructed?"

Bob nodded somberly.

"Then you know they were very small. They were in a room inside the punishment facility, which was also dark. People were taken there for any reason that provoked the guards. In my case, leading an escape attempt would obviously be enough to land me there." He sat quietly awhile and took long gulps of ale.

Bob wondered if he would continue.

"When you went in," Atcho began, "the guards would open the box, and you had about two seconds to figure out how you were going to sit in it, because once in and they had closed it, you weren't coming out for a very long time—in my case, most of eight months."

Bob shook his head, and his face showed that he felt the horror.

Atcho was quiet again. "You couldn't adjust your position," he finally went on, "there wasn't enough room. You can't lie down, sit up, sit back, or kneel. Within minutes, your joints and muscles are aching because some are already stretched or mashed in peculiar positions." He fidgeted, and then continued with obvious reluctance. "If the guards were very angry with you, they made sure you drank a lot of water before you went in, because ..." He stopped and looked steadily at Bob. "... in the box there is no latrine, no exit, no relief." He was quiet a while longer and nibbled on a piece of bread. "They fed us through a slot." He gestured at the pub grub on the table. "There's more food here right now than you might see in a week."

Bob studied Atcho's face. It was stretched taut.

"Shall I go on?"

Bob nodded.

"Within hours, you think there can be no greater pain. It sears through every muscle and nerve in your body. At first, you can't sleep; some limbs become numb. You pee on yourself and shit on yourself because you have no choice. The stench is unimaginable, and the fumes fill your head and make your crazy. Then you vomit. Finally, you doze off from exhaustion—and when you wake up, the pain is excruciating by magnitudes beyond what it was when you went to sleep."

"Maybe that's enough, Atcho," Bob said kindly.

"No," Atcho retorted, and his ferocity surprised them both. "You asked to hear this, so do me the courtesy of listening. And then I have a few questions for you."

Bob leaned back in his seat.

"Every now and then—I really don't know the frequency—every now and then, they'd open the box and pull you out to hose down you and the box." He looked down at his feet. "Within hours of going in, the filth wore sores into your legs and buttocks, and they'd become infected. When they took you out to clean you and the box, you'd try to straighten your arms and legs, and they were all but frozen into their forced positions. Then, when the water hit the infected sores ..."

Bob saw the relived agony on Atcho's face. "I get the picture," Bob said softly. "I'm so sorry for what you went through. What did you want to ask me?"

Atcho's cheeks quivered. He felt his throat constrict, and when he tried to speak, he found that he could not. He withdrew a moment to compose himself, and then leaned forward and forced out one word. "Why?"

Bob looked confused. "What? Did you ask me why?"

Atcho nodded and put his palm up to request a further moment. "Why were we deserted?"

Bob looked startled. "You've read the histories. You know why Kennedy pulled out. From what I gather, you had reached the same conclusions in Jaguey Grande."

"I'm not talking about the Bay of Pigs," Atcho said hoarsely, and Bob saw that he seethed with anger. "I'm talking about Cuba. Why was Cuba abandoned?"

Bob reeled back in surprise. "I don't know any more than you do. I was a child when all that occurred."

"As you say, we are father-in-law and son-in-law, and we ought to be able to at least have this discussion."

Bob saw that offering protest now would not work.

"There was a holocaust going on ninety miles from Key West." Remembered despair filled Atcho's face and contorted it in bitterness. "Cuba was a loyal, friendly ally. Since Castro took over in Cuba, the US has taken military action in the Dominican Republic, Grenada, and other places around the world—you even put a man on the moon. How many resources were used for that? But our people, our culture, our country were left to destruction by a madman."

Bob sipped his beer. "I don't pretend to be an expert on Cuba, but didn't the cruelty of Batista have something to do with what happened down there?"

Atcho shook his head. "Very little," he said vehemently. "Research the history. Cuba was strong. The economy was good. A demagogue came to town and fomented class warfare. The object was always power."

"I don't know how to respond. You know that what you just said runs counter to popular view."

"I know." Atcho leaned forward, and all but hissed, "I lived it, and so did a lot of the people you know. Our story never gets told. And we ask ourselves why—why were we and our country abandoned?"

"I don't have an answer." Bob shook his head. "I wish I did."

"Here's the main issue." Atcho had regained his composure. "One that Cubans in the US fear most." He paused for emphasis. "It can happen here."

Bob studied Atcho's face, and his own took on a doubtful expression. "Is that what worries you? Is that what keeps you awake at night?"

"I've probably said too much already." Atcho appeared resigned. "Those of us who lived it recognize things we've seen before. I love this country as much as I still love Cuba, but the US is not immune to evil men promising utopia." He sat back, and Bob saw from his expression that he did not intend to address the subject further.

"I have one more question," Bob said. "Different subject—no more serious stuff. You prompted it when you mentioned putting the man on the moon."

Atcho looked at him quizzically but offered no protest.

Bob watched him a moment longer. "I've seen you staring at the moon many times. It's more than just enjoying the beauty of it. You almost seem —well, reverent."

Atcho relaxed and smiled, almost introspectively. "Ah, the moon," he said, and he seemed to have moved into a world alone. "You know, despite appearances, I cared for my baby daughter very much. I found myself on a boat once—when we were brought from the Isle of Pines. I found a place where I could pretend I was alone. We made the voyage in the middle of the night, and the moon was full—and I looked up and saw it in all its majesty, and I wondered, is my little girl seeing that wonderful beauty at this very moment?

"The thought occurred to me that that brilliant moon was the only thing in the universe that Isabel and I could share at the same time." He sat quietly. "So, yes, the moon is very important to me."

He laughed, and there was irony in his voice. "But guess what?" He leaned forward with a sad smile. "The moon doesn't care."

Bob started to say something, but Atcho stopped him. "I've often thought about whom to blame for all the evil in the world, or for that matter, whom to credit for all the good. And the fact is that a thousand years from now maybe, or a million years, it won't matter. But guess what? The moon will still be there, doing the same things it's doing right now. And so, at times when I become bitter, I look up, and I think about that, and I think that, for all the good it would do, I might as well curse the moon. That's how I get to sleep at night."

They remained quiet a few minutes. Then Bob said, "Thank you for coming. More than ever, I feel proud to be in your life." He caught himself as Atcho looked up, and a grin spread across his face. "Don't you dare tell anyone. I'll deny it."

Atcho smiled and acknowledged the crosswise compliment with a nod. "Let me tell you one other thing," he said. "You know we Cubans love our rum and coke."

Bob nodded with a grin.

Atcho went on, "We call the drink we love most, 'Cuba Libre.' You know that means 'Free Cuba.'" Bob nodded again, and Atcho continued. "Then you've probably heard Cubans in the US laugh and call it *La Mentirita*. That means, 'Little Lie.' The world thinks Castro is a hero, and that Cuba is free. We Cubans know that's a little lie."

They were both silent for a few minutes, then Atcho looked at his watch. "What do you think? Have we solved enough of the world's problems for one day?"

Bob nodded. "I'll do the best I can with Isabel."

"I'll deal with my own demons. Let's get out of here."

30

Ten days later, in the early morning hours, Govorov called. “Atcho.” His low, grating voice brought Atcho instantly awake.

He rubbed his eyes. “Do you always have to call in the middle of the night?”

“This is the best time to ensure privacy. Besides, it’s been a while since we’ve spoken. You should be happy to hear from me.” When Atcho did not respond, the general continued. “Congratulations on a splendid showing at the State of the Union address. I saw the videotapes. You looked very distinguished, and most heroic.”

“What do you want?” Atcho’s mind sharpened. There was something vaguely familiar in Govorov’s intonation of certain words.

The Russian sighed into the phone. “You’re hopeless when it comes to common courtesy. Well, no matter.” His mocking tone reverberated. “I have good news. We have a mission.”

Cold talons seized Atcho’s stomach. “What am I supposed to do?”

Govorov laughed. “I can’t tell you yet, but when I do, you’ll agree that it was worth the wait.”

“When?”

“Soon. We’re still working out details.”

Atcho was silent.

"Don't be impatient." Govorov's tone sharpened. "By the way, I hear you attended a reception after the president's speech."

"Who told you?"

"Don't be cute. I've allowed a lot of latitude, but there's a limit. Check with me before going to events not expressly cleared by me. Is that understood?"

Atcho remained silent.

Govorov's voice took on a threatening quality. "Do you understand?"

Atcho stared into the phone.

"Atcho, do you understand me?"

"Yes," he snapped.

"Good. I'll be in touch."

With the dial tone ringing in his ear, Atcho stared into the night. Since the general had always encouraged his attendance at social gatherings, he was surprised at the man's reaction to the reception. Cold sweat broke out on his brow. For seven years, he had known a mission was coming. He still had no plan.

31

"You look distracted," Sofia remarked, playfully reproachful. This was their fourth time seeing each other since the State of the Union reception, and Atcho had looked forward to seeing her immensely. Govorov had ruined that for him last night.

They sat in the outside area on the roof of an elegant seafood restaurant in the middle of a busy marina on the Potomac. Atcho loved this spot. Although bustling, it was not crowded, conversation was typically light, and the tall sailboats bobbing at the docks provided a pleasant feeling of movement. The only drawback was that politicians and other powerbrokers frequented it too, for the exact same reasons.

"I'm a bit preoccupied," Atcho said. "I had something unexpected come up in business." He had tried to call and cancel with Sofia but had been unable to reach her.

She scrutinized his expression. "Do you want to talk about it?"

He shook his head. "I wish I could." He found the feeling more genuine than he had intended to indicate. "Some things I have to take care of." He looked at her. She had drawn back a bit. "It has nothing to do with you." His fervor surprised even him. *Careful. Don't let your feelings run away with you.* He changed the subject. "Tell me about yourself. You know all about me, but I know almost nothing about you."

"Ah, changing the subject?" Sofia laughed, her green eyes flashing. "What would you like to know?"

Atcho felt his spirits rise. Sofia had that effect on him. "Everything. We've spent the last three times together talking about me, the Cuban Revolution, what prison was like, and Isabel." He stopped and squinted at her. "We haven't talked about you at all. Am I that much of a chauvinist pig, or are you hiding a dark and lurid past?"

The music of Sofia's laughter raised his spirits further. "As near as I can tell, mister," she smiled mischievously. "you are robbing the cradle. I'm about twelve years younger than you."

"But I'm so well-preserved," Atcho returned, without missing a beat. They both laughed. Then Atcho became serious. "I want to know about you," he said.

"Thank you. I mean that sincerely." Her face acquired a sad expression. "I should tell you first of all that I am a widow."

"*Madre de Dios.* I feel so foolish."

"No, no, it's OK." Sofia reached across and touched his hand. "Really, it's OK."

"You've put so much into comforting me."

"I could, because I had been through the pain. I came out the other side, and I didn't lose my home and my country—and I didn't go to a dungeon."

They sat quietly.

"I don't tell many people about my husband," Sofia said. "I loved him, and ..." Her eyes brimmed, and she stopped. She collected herself, and after a moment she said, "I just thought we should get through that bit of information. It had to come out ..." She caught herself, and proceeded cautiously, "if we're going to keep seeing each other."

Startled, Atcho felt warmth overtake him. He sensed redness rising in his cheeks. "Are we seeing each other?"

Sofia laughed and used a napkin to dab away her tears. "Silly man. You've asked me out four times. What did you think we were doing?"

They lingered over soft-shelled crab and sparkling white wine. Sofia told Atcho that she had graduated from Yale and had married an Army officer soon after. Seven years after their wedding, he had been killed in a black ops incident that no one would talk about. "I joined the diplomatic corps just out of college, and I've been with it ever since." She had been in Havana six months when she met Atcho. "I've served in Geneva, Madrid, and at the State Department here in Washington."

"What do you do there?"

"I'm a division director in the Office of Intelligence and Research."

Atcho gulped and hoped his expression did not communicate sudden anxiety. "A keeper of state secrets," he quipped. "Should you be telling me this?"

"The organization is no secret. It's a matter of public record. You can find me in the directory. I oversee analysts."

"Still, that sounds impressive. Why would you have anything to do with an old reprobate like me?"

"A glutton for punishment, I guess."

Atcho loved her brilliant smile. He relaxed in a way he could not remember. With minor reluctance, he asked to see her again the following week. *I can always cancel.*

As the week passed and he heard no word from Govorov, he looked forward to seeing Sofia again, and when they said their goodbyes, he asked her out again for two days later. Soon, they were together regularly. *Govorov could drop dead anytime. I won't stop living.*

Shortly after settling in Washington, Atcho had taken up flying. He loved the view from the air of the landscape below: the stately monuments of the capital city, the verdant valleys of Virginia and Maryland, and the broad blue ribbon of the Potomac wending to the Chesapeake Bay.

One day, after they had been dating for several weeks, Atcho rented a plane and piloted Sofia through northern Virginia, across scenic Shenandoah Valley, and through the Blue Ridge Mountains. As they parted ways that evening, Atcho realized that regardless of how much time he spent with Sofia, it was never enough. As soon as he turned to leave, he felt an ache, and began to anticipate their next meeting.

I'm in love. As soon as he thought it, he felt guilty for the implications for Sofia, and for Isabel.

Since his daughter's birth, his familial attention had focused on her. In effect, she had replaced his late wife in absorbing his affection. Despite the fact they had been estranged, he cared for her deeply. *She is the object of the threat that Govorov holds over me.* His thoughts returned to Sofia. *We'll see where this leads.*

32

Atcho saw Isabel and Bob rarely over the next few weeks. Since their conversation at Cowan's Irish Pub in mid-May, and as he had done regularly since the reception, he called Bob to learn how Isabel was doing.

Today, Bob seemed unusually upbeat. "Come by the house," he boomed. "Isabel agrees. I told her there's no way she can keep you from your grandchild."

Atcho stared at the phone, unsure he had heard correctly. "What did you say?"

Bob laughed. "You heard me, Grandpa."

"W-when?" Atcho stammered.

Bob chuckled again. "The baby's due in January. We hadn't told you because we were afraid of another miscarriage. The doctor says everything is progressing fine." His voice took on a serious tone. "This had a lot to do with Isabel's outburst. We were seeing the doctor before conception, and she had scheduled a visit for a few days after the reception. She was deathly afraid he would say she could not have a baby."

Atcho mulled that over. "She has good reason to hate me."

"Don't get morbid on me," Bob's voice boomed again. "You're going to be a grandfather. Listen, General Clary just returned from a trip to Geneva and Moscow. He's working on that arms treaty. He's having a barbeque at his house next week and asked us to invite you. Why don't you come, and bring Sofia with you?"

Atcho's head swam. He should be thrilled. This news about Isabel, welcome as it was, increased his discomfiture. And the invitation for social contacts with senior military officers brought him closer to a situation ripe for compromise.

"Atcho? Are you there?"

"I'm a little overwhelmed."

"I'll tell the general to expect you."

"I don't know."

"I won't take no for an answer. Clary doesn't know about the baby yet, so we're going to turn the occasion into a celebration." He paused. When he spoke again, his tone was serious. "I think you owe it to yourself and Isabel." His voice became light again. "You might get to see another side of your daughter."

Atcho's heart skipped another beat, even as Govorov's warning about social events rang in his mind. But he could not call the general, and he could not pass up the opportunity to be with Isabel on a special occasion. *Hell. Govorov will love the idea of my carousing with top military brass.*

"OK, we'll be there."

Sofia was elated at the news of Isabel's pregnancy and by the invitation. "That's great," she said, but she sensed he had reservations. "There's no way you can't go to this party. It'll be great for you and Isabel to enjoy something together that you're both happy about. Bob wouldn't steer you wrong."

Atcho realized with trepidation that he and Sofia were now a couple. They had developed an emotional attachment—*to the extent that she feels comfortable commenting on my family affairs. I'm a fool.*

33

"Welcome." General Clary clasped Atcho's hand. "Sorry I wasn't here to see you honored by the president. That was well deserved. I've seen the tapes." He turned to greet Sofia. "Bob told me about you," he said graciously. "I can see he didn't exaggerate." He turned back to Atcho, "congratulations on the baby. I'm thrilled."

A plump woman greeted them. Her brown hair was cut short, she wore a wide, friendly smile, and she exuded a festive demeanor. "Congratulations on the grandchild. I'm so happy for you." She extended her hand. "I'm Peggy, Paul's wife. Let's get you outside to the food and drinks. Bob and Isabel are already out there."

The house was spacious and comfortable, with soft, well-upholstered sofas and chairs, and finely carved dining-room furniture. It seemed to reflect Peggy's personality.

As they went out the door to the backyard, a petite teenage girl entered. "This is my pride and joy," Peggy exclaimed and threw an arm around her daughter's shoulder. "This is Chrissy." Her eyes sparkled with pride. "People think she looks like me."

"Mom," Chrissy protested. She accepted the show of affection with humor and continued through the door.

"That's National Merit Scholarship material," Peggy enthused.

Atcho caught himself thinking about the general's family. Oddly, he had never perceived of Clary in a family setting. He chuckled.

A whiff of hot coals and barbequed beef wafted on the air. In the backyard, guests had gathered. Atcho noted several senior military officers and a few well-known political figures. He saw Bob and Isabel talking with friends in a vine-covered gazebo near the grill. He looked at Sofia. "This might be a cold reception.

Seeing them, Bob started toward them. Isabel looked up. When her gaze met Atcho's, she held it nervously, and then smiled. "Hello, Papá."

Atcho felt a slight thrill. He thought he had heard warmth in her tone.

Isabel took Atcho by the arm and excused herself from the others. When they were alone, she said, "I'm so sorry. Bob told me about your conversation."

"That's in the past," Atcho said, touching her cheek. He started to guide her back toward the other guests.

She touched his arm. "Wait a moment, please." She fought emotion. "I don't understand everything that's happened, and I know you've been through incredible pain. I want to say that you're welcome in our house anytime. My baby needs a grandfather—and I need my father."

Mindful of where they were, Atcho slipped his arms around her waist and hugged her tightly. "I love you, Isabel," he whispered.

After a few minutes, they made their way back to the party, Clary approached. "Atcho, how about a drink?" They headed for the bar while Sofia returned to her husband.

"Bob says you're quite a pilot," Clary said as he walked with Atcho. "He mentioned you've worked your way up to small private jets."

"It's a hobby. I recently soloed in a jet. I do it to keep busy in my off hours."

"That's great," Clary said. "We should fly together. I've kept up my private license over the years, too." He grinned sheepishly. "The Air Force wouldn't let me fly their planes because of my eyes."

Atcho tensed. The general invited friendship, precisely what Atcho hoped to avoid. But there was no plausible reason to refuse. "Sure," he said simply. He would excuse himself later.

"Good." Clary clapped a hand on Atcho's shoulder and steered him toward a group of men.

Atcho regarded them with growing dismay. He recognized each of them. They were all generals.

"Gentlemen," Clary said. "Meet my new flying buddy."

"Very pleased to meet you," one tall, lean general said. "I'm Joe McKesson." Atcho shook his hand. This was the chief of staff of the Army.

"I'm Carl," another said. "I saw you at the State of the Union address. This is really a privilege." Carl Fox was the national security advisor.

In the circle were other men of equal stature, all complimentary and friendly.

Atcho accepted their comments dutifully, and laughed along with jokes and conversation, but he was careful not to invite further familiarity.

Despite the uneasiness of socializing in such high-powered company, the afternoon passed well. Someone asked Clary about his opinion on Soviet sincerity in peace overtures. Was an arms-reduction treaty realistic? If an accord were reached, would the secretary-general of the Soviet Communist Party sign the agreement?

Careful to indicate that he could not state an opinion based on classified information, Clary responded vaguely. "I can only say that if the president did not believe in what we are pursuing, he would not have us spending so much time on it. He's the guy who invoked the Russian proverb: *Doveryai, nye proveryai.* Trust, but verify."

Atcho avoided active participation in the discussions despite his interest. As the sun waned, he nudged Sofia. "It's time to go."

She nodded. They thanked their hosts and said goodnight to Bob and Isabel.

34

Sofia sat quietly as they drove to her apartment. After a while, she slid close to Atcho and placed her head on his shoulder. "This has been a wonderful afternoon. I'm glad that Isabel warmed up to you." Her face took on an inquisitive expression. "General Clary is the man who came to see you in Havana, isn't he?"

Atcho chuckled and nodded. "He was pretty upset with me then."

"I know. I heard several versions of the story."

Atcho glanced at her curiously.

After a few moments, she said, "One thing I've wondered about. Why was that picture left behind in the square in Havana?"

"What?" Atcho asked absently.

"The picture of Isabel found in the square the night you tried to rescue her. Why was it there?"

An almost imperceptible warning buzzed at the back of Atcho's mind. "What do you mean?"

"The kidnappers had Isabel in the Jeep with them when they came to the rendezvous, so the photograph served no purpose. From what I hear, the picture was new. If it had been dropped in the square, wouldn't it have been smudged or wrinkled? Why didn't one of the local officials find it?"

As Atcho contemplated the question, the warning faded. Sofia's observations caught his interest, but details of the episode were buried in memory. They seemed to have little to do with his current situation. He shrugged. "You might have a point."

When they arrived at the curb in front of Sofia's town house, Atcho cut the engine and put his arm around her shoulder. Sofia kissed him lightly. "Would you come in for a while? There's something I'd like to tell you."

Atcho searched her face but found no indication of what she wanted to say. As they moved up the walkway, he sensed a mental warning again. *She's going to end this. Hell. Now is as good a time as any.*

As he entered the town house, the scent of fresh flowers greeted him. The home was decorated in a contemporary country motif, complemented by fine pieces of Old World charm. Atcho looked around as he settled onto a sofa.

On the other side of the room, Sofia poured two glasses of wine and put on soft music. She crossed the room, handed one of the glasses to Atcho, and sat next to him.

Atcho's heart pounded. They clinked glasses. "Cheers."

Sofia sighed, acquired a matter-of-fact expression, and placed her glass on a low table in front of them.

Here it comes. "What is it?"

"I haven't known you long," Sofia said. "On the other hand, I've known you for about seven years."

"That's true."

Sofia struggled for words. "People care for you. But you don't have close friends."

"Go on," he said, his expression blank. *Where is this going?*

Noting his expression, Sofia hesitated. "I'm not doing this well." She placed her hands on Atcho's arm. "I'll tell you straight out. I love you, Atcho. I've loved you since we were together at the Swiss Embassy in Havana. I had never seen a man with such character, strength, and compassion, who hurt so much. Your sorrow haunted me. I couldn't get you out of my mind. I worried when you didn't come back to the embassy and looked for you every day."

Shock registered on Atcho's face.

Realizing that she rambled, Sofia stopped. Tears ran down her face. "I'm sorry. That's not what I was going to tell you. I think you should know how I feel so you'll understand what I'm trying to say." She wiped her eyes. "Atcho, you are both an open book and a mystery."

Stunned, Atcho sat in silence. "What does that mean?"

Sofia gripped his arm. "You're a well-educated man of strong character, demonstrably courageous, and a leader that others follow willingly. You're intelligent, hard-working, compassionate, and comfortable with social graces. You live in a free country where you've become wealthy, and the highest office in the land honored you. Your relationship with your daughter was strained, but it's been warmer than between many parents and their children. And we both know that you could have any woman in the country.

"Despite all that, you carry sadness around, and you won't let anyone get close to you."

Atcho went to pour a fresh glass of wine. His hand trembled. "Why are you saying these things?" He tried to sound angry, but he was too dumbfounded.

Sofia rose from the sofa, crossed to him and touched his shoulder. "Twice I watched you struggle with incredible pain. Both times I saw a man whose suffering had gone beyond what most people could bear.

"I lived in Havana. I helped political prisoners as they came through the Swiss Embassy. I know how they react. I saw their transformation from incarceration to freedom. Frankly, you act like a man still in prison."

Atcho whirled. "What do you mean?"

Sofia shrugged. "You avoid personal relationships. You're skilled at your work but find outside activities that don't include other people. You attend social events but use the contacts only to enhance your business, and you do that halfheartedly."

Atcho studied Sofia's face. "Why tell me this now?"

"For two reasons. First, to let you know you have friends who care about you and would help if you'd let them." She hesitated, and then looked steadily into his face. "And, because I love you more than I ever thought possible. I want your suffering to end."

Atcho stood motionless. "Did you really look for me in Havana?"

Nodding, Sofia smiled. "Some refugees saw you leave with several other men for the Peruvian Embassy. When I heard about the shooting and your disappearance, I didn't know if you'd gone into the embassy and stayed, or if you'd been shot. When you came out of Cuba six months later, I had been transferred to Switzerland. I know there was press coverage when you arrived in Miami, but I didn't see it in Geneva. Since your real name was used in news reports, and I knew you as Manuel Lezcano, I wouldn't have known that was you anyway. Until someone contacted me about the reception, I thought you were completely gone from my life."

Atcho regained outward calm. "How did they find you?"

"Several refugees I helped remembered me. When the reception was planned, the organizers wanted to invite anyone who had been part of your past in Cuba. I wasn't hard to find."

Atcho thought a moment. "Whose idea was it to have the reception?"

"The guy you call Burly put it together. He became fond of you in Jaguey Grande. Somehow, he learned the president would present you to the nation. He thought that people who fought beside you might like to honor you as well. He was right. Everyone who knew you in Cuba was touched by your dedication and courage and wanted to be there that night. I saw you on television during the president's address. Nothing could have kept me from that reception."

She embraced him. Soft lights played over her ivory skin and long, dark hair. She caressed his lips with her own. "I adore you."

Atcho stood rooted to the floor while memories and fears of the past, and visions of a desolate future whirled through his mind. He caught a fleeting image of a dark figure in the moonlight grinning over Sofia's limp body.

She put her arms around his neck and pressed against him. "Kiss me."

His resistance melted as he drew her to him. "I love you," he whispered.

The instant the words passed his lips, the pain and stress of years rolled away. One second later, they rolled back with double their ferocity. The insistent warning reverberated again in his mind. He shut it out.

35

Atcho's eyes blinked open. Moonlight streamed through the bedroom window. He tensed as he heard again the warning in his mind. He sat up. Next to him, Sofia stirred.

He slid out of bed, crossed to the window and stared into the night. Had he been duped again? Atcho glanced at Sofia and began to dress.

"Atcho?" Sofia called. He made no reply. "What are you doing?"

Atcho whirled around. "Who are you?" he growled.

"What?" Sofia was still half-asleep.

"I asked who you are?"

"What do you mean?" Distress tinged her voice.

"I want to know who you work for. CIA? FBI? Army intelligence?"

"What are you talking about? I work for the State Department. You know that."

"Well, Miss State Department, I have a few questions." He flipped on the light.

She pulled the sheets around her and stared at him.

"How did you know about that picture?"

Stunned, Sofia did not answer. She stared in disbelief.

"How did you know about the picture of Isabel? I never told anyone about it. Juan is dead. Clary knew what it was, but he didn't handle it, and no one else saw it. How do you know about it?"

"Quite a few people know about it," Sofia answered quietly. "I've heard your story in several places." She stood and reached for her robe.

"I hope you come up with a better line than that."

"That's the truth." She held her anger in check. "What do you think everyone was talking about at the reception? It sounded like someone had found a Cuban Davy Crockett. There's the story of how you killed a lieutenant with a knife, then faced a Russian officer. Then there's one about stealing a tank and driving through a firefight."

Her sarcasm matched Atcho's. "I almost forgot. You had to hitchhike through enemy lines to the battle, because you were off trying to rescue your daughter from kidnappers when the invasion began. And, you single-handedly defeated a squad of soldiers. And don't forget about the attempted escape—which actually succeeded because one guy got out and spread the word about the Isle of Pines."

She tapped her foot while tightening a cloth belt about her. "Shall I go on? There are stories I'll bet even you haven't heard."

She stopped as his expression changed from anger to chagrin. "Separating truth from fantasy about you is not difficult," she went on, more gently, "but there is a part that puzzles everyone. I think it explains your strange behavior." She scrutinized his face. "Why did you stay in prison under an alias all that time? But for that, you might have been released years earlier."

He remained silent, bewildered.

Sofia crossed to him, put her arms around his neck and kissed him. "As for your original question, I think Burly told me about Isabel's photograph. Didn't you and Juan spend a lot of time with him?"

Shamefaced, Atcho nodded.

"Maybe Juan told Burly about it. You've been the hot topic of more than one conversation." She pulled his face close to her own. "Come back to bed."

Atcho shook his head sadly. "I'd better leave."

Sofia jerked her head. "This doesn't change anything. I knew a long time ago that something was wrong. I love you."

"Too much," he replied, while tucking in his shirt. "That's why I can't stay."

Sofia crossed to the bed and sat down. "I want to tell you something. I loved my late husband with all my heart."

Atcho raised his head.

"He was like you in many ways. I told you he was killed in a black operation."

Atcho nodded.

"I told you that because I want you to know that I understand danger, and sacrifice." She looked into his eyes. "The people who love you know something is terribly wrong. Won't you please let us help?"

Atcho felt his heart being ripped from his chest. He embraced Sofia gently and kissed her cheek. "I can't," he whispered. "I have to go."

Tears ran down Sofia's cheeks. "Will I see you again?"

"I think not."

As he turned toward the door, Sofia choked back sobs. "I'll be here." Her eyes took on a determined look. "Know this. I've loved you for a very long time. I don't sit around and let things happen."

36

An hour later, sitting in his own apartment, Atcho cursed himself for hurting Sofia. *What did she mean when she said, 'I don't sit around and let things happen'?*

He was exhausted from lack of sleep. He tried to drive thoughts from his mind, but they kept intruding. When Sofia had said he was an open book, she approached the truth. In a matter of weeks, she observed the same discrepancies in his story and arrived at the same conclusions that Isabel had. He wondered how many others had done so. Time was running out. *Time to go on the offensive.*

How?

Suddenly, he sat up. He reviewed the events and conversations of the past few months. Then, he walked through darkness to his desk and turned on a light. Scanning his phone directory, he located entries for Burly and Rafael. After memorizing the numbers, he tore the page into pieces, took them to the bathroom, and flushed them.

At six in the morning, he took his regular jog. Under a full-length running suit, he wore a pair of shorts and a T-shirt.

Because he believed he was often being watched, he had been religious about maintaining an exercise schedule. He had learned at the camp outside of Moscow that being careful about establishing behavior patterns allowed freedom of movement. By mixing routine and varied habits, he could find pockets of time to exploit in plain sight.

He ran three to five miles on most days but varied the route so that he never ran the same course two days in a row. Over the years, he had noted wide expanses of open ground where he could be observed from a distance. He also knew where congestion hid him from view.

This morning, he used this knowledge to check for followers. He saw none but kept up his guard. Starting at a fast pace, he headed toward an area where commuters waited for buses.

He jogged through the crowds, creating as little disturbance as possible, Above the sounds of rush hour, his mind flashed to the soccer game pictured in his yearbook. He remembered spectators urging him on. “Atcho! Atcho!” they had cried. He had responded, sweat flowing down his face and arms as he drove the ball toward the goal.

How differently his future had appeared then. He had been nearing graduation, preparing to marry the beautiful Isabel, for whom their daughter had been named. His ambition then had been to work with his father to oversee the family plantation.

A blaring horn returned Atcho to the present. He looked around. Certain that no one pursued, he entered a public restroom. When he emerged in shorts and a T-shirt, he ran toward the Potomac River, where many people went for morning exercise. Once there, he ducked into a hotel where he could use a public phone booth with little probability of being seen.

“Come on,” he muttered anxiously on the fifth ring.

He was about to hang up on the sixth when he heard a sleepy voice. “Hello?”

“Burly. It’s Atcho.”

“I know,” Burly yawned. “No one else calls me Burly.”

“I don’t have much time,” Atcho interrupted. “You told me once that if I needed help, to call.”

“What’s wrong?”

“I can’t say. Please trust me, and no police, CIA, FBI, or anybody else.”

“I hear you. Can you tell me anything?”

"There's an informant, and I don't know who it is. Isabel could lose her life."

Burly whistled into the phone. "Is that still going on?"

"Don't ask. Will you help?"

"Of course. But I'm retired. What can I do?"

Atcho felt a surge of relief. "Do you remember Rafael from the reception?"

"I should say so. I trained him in Guatemala."

"Here's his number." He said it slowly, giving Burly a chance to write it down. "Tell him to assemble and arm a platoon of the best men he knows. They must be discreet. No mercenaries. We need trustworthy men to train in one of those survival camps in Florida. They should be ready as quickly as possible.

"Help him establish a false identity in a Midwestern city. He should initiate a real estate transaction with me, using the alias. That'll give us a legitimate reason to correspond. But he can't try to deal with me in person. The risk is too great. Have a phone line patched directly to wherever he is and monitor it around the clock. Get me a cell phone that someone else pays for. Use Rafael's new identity to rent an office to use as a safe house in one of the buildings along the river here in DC. Leave the phone there. I'll pick it up later. Tell Rafael I'll reimburse him for expenses. The same goes for you. I'll be in touch."

"Wait. Is this why you've been so uptight? Why didn't you ask for help before?"

"I never knew who the informant is. I still don't. But I know who it isn't. I need to set up an organization that hasn't been infiltrated." A question forced its way into his mind. "Burly, did you ever mention a picture that was brought to me in Havana?"

Burly was quiet a moment. "I first heard about it from Paul Clary. You shook him up when you kept him overnight. Juan told me the story. He wondered why the picture wasn't found by security police when they removed the bodies and Jeeps, and why it looked so new."

"Did you ever mention it to Sofia Stahl, the secretary who helped refugees at the Swiss Embassy?"

"I might have. I told the story to some people the night of the reception. I think she was in the group."

Relief. "Thanks. I have to go."

After hanging up, Atcho retraced his steps, taking similar precautions. As he ran, he enjoyed a familiar, long-forgotten sensation. For the first time since his visit to the train station at West Point during the class reunion, he felt a measure of control over his own life. He relished the feeling and his confidence grew. Finally, he could strike back.

37

A month passed. Govorov called to say that the mission had been postponed. "Don't despair," he mocked. "Your day will come." After that, as always, he called at regular intervals, late at night. Since the first phone call from Govorov years ago, Atcho had searched his mind to place the pronunciation of certain words, and slurring of others.

Another month passed. Burly and Rafael completed Atcho's instructions. Having received the key to an office situated near the river, he stopped in during one of his morning runs.

The suite was bare except for a plain desk and chair that had been abandoned by previous tenants. Its largest office was triangular, with a long point overlooking a marina on the Potomac.

The peculiar shape of the building allowed excellent observation of every approach. Behind it, and visible from a back window, was a parking lot. Burly had done a great job. In this office, he could store equipment, or hide.

The cell phone was there, inside the desk. Atcho placed calls to both Burly and Rafael, pleased to learn that the platoon was organized and ready to move on order. "You're going to have to trust me," he told Rafael. "My instructions must be carried out quickly, and without question."

"Every man in the group fought at the Bay of Pigs," Rafael responded. "They remember you. When you call, we'll be ready."

Atcho gave him Bob and Isabel's address, and those of Bob's immediate and extended family. He gave instructions and promised as much lead time as possible.

Rafael suggested a two-step procedure. When he thought the time was near, Atcho should issue a warning order. On receipt the men would travel to their positions. At Atcho's final order, they would execute.

"What do we do if you're isolated and can't reach me?" Rafael asked.

"If you receive word that I cancelled all my appointments, send the men to their waiting positions." They had little room for error.

Atcho had studied the plan over and over. The stakes were appalling. Should he fail, not only were Isabel and her family at risk, but criminal charges would likely be brought against men who would have risked their lives and freedom for him. The lingering hope of a normal relationship with Isabel and a life with Sofia would be lost forever.

38

More months passed with only check-in calls from Govorov. In the interim, Atcho pushed his tormentor out of his mind as much as possible to concentrate on business.

Then, during the first week of December, the general called. "Atcho, you've sounded different the last few months."

"I'm impatient. Are you finally going to tell me what I have to do?"

"You sound eager."

"I'm leading a sedentary life. I could use adventure. Besides, I might find and kill you."

Govorov chuckled. "I've always admired your spirit. You never give up. I'd welcome a face-to-face contest. You'd be a worthy opponent." His tone became stern. "It's time for you to train for your mission. Tomorrow morning, you'll fly to Idaho."

Atcho was stunned. "I can't leave tomorrow. Have you forgotten that I run a business?"

"Have you forgotten that you run it at the convenience of the Soviet Union? You'll go to Idaho and be there a week."

Atcho continued to protest, but Govorov remained unmoving.

"At least let me call my secretary to cancel my appointments. I'd like to have the business to come back to, and you don't want to call attention to unusual behavior."

The general acquiesced. "You'll be watched from now on. Do I need to remind—"

"You've explained consequences clearly," Atcho snapped. "You monitor my phone, and bug my office, apartment and car. What am I supposed to be able to do?"

The Russian laughed quietly. "If there's something to be done, you're the one I'd expect to do it. You should be flattered by my confidence."

"What will I do in Idaho?"

"Don't be impatient. You'll find out. Be sure you're on the flight to Boise." He gave the trip details while Atcho listened in resigned silence.

Early the next morning, Atcho called his secretary. He gave her a list of tasks. Suspecting that she might report to Govorov, he made the list long, with mundane items included. Among them were instructions to call Rafael's alias and cancel appointments.

When he left his apartment, two men waited for him. "You ready to go hunting?" one of them asked.

Atcho stared at them. Based on appearance and accents, he would have guessed they were from Kansas or some other Midwestern state. He knew better. "I'm ready."

The flight to Boise was uneventful, as was the ride to their destination, fifty miles north of the city. Darkness gathered as they drove up to a log cabin. Apparently built to cater to hunters, its walls reflected light from a fireplace before a warm rug. Atcho wished he could enjoy the peaceful surroundings.

The next morning, he and his guards began a schedule that was repeated every day for a week. They rose early and drove to a platform built in a flat area. The structure was thirty-five feet tall, and a window had been constructed on one side. They provided him with a Winchester M70 rifle with high powered scope. Made with a long barrel and a low kick, its reputation was a rifle for deadly accurate shots.

Several hours each day, even as cold wind whipped through his clothes, Atcho fired repeatedly at a bull's-eye dragged on a sled behind a pickup truck. By the end of the first day, his shot groups were tight around the center of the target.

Then he practiced for speed. He brought the rifle to his shoulder, sighted through the scope and fixed the crosshairs on the small black circle. By the end of the third day, he brought the rifle on line and fired in one fluid motion.

On the morning of the fourth day, one of the men handed Atcho another Winchester M70. "You'll see the first one again at the mission site. Boresight this one and keep practicing."

At the end of the week, they left for Washington. On the plane, Atcho stared silently out the window.

They were in the air for a short time when he spotted a headline on a newspaper held by another passenger. Soviet Premier Gorbachev was in Washington, DC to sign the arms treaty recently approved by the US Senate. Atcho wondered how General Clary felt about the accord.

Of more immediate concern was Rafael's progress. By now, every member of Bob's family should be under observation. That would only be true, however, if Rafael had received the message from Atcho's secretary.

Shortly before midnight, he and his escorts arrived at his apartment. While his guards made themselves comfortable in the living room, he fell wearily into bed. *They're not letting me out of their sight.*

He reached down by the nightstand and felt his briefcase. Inside was the cellular phone Burly had provided. Atcho wanted to find out if Rafael had succeeded in the first part of the rescue plan, but since the room was probably bugged, he dared not make a call on either the cellular or the landline.

Wondering if his escorts were asleep, he stared around his darkened room. He had lived in this apartment since arriving in Washington. Despite his wealth, it was sparsely furnished. Decorating had not entered his mind. Yet now, he contrasted the charm of Sofia's town house to the bare walls and floor of his own room. He thought of the stately elegance of Clary's house. For a moment, he forgot about his bleak future, and merely longed to stop living like a hermit. Then, despite himself, he dozed.

The harsh ring of the landline phone jarred him. When he picked up the receiver, he heard Govorov's cold voice. "It's good to have you safely back in Washington."

"What now?" Atcho switched on the lamp by his bed. On impulse, he reached for his briefcase.

"I was pleased with reports of your marksmanship."

"That's great. Are you going to let me sleep?" He fumbled to open the attaché, hoping the men in the living room stayed there.

"I'm surprised at you. You've been anxious to find out about your mission. Aren't you curious?"

"Why did you take that first rifle away?"

Govorov laughed. "I thought that was obvious. We needed to put it where you'll need it while no one was looking."

"I don't want to shoot anyone. I'm not a murderer." Moving the cellular phone where he could see it, he tapped out Burly's number.

"You didn't have a problem taking care of that squad in Cuba," Govorov said. "And I watched what you did to that lieutenant in Havana. You stuck him with a knife."

"Those circumstances were different, and you know it."

Through the cellular phone, he heard Burly's line ringing. In the other room, a chair scraped. *Come on, Burly.*

"Enough chatter," Govorov said. "I promised you a worthy mission?"

"Keep it to yourself."

On the cell phone, Burly spoke. "Hello."

On the landline, Govorov affected a jocular tone in his hoarse, whispery voice. "Is that any way to act after waiting all these years?"

"Atcho, is that you?" Burly asked on the second phone.

Atcho covered the mouthpiece on Govorov's line. "Yes," he said to Burly. "Move."

"What?"

"I said move." He heard Burly inhale sharply.

Outside the bedroom door, footsteps approached. Cold sweat broke out on Atcho's forehead.

"Understood," Burly said.

"Atcho, are you there?" Govorov asked impatiently.

"I'm here." Heart beating furiously, he shoved the cellular phone beneath his blankets. "As we speak," he said sarcastically, "my companions are paying me a midnight visit."

The door swung open, and one of the guards appeared. Rubbing his eyes, he regarded Atcho dubiously.

"It's Govorov." Atcho held the receiver out to him.

The guard spoke into it. A moment later, he handed it back and left the room, closing the door behind him.

Atcho breathed a sigh of relief. "Can I go now?"

"You're being far too flippant." Govorov's tone was stern. "We expect performance. We'll get it, or you'll watch your daughter die."

Atcho suddenly felt very calm, and deathly deliberate. "What is it?"

He heard the general take a deep breath on the other end of the line. "You know that our general secretary is here to sign the disarmament agreement?"

"So?"

"Not everyone in the Soviet Union thinks the treaty is in our best interest."

"What am I supposed to do, shoot our president?"

Silence.

Dread coiled in Atcho's stomach and snaked into his chest. "Is that it?" he whispered. "You want me to assassinate the president of the United States? You want me to kill Ronald Reagan?"

"No," Govorov hissed. "Your president will be in office only another year. Nothing would be gained by that. At ten o'clock tomorrow morning, you will shoot—and kill General Secretary Mikhail Gorbachev of the Soviet Union."

39

Atcho slept no more that night. Nerves heightened, survival instinct honed to a knife's edge, he lay flat on his back staring at the ceiling. Hours dragged by.

Almost immediately after Govorov hung up, he risked discovery by redialing Burly's number on the cell phone. Whispering his inquiries, he learned that Rafael's men were in position. Burly had provided false FBI identification and a cover story for them to help calm their charges.

No one knew where Isabel and Bob were. When the men assigned to protect them arrived, the house was empty. A neighbor said that they had rushed from home in their car.

"Did anyone follow them?" Atcho asked.

"Not that anyone saw. But several minutes after our guys got there, a sedan with two men drove up and parked in front of their house. One got out and knocked on the door. He seemed upset when there was no answer."

"Was there anything strange about the car?"

"It was a rental. But our guys turned a listening device on the men. They were speaking Russian."

Atcho's pounding heart slowed at the news. For a second, he felt resigned to his fate. Then his spirit stirred. He told Burly he would keep in touch.

One overwhelming factor stood out in his mind. Time was running out. *Tomorrow morning,* Govorov had said. *At ten o'clock.*

As he lay in darkness, Atcho went over what Govorov called their "final" conversation. "Kill Gorbachev?" Atcho had repeated. "Are you crazy? Do you want to start World War Three?"

"I assure you that will not happen."

Atcho hated the rasping, whispery voice. And again, the almost familiar pronunciation and word choices nagged at the back of his mind.

"What's wrong with you people?" he had yelled furiously. "What reason could you have for wanting to kill your own leader?"

"I told you. Not everyone believes this treaty is a good thing. Add in *Glasnost* and *Perestroika*—the so-called 'New Openness'— and he's lucky to have lasted this long."

Atcho subdued a reaction. "Why here? Why me?"

Govorov's response was measured. "If he's killed here, that will stop the treaty from being signed. As for you, you're an excellent marksman, you fit the profile, and you're available."

Understanding dawned. "I fit the profile," he said calmly. "Embittered Cuban patriot, resistance leader, and West Point graduate. I've been honored by the president." He paused, mulling an obvious conclusion. "There will be no escape for me."

"That's right.".

Atcho felt numb. "You couldn't have foreseen this. Khrushchev was still in power when you warehoused me. Brezhnev was still around when you allowed me to emigrate. You saved me all these years for rare missions. Aren't you afraid you might lose a valuable commodity?"

"Frankly, you've been a disappointment. Your withdrawn behavior keeps you from the types of people I wanted you to meet. You learned too well how to be a *plantando* on the Isle of Pines. You contradict everything I say and take no advantage of opportunities to develop contacts pushed under your nose. General Clary and his guests at the barbeque are a case in point. As a result, you've been unsuitable for every mission that came along. But, you *are* uniquely suited for this one."

He added, "I forgot to congratulate you on your expected grandchild."

There was no warmth in his voice. "It's good to know that you have added incentive."

Atcho ignored the dig. "How do you expect me to get past the Secret Service? They'll check the buildings well in advance."

"That's why we changed out the rifles. The first one is in place. You know I'm thorough. Security will be tight, but Gorbachev will be in a passing motorcade. Precautions will not be as stringent.

"You own and manage a building on the street where his motorcade will go by. You have every right and reason to be there. A suite is vacant because one of our organizations rented it for this purpose. The rifle is in the center windowsill."

Atcho rubbed his forehead tiredly. "What if I refuse, or miss?"

"That wouldn't be wise, if you value Isabel's life and ... No need to press the point. The general secretary will be killed whether or not you do it. You're not the only sleeper agent in the United States, or the only one assigned to this mission. Don't be a hero. You won't save your own life, but you can save others that are important to you."

He paused, and when he continued, his voice took on an officious tone. "You are now a prisoner in your apartment. Early in the morning, you'll be escorted to the place where you'll complete your mission." Then came a sardonic touch of humor in the hoarse, whispered words. "Think of it as a strike against your oppressors."

"You're my oppressor," Atcho snapped. "You connected Eduardo and Atcho and rode that knowledge for all it was worth, and it wasn't worth much."

"You underestimate the contribution you are about to make."

"You mean the start of the next world war."

"The leaders of our faction don't seek war. We simply don't want democracy in our country. And we don't want too much peace. I think your own defense industry would agree with us on that."

"Are you going to help hunt me down?"

"You'll get a head start. We'll have to keep up appearances."

"Aren't the windows of the premier's limousine bulletproof? How am I going to get a clear shot?"

"You'll get a shot. Be ready. Anything else? I have to go."

"One more question. How did you connect Atcho and Eduardo?"

Govorov laughed. "I'm going to miss you. I can't answer that. You'd learn too much, and I enjoy living. Good luck and goodbye."

The phone went dead.

During the long night, the conversation with Govorov played over and over in Atcho's mind. *You're missing something. Find it.*

40

At nearly eight o'clock, sunshine streamed through Atcho's windows when his two guards entered the bedroom. He made no protest. He showered, dressed, and drank a cup of coffee. Then he picked up his attaché case and prepared to follow his escorts. The cell phone was concealed inside his jacket.

One man grasped the attaché. "What do you need this for?"

"I have work to do when you're finished with me," Atcho replied. The guard looked dubiously at him, opened the case, and rummaged through several real estate documents. He grinned at his partner and handed the briefcase back to Atcho. "Yeah, you'll need to complete this work," he said sarcastically.

Atcho crossed the room, set the case on a coffee table, and lifted the lid to mask his actions. He straightened files. When both escorts looked away, he placed the cell phone inside. He also put in a small bag he took from another pocket. It contained a vial of oil and a pair of surgical gloves.

Minutes later, they sped through the capital city. Soon, they turned onto Pennsylvania Avenue. Tranquil and inviting against thick grass and neatly trimmed winter plants, the White House stood surrounded by a black cast-iron fence.

Recalling his reaction when he saw the Kremlin, Atcho decided that the

White House represented a deadly combination of good intentions, poor planning, and naïveté. Here, as in the Moscow, orders had been issued that had devastated his homeland.

A few blocks further on, the car pulled in front of his office building on Pennsylvania Avenue. "We'll be watching the exits," one of the men said. "Don't leave before you finish."

Atcho emerged from the car carrying his briefcase and entered the building. A Secret Service agent checked him over.

"What's this?" he asked, holding up the surgical gloves and vial of oil.

Atcho grinned. "My office door keeps squeaking and I can't get maintenance to fix it, so I'm doing it myself."

The agent reviewed his identity documents, checked his name on a list and let him pass.

Avoiding the manager's office, Atcho went instead to a closet on the second floor. Finding it unlocked, he entered, closed the door, and pulled out the cellular phone.

Burly answered on the first ring. "Is that you, Atcho?"

"Have you found Isabel?"

"No."

Icy fingers constricted Atcho's chest. "How are Rafael's men?"

"They're fine. The FBI ID and cover story worked. The subjects are safe and cooperating."

Atcho glanced at his watch and inhaled. The Soviet motorcade was due to pass in sixty minutes. "You have one hour to find Isabel. Do you hear, Burly? One hour. Check the hospitals. Call Bob's office. But find her." His voice hissed with urgency.

"Shouldn't you tell us what's going on? We might have suggestions?"

"Not until I know who the informant is," Atcho said coldly.

"Do you suspect me?" Burly's tone was incredulous.

"I know it's not you. But you might inadvertently say something that could cause damage." On impulse, he asked, "Is Mike Rogers still in the Secret Service?"

"I don't know."

Atcho's mind raced. "Find out. We'll need to contact him with only a moment's notice. If you can't reach him, get someone with authority who'll respond quickly."

"Anything else?"

Atcho glanced at his watch again. Another minute had passed. "Get going. Call me as soon as you hear anything."

Shoving the phone into his briefcase, he slammed the lid down. He peered into the hall. Seeing no one, he crossed to the stairs. Taking them two at a time, he reached the fourth floor and followed a corridor to the front. There he found the vacant suite.

Inside, the office was plain and bare. Moisture had gathered in corners around the ceiling, and paint peeled from the walls. A heavy, musty odor permeated the room.

The only piece of furniture was an empty desk. On the opposite wall was the window Govorov had mentioned overlooking Pennsylvania Avenue. Atcho searched for bugs. If there were any, he needed to find them before using the cellular phone again.

Finding none, he studied the window. It opened inward and had two columns of glass on each panel.

Staying in shadows, he looked up and down the street. The view was excellent in both directions. Trees directly in front and to his right had been trimmed, ensuring an unobstructed shot. *Govorov prides himself on thoroughness.*

Following the general's instructions, he tugged on the sill. After some exertion, it moved. He lifted the wood out of the way. Inside, carefully wrapped in waterproof material, was the Winchester M70 and scope he had first used in Idaho. With them was a tripod.

He unwrapped them. Then he moved the desk to the center of the room a few feet from the window. From his attaché, he removed the surgical gloves and the vial of oil and used them to rub down every inch of the rifle with his handkerchief. When finished, he opened the windows, and sat down to wait.

Twenty minutes had passed since he'd talked to Burly. He stared idly at the ceiling, his thoughts turning to Sofia. An eternity seemed to have passed since he last saw her. He shook his head in disgust as he recalled their last evening together. *How could I have been so stupid?*

He thought about the conversation that had triggered his outburst. She had raised questions about the picture found at the site of the firefight in Cuba. He searched his memory for details of that episode, trying to remember the vague concerns that had prompted him to keep Paul Clary captive overnight. And he recalled once more the terrible night he first met Govorov.

What you look like is what we want to know, the Russian had said. After that, Atcho had been manipulated, but with no attempt to capture him until he had walked into the operations center at the Bay of Pigs. How had Govorov established a positive identification? Had someone in the resistance group betrayed Atcho? That was possible, but at that time only his sister Raissa, her husband, and Juan knew that Eduardo had survived the fire. Given his brother-in-law's resentment of Isabel, he was a possible suspect, but what reason would he have had to risk contacting the Russians?

The phone rang. "Still no word of Isabel," Burly said. "I talked to Mike Rogers. He said he'd help but wants to know what's going on."

"Tell him thanks, but I can't say anything more than I have already. Keep trying to find Isabel." He glanced at his watch. Only twenty minutes remained before the target was due. "Burly, do you have more than one phone line into your house?"

"My home phone has call waiting, and I have a cell phone in the car. I can bring it inside."

"Do it. Call Rafael. Tell him to let you know at once when Isabel has been located. Impress on him to call immediately. Then, contact Mike Rogers and instruct him to keep your line open. Tell him to establish channels with every active operation in the city. He must be able to react within seconds. When you have all that completed, call me on your cell phone, and keep that line open to me. You've only got ten minutes. Do you have all that?"

Burly repeated the instructions and hung up.

Wrestling again with memories, Atcho waited. Govorov's words rang through his mind again. *What you look like is what we want to know ... We took your picture routinely with other prisoners, then we saw Manuel's photo, and voila.*

Atcho sat up.

Govorov couldn't recognize me in Havana because I was too beaten up. But after my capture, he knew that Manuel, Atcho and Eduardo were all the same person.

While he was recuperating in Havana, Paul Clary saw him, and something about the man had made Atcho uneasy. But they had not known each other. In order for Clary to be suspect, he would have had to know, before they met, what Atcho looked like, and about his nickname. He and Clary were approximately the same age. The general had graduated from Princeton. As a cadet Atcho had met students from there on several occasions. But in those days, only his father in Cuba and classmates at West Point had used his nickname.

Then Atcho remembered what had bothered him about Lieutenant Clary. The young officer had accepted a great deal of risk to deliver a photo that was of no use in resolving a situation the United States Embassy would normally avoid. Also, his personality had transformed with little provocation.

Govorov's words rang again. *What you look like is what we want to know.* The only thing Clary accomplished by his visit was seeing Atcho. "But Major Richards verified his story," Atcho murmured. The phone rang again. Scarcely believing that another ten minutes had elapsed, Atcho answered it.

"Everything is set," Burly said. "And, we think we know where Isabel is."

"That's not good enough. I have to know, beyond a shadow of a doubt, that she's safe." He paused in deep thought. "Do you remember Major Richards in Havana?"

"Yes. He retired in New Mexico."

"Call him and find out how he came by that picture of Isabel."

"What's up?"

"No time to say. Find him. Quick. And call me back in five minutes. Call immediately if you hear from Rafael." Burly hung up.

Atcho went back to his ruminations about the nature of the informant. The person had to have known him years ago, and still be close to him. On several occasions, Govorov had been aware of information that Atcho was certain he had mentioned only to Bob. But his son-in-law had been a small child when Atcho and Govorov first encountered each other. That ruled him out.

I tried to keep you away from the battle area, the Russian had sneered. He had known the date of the invasion at least two weeks in advance. Neither Brigade 2506 nor the resistance fighters had had that information.

Another thought entered his mind. When Atcho attended the West Point homecoming, Govorov knew almost immediately about his activities and conversations. Through Bob, Clary could have learned about those things without appearing suspicious and relayed the information to Govorov.

Atcho remembered Govorov's scolding for having attended the reception following the president's address. Several weeks had passed between that event and Govorov's call. General Clary was traveling to Geneva and Moscow at that precise time. He had not been around to keep anyone apprised of Atcho's activities.

Several times, since last April, Clary had flown with Atcho. Always congenial and most courteous, Clary had also been quick to introduce him to every senior military person he knew, precisely the people Govorov wanted Atcho to meet. Referring to Atcho's reluctance to develop high-level contacts, Govorov had said, *General Clary is a case in point.*

Atcho stood and paced the floor. He was certain Clary was the informant—*no, he's a spy*. He crouched by the phone. *I have to tell Burly*. Then he hesitated. *How could Clary have connected Atcho and Eduardo? He had to have done it before seeing me in Havana.*

He looked out the window. The usual crowd of passing pedestrians had grown. Many stood waiting expectantly. "They're gathering to see Gorbachev as he passes," Atcho murmured. Dread seized him. He glanced at his watch. Only five minutes remained to the appointed time.

The phone rang. "All channels are open, and waiting for your instructions," Burly said. He had no additional news other than that Major Richards was being contacted.

"All right," Atcho said. "I have my phone set for hands-free operation. Now, I need quiet. Yell if you hear anything." Burly acknowledged.

Atcho pulled the desk into shadows next to the wall to the left of the window. Then he attached the tripod to the rifle and set it on the desk. He took a solid firing position and peered through the scope.

Far down the street, motorcycle police rode toward him, followed by a convoy of black limousines.

Atcho lowered the rifle. In cold fascination, he watched the procession. *I wonder what the headlines will read tomorrow morning.* Recalling the caption in the West Point yearbook under the picture of his soccer game at Princeton, he grunted. He imagined a newspaper with the banner "ATCHO SCORES!" in bold letters. Seizing control of his wandering mind, he looked outside again.

Down the street, the crowd grew as motorcycles purred by in slow procession, followed by the column of limousines. Moments later, the first policemen rode past Atcho's position.

Movement in the building across the street caught Atcho's attention. He glanced over. Hidden in the shadows behind a window was the figure of a man. The steel barrel of a rifle extended from his hands.

Atcho remembered Govorov's words. *You're not the only sleeper agent in the United States, nor the only one assigned to this mission.*

Atcho felt his last hope drain away. Even if Isabel were saved in time, the general secretary would die, Atcho would be accused, and the world could be plunged into war. *I wonder how many other snipers are on this.* He stared at the motorcade.

A puzzled look crossed his face and morphed to shock. The procession slowed to a halt.

Atcho picked out the ZiL limousine with distinctive markings indicating the presence of General Secretary Gorbachev. He watched in disbelief as the vehicle glided to the curb. Sharply dressed men scurried to open the back door.

You'll get a shot, Govorov had said. Apparently, members of the conspiracy had convinced the general secretary to meet ordinary Americans.

Atcho leaned into his firing position and aimed at the open door of the car. Seconds passed. A man emerged, then another.

Atcho recognized the second man. He was of medium height and build, slightly rotund, with a congenial but stern expression. He was bald, and a red, elongated birthmark ran from above his right brow to the top of his scalp.

As Atcho watched in amazement, Mikhail Gorbachev threw his arms open, smiled broadly, and strode across the street to shake hands with eager citizens of the United States. Atcho's heart beat furiously as he aimed the rifle. Gorbachev's smiling face filled the scope. The crosshairs divided his head into quadrants centered on the red, elongated birthmark. All noise except Atcho's heartbeat seemed to fade as he tightened his grip.

Nothing existed except the rifle, and the premier's magnified face.

Almost imperceptibly, Atcho took in a deep breath and began to let it out. He placed his finger against the trigger and gradually increased pressure, resisting an urge to anticipate the explosion that would announce the completion of his mission.

Another man moved in front of the lens. Atcho cursed and lowered the rifle. He wiped perspiration from his brow and adjusted his position against the wall. Then he pulled the rifle back into his shoulder, sighted through the scope, and watched for Gorbachev to reappear.

Atcho's mind flashed back to the soccer game pictured in the yearbook. He heard his fellow cadets shouting encouragement from the sidelines as he ran downfield toward the goal posts. "Atcho! Atcho! Atcho!" they chanted.

Suddenly, Atcho stiffened. Princeton. The thought hit him like a bolt of lightning. His mind zeroed onto the picture of the spectator who had seemed familiar when he had studied the photo at the West Point library during his class reunion.

Paul Clary. He had attended that game. That was how he had known the name "Atcho" and that it belonged to Eduardo Xiquez.

Gorbachev walked into view. Atcho took aim. His finger pulled steadily against the trigger. Visions of fire consuming his beloved parents and home swirled with images of a dark figure clutching tiny Isabel on a cold, moonlit night. His brain flooded with memories of fearful crowds huddled together against deadly gunfire, while a bullet-ridden infant fell from the sky. "*Gusanos. Gusanos. Gusanos.*" The morbid chant sung by loyalists at the Peruvian Embassy on that terrible day mixed with Govorov's mocking laughter.

He remembered the hard labor in the marble quarries on the Isle of Pines. He relived the fading hopes of abandoned soldiers on a lonely beach in Cuba. Memories of cruel dungeons in *La Cabaña* replayed in vivid detail.

"This earth isn't worth saving," he muttered. He peered through the scope at the long, red birthmark. His concentration intensified. He set his jaw, steadied his aim, and pulled on the trigger again.

41

New visions danced before Atcho's eyes. Crowds of pedestrians in Red Square were superimposed on a similar scene in Washington. The majestic beauty of West Point merged with the tranquil mountains of Idaho. Images of Isabel, Sofia, and Bob appeared, smiling. Then their skins burst into flames and melted from their bodies. Burned-out cavities appeared where their eyes had been.

Mushroom clouds seemed to swell in front of Atcho, followed by haunting pictures of cataclysmic destruction, previewed fractionally in Nagasaki and Hiroshima. Juan appeared, a ghostly apparition, his calm eyes looking seriously at Atcho. "You cannot be impulsive," he said, and disappeared. Then, Atcho's father appeared, leading a long, gray line of proud, illusory figures.

"Duty, honor, country," he whispered. "You can't start World War III." The strong chords of the West Point song sounded through his mind. "... or living, or dying to honor, the Corps, and the Corps, and the Corps."

Atcho dropped his head and lowered the rifle. "Listen carefully, Burly," he yelled hoarsely into the phone. "Tell Mike Rogers to get Gorbachev back in the car. Do you understand? The Soviet general secretary must go back inside the car. Now. There's going to be an attempt on his life."

Atcho sensed movement in the window across the street. A rifle barrel pointed at Gorbachev.

Atcho jerked his weapon to his shoulder, centered the scope on a dark mass in the shadows, and fired. The report reverberated from the walls.

"What was that?" Burly yelled.

"Never mind. Tell Mike to do as I said." Atcho crouched and peered over the windowsill. Across the street, the rifle barrel was visible, pointed skyward. The dark figure had disappeared. *Poor bastard. I wonder how Govorov kept him under control.*

Below, people looked around, confused. Then they focused their attention in Atcho's direction. He looked at the motorcade. Men in dark suits surrounded the general secretary. They hurried him to the limousine and masked his entry into the back seat. Then, the procession raced off toward the White House.

"Burly, are you still there?"

"Yes."

"Have you heard from Major Richards?"

"Yes, a minute ago. He said he never saw that picture. Paul Clary brought it to him in an envelope, told him what it was, and suggested he try to get it to the resistance movement." Burly paused. "Is Clary the informant? Is he a spy?"

"Can't confirm yet. I gotta go."

Before he could hang up, Burly yelled through the phone, "Atcho, she's safe. We have Isabel. Do you hear me, Atcho? Isabel is safe."

Atcho froze. "What?" he asked in a daze.

"Isabel is safe."

"Are you sure?"

"Yes," Burly yelled. "We have her. She's safe. And I have more news."

"Not now. I've got to move." He shoved the rifle back into the hollow wall and replaced the wooden sill. "Stay close to the phone."

He hung up. His heart beat furiously. He looked at his watch. Scarcely two minutes had passed since he had spotted the police moving down the street. He returned the cell phone to his attaché case and yanked the desk back into its original position. Then, he strode to the door and stopped to survey the suite.

Except for the open windows, everything appeared as he had found it. Even the smell of gun smoke had been dissipated by free-flowing air. He peered into the hall. It was empty. He cleaned the doorknob of fingerprints. Then he walked down the corridor, into the restroom.

Moments later, he heard footsteps of men running in the hall. "Open up," someone yelled. Loud thumping sounded as the door to the vacant suite was broken down.

Atcho crossed the floor and stood in front of a urinal. Seconds later, two men burst through the door. "Don't move an inch. Who are you? What are you doing here?"

Atcho turned slightly.

They held pistols, pointed at him.

"I own the building. Do you mind if I finish what I'm doing?"

One man flashed a badge. "Did you see or hear anything strange up here?"

"When I came off the elevator," Atcho replied, fixing the front of his pants, "I heard a sound like the backfire of a car. I came down the hall, and a guy pushed past me into the stairwell." He continued to fiddle with his zipper.

"Was he carrying anything?"

"Come to think of it. He had something wrapped in blankets."

"You stay with this guy," the agent instructed his partner. "I'll check out the stairwell. See what's in the briefcase."

He left while his companion reached for the case.

Atcho swung his hand down, caught the man by the back of the neck, and rammed his head into the wall. The hapless agent dropped like a stone. Atcho grabbed the man's pistol and shoved it into his belt. He pulled the earpiece and radio from the limp figure, adjusted them on himself, and picked up the agent's badge. Finally, he dragged the man into one of the toilet stalls and closed the door.

Hurrying to the elevator, Atcho displayed the badge to more agents swarming there. He pushed a button and descended to the first floor. When the doors opened, a mass of agents and policemen jammed onto the elevator.

"They've cornered someone on the roof," he told them, and held the badge before him again.

Outside, Atcho continued to use the Secret Service credential to move through the crowd of curious onlookers. He walked purposefully until he rounded a corner. Then he put the emblem in his pocket and pulled the radio wire from his ear.

Two blocks further on, he hailed a cab. He gave instructions to his home, sank into the back seat, and closed his eyes. His body felt heavy as weariness overtook him. Blood rose to his head, making him hot and dizzy.

He reopened his eyes and watched tall buildings pass by. His task was not complete. Isabel and Bob were safe for the moment, as were the rest of Bob's family. But federal officers were needed to continue protective custody until Govorov's apparatus was neutralized. Rafael's men could not be expected to continue their pretense much longer. Burly would have to use his influence to secure adequate federal protection.

I'd better call Burly. Then he sat up in dismay. He had left his attaché in the restroom, complete with phone and real estate documents that would identify him. "Pull over," he told the driver.

After paying the fare, he hurried along the busy street until he found a phone booth. There, he dialed Burly's number.

"Where are you?" Burly demanded. "Everyone's looking for you. They found your briefcase in a restroom where you beat up a Secret Service agent. Mike Rogers wants to talk to you."

Atcho sighed. "I figured that. We still have work to do. Keep stalling Mike. I'll call him later. Meanwhile, bring in federal authorities to relieve Rafael's men." He thought a moment. "Get word to the Russians that General Govorov was a major conspirator. And tell Mike to look in the building directly across from the one where I was. He'll find a body there that might shed some light. Rent another phone and car for me. Do that before Mike's men start watching your every move. I'm going to the safe house."

42

Atcho paced. Six hours had passed since he had arrived at the office along the north bank of the Potomac, and there had been no sign of Burly. Without a phone or radio, he was cut off from outside news. Undoubtedly, he was the target of a manhunt. Mike Rogers and other officials would press Burly and Rafael for anything they knew about Atcho's movements.

He glanced out the window. He could not stay in this place any longer. The probability of discovery was greater with each passing minute. *I expected to kill Gorbachev and be captured,* he realized in surprise. He was not yet willing to stake his future on the fickle justice system.

Shadows lengthened as he left the safe house. He no longer felt secure there. He moved with rush-hour pedestrians scurrying toward evening activities, watchful for anyone who seemed more than casually interested in him.

Soon, he approached a commercial area near the marina, and entered a boutique. Moments later, wearing a casual, inconspicuous outfit, he emerged and hailed a taxi. He sat directly behind the driver where his face was hidden from view. The pistol and badge he had taken from the Secret Service agent were under his jacket.

"Have you heard anything in the news about the Soviet official's visit?"

"Not much," the driver responded. "Some guy scared him bad this morning. Right when he stops to shake hands with people, this car crossed an intersection a block away and the engine backfired. They got everybody thinking for a few minutes that it was an assassination attempt, because it sounded like gunfire, ya know. But things settled down pretty quick."

Whew. They covered that neatly. He settled into the seat and watched scenery glide by through gathering darkness.

The taxi crossed the Potomac, turned east, and drove along Washington Parkway toward Alexandria. It wound through back streets until it entered a fashionable neighborhood.

Atcho ordered the driver to pull over, paid him, and exited. He approached the door of a house and watched until the cab disappeared. Then he walked quickly back to the street and, clinging to shadows, made his way to an alley. Cautiously, he maneuvered through the few remaining blocks toward General Clary's residence.

He circled, noticing several dark cars parked at various locations around the block. Thankful that early darkness and frigid winter temperatures kept people in their houses, Atcho scurried across the remaining street, and ducked into Clary's backyard.

The house was dark except for a flickering glow in the downstairs den. Atcho crept to the sliding glass door and peered inside. Against the light of a television, he saw a man sitting in an overstuffed chair. Drawing the pistol from his belt, he pulled slightly on the door. It was unlocked. He jerked it open and lunged inside.

"Don't move," he snarled and pointed the pistol at the figure in the chair.

"Comrade Xiquez," an unfamiliar voice said. "How fortunate."

Atcho continued to point the pistol at the man while backing against a wall. With his free hand, he felt for a light switch.

"We wondered where you might show up," the man continued. "This seemed one of the most likely places, so we kept this house under surveillance."

"Who are you?" Atcho found the switch and turned on the lights. "Where's Clary?"

The man ignored the question. "Call me Ivan," he said, rising and extending his hand. He was nondescript, dressed in a plain, dark suit. "I am a comrade in the KGB."

Atcho stared. "I'm no comrade," he said after a moment, ignoring the extended hand. "You stay where you are until I have some questions answered."

A picture of his own face appeared on the television screen. A reporter spoke. "In a curious twist to the story about the backfired engine that upset the Soviet leader today, this man is being sought by local authorities in connection with several real estate irregularities. His name is Eduardo Xiquez, and he goes by Atcho. You might remember that last January the president honored him during the State of the Union Address. Ironically, he owns the building that the premier was passing when the incident occurred. If you have information concerning his whereabouts, please contact authorities."

Atcho glared at Ivan.

"You might as well listen," the KGB officer said. "You won't receive help from the Americans."

"Where is Clary?"

Ivan shrugged. "I understand your hostility, and your caution. You have nothing to fear from me. As for General Clary, he's gone."

"Gone where?"

"I wish we knew. Do you mind if I call you Atcho?"

Atcho continued to stare at Ivan, pointing the pistol at his chest.

Ivan sighed. "If we wanted to harm you, we could have done so from the moment you left the taxi. My men reported your progress since you entered the neighborhood. While you crouched at the back door, you were the target of a high-powered rifle no more than fifty feet away. If I wave my hand, you'll be shot from three directions. Now, would you please put that weapon down? As strange as this might sound, our interests are identical."

Atcho looked about the room, then back at Ivan. Finally, he returned the pistol to his belt.

Ivan looked relieved. "I'm authorized to offer you every asset at our disposal to help find the general. I am in command of this operation, but as the Americans would say, you're running the show."

Atcho looked at Ivan, stunned. "Running the show? What show?"

Ivan chuckled. "I thought you were familiar with our capabilities. We have men watching airports, bus stations, train depots, and every means imaginable of leaving the city. The general's friends and acquaintances are under surveillance. We coordinated with American authorities to find Govorov."

"So Govorov is also missing?"

Ivan looked at him strangely. "Let me ask you a question. You came here looking for Clary, so I assume you've learned of his activities. Have you mentioned them to anyone?"

Atcho was suddenly cautious. "What am I supposed to have learned?"

"Let's not mince words. You came to kill Clary, so you must have guessed his role in all this."

Atcho held Ivan's steady gaze. "So?"

"I repeat. Have you mentioned to anyone what you've learned?"

Atcho hesitated. "One person. Why?"

Ivan stood and paced. "It doesn't matter. The truth will soon be out."

"You mean that General Clary spied for you guys. Yep. The cat's out of the bag."

Amused, Ivan looked at Atcho. "You haven't figured out the rest of it, have you?"

"You mean that Clary and Govorov are the same guy?"

"How did you guess?"

Atcho shrugged.

43

"This is my show?" Atcho asked.

"Yes," Ivan replied, startled at the transformed man before him. Atcho had come into the room with an air of desperation. Now, he was fully in command.

"Why?"

"Because you won't let him escape. You have the most reason for wanting him."

"Let's go. My friend Burly won't be able to keep the dogs at bay forever. Assign a few men to keep watch here. And get me a cell phone."

Moments later, Atcho and Ivan were in the back of a sedan speeding toward the capital. Atcho picked up the telephone Ivan provided, and called Burly.

"Where are you?" Burly asked. "I ran into difficulties."

"I figured," Atcho interrupted. "I can't tell you where I am. Are you still in touch with everyone?"

"You'd better believe it. Mike's here, and so is Rafael. They set up a command post in my house, thinking you'd call in."

"Tell Mike not to bother tracing this call. And tell him to call off the dogs if he wants my cooperation. I want to hear a retraction of that news story. Then I'll contact you again."

"I'll relay the message. Mike's pretty sore, though. He made me reveal everything about the threat against your family."

"Thanks." Atcho smiled wanly. Clary had apparently gone unmentioned. "How's Isabel?"

"She's fine. Oh. I have something else to tell you."

Just then, Ivan nudged Atcho. "We think we've located the general," he whispered.

Atcho nodded and spoke back into the phone. "It'll have to wait, Burly. I'll call as soon as I hear that retraction." He hung up and turned to Ivan. "Does your driver speak English?" Ivan nodded. "Tell him to scan commercial radio stations and let us know when he hears anything about me." He waited for his instructions to be carried out, then asked, "Where is Govorov?"

"At National Airport. He's taxiing down the runway in a private jet right now. He used an alias to charter it. One of our men spotted him, but not soon enough. He's taking off now."

Atcho sat forward, his brow furrowed in thought. "There's only one place he can go," he mused softly. He turned to Ivan. "We're about ten minutes from National now. Tell your men to have another jet fueled, warmed up, and ready to fly by the time we arrive."

"But we don't have a jet. And we can't rent one. None of our men have the credentials."

"Take one," Atcho ordered. "Your guys know how to do that. Tell them to do it quietly. We don't want a SWAT team roaring in there. I'll fly the plane."

While Ivan conferred over the phone, Atcho leaned back and looked up at the night sky. The moon had risen, full and brilliant. Atcho sucked in his breath. "You came for the final act," he muttered, addressing the silvery globe. "How considerate."

The driver motioned. Atcho sat up to listen to the radio.

"This just in regarding the story about Eduardo Xiquez, the real estate businessman. Authorities have egg on their faces. Xiquez was vacationing when his briefcase was stolen. When it was retrieved, documents found inside related to fraudulent real estate transactions. However, they belonged to the thieves, and Xiquez has been cleared."

Atcho grabbed the telephone. "Let me talk to Mike," he told Burly.

A moment later, the familiar Texas drawl of Atcho's West Point roommate came over the line, tinged with an anxious note. "What in hell are you doing, Bud?"

"Do you have channels all the way to the top?"

There was a momentary silence. "Do you mean to the very top?"

"We don't have time to play, Mike. I mean to the president."

Mike paused again. "They're open up and down the line."

"Good. Do exactly as I say."

"Well, now, that kinda depends—"

"We don't have time for that. There was an attempt against the Soviet leader today. We both know what would have happened if it had succeeded. I know where one of the principal conspirators is, and where he's going. I need your help to bring him in. I already have the full cooperation of the Soviet effort. Now, will you do as I say?"

Mike whistled into the phone. "Well, Bud, I admire the way you get around. Let me check." Moments later, he came back on the line. "Okay, partner, you got it, short of nuclear war."

"Don't take what I'm going to say personally, Mike, but I need more than your word. If this story hits the press, you can kiss the arms treaty goodbye. The Cold War will be set back at least ten years." He let that sink in. "If something happens to me, a complete, written account will go to fifty newspapers in this country and overseas." That statement was not true, but it was the best defensive scheme Atcho could come up with on short notice. "I'm the only one who can close this up quietly. Are you sure I have complete cooperation?" The knuckles on his hand gripping the phone had turned white.

"Wait," Mike said.

Atcho looked around. They had arrived at National Airport and were driving along a road to a group of hangars set apart from the main terminal. Through a chain-link fence, a private jet was silhouetted against the night sky surrounded by dark sedans.

Mike came back on the line. The "good ol' boy" tone had disappeared. "It's your ball game. What do you want?"

The sedan rolled to a halt. "First, put the eastern seaboard on full military alert."

Mike whistled again. "You sure don't ask for much. What else?"

"Do it, Mike. I'm borrowing a private jet—but the owner doesn't know it. We'll be lifting off from National in two minutes. I want a straight-line flight plan from here to Havana. Tell the Soviets to arrange my entry into Cuban airspace. If need be, the general secretary can call Fidel. I should arrive in two to three hours."

"Anything else?"

"Another jet took off ten minutes ahead of me. Send a couple of fighters to tail him but instruct the pilots to give no indication of their presence."

"Do you mind telling me why you want the alert?"

"Because I think he'll fly south, but he might do something else. And he's smart enough to fly below radar. Maintain as much radio silence as possible. He'll be monitoring the frequencies."

"Why don't we shoot him out of the sky?"

"I can see the headlines," Atcho said sarcastically. "*Navy shoots down civilian aircraft over international waters. Cover-up suspected.*

"Besides, the Soviets would appreciate your not dispensing with their General Govorov before they've had a chance to question him about others in the conspiracy." He paused. "By the way, your guys would probably like to find out how much damage he's done to our national security. He's also known as General Paul Clary."

A long silence ensued, and then Mike spoke again. "Understood. Play it your way."

"I'm boarding the plane now. Get a direct, secure channel so we can talk while in flight." He hung up and looked across at Ivan.

The KGB officer regarded him with awe. "Do you realize that you gave orders to the heads of two superpowers? You're running the military forces of one, and the intelligence apparatus of the other?"

"I hadn't thought about it in those terms."

44

Two hours later, Atcho watched the lights of Miami float beneath him. Ivan sat in the copilot's seat, alternately watching flickering instruments and staring into darkness beyond the windshield. Fatigue weighed on him. He fought to stay alert. "Mike, are you there?"

"Yes. Everything is set. There'll be a welcoming party of sorts when you land."

"What about the general?"

"His flight path is just as you predicted. You'll both land at Camp Columbia. Contact the tower before entering Cuban airspace. The general should land about twenty minutes after you do."

"Roger." Atcho was glad to have taken the direct route. "If I need anything else, I'll call. Otherwise, I'll be in touch when this is over."

"Good luck."

Atcho acknowledged the sentiment and began a shallow descent. Twenty minutes later, he settled the sleek aircraft onto a runway at Camp Columbia and powered it to a halt. A pickup truck pulled in ahead of it and signaled for Atcho to follow. Soon, they maneuvered in front of an isolated hangar. Immediately, they were surrounded by armed troops.

Followed by Ivan, Atcho opened the door and descended. An officer met him at the bottom of the stairs. "I am Eduardo Xiquez," Atcho said, and introduced Ivan.

The Cuban officer introduced himself. "My instructions are to render assistance. The other plane is on final approach."

Atcho turned and looked toward the other end of the runway. High in the sky and descending rapidly, a pair of landing lights indicated the path of the craft as it settled to the ground. Then, the rumble of engines became audible, and grew in volume as it touched down. It coasted to the same spot where Atcho had stopped, and then followed the pickup to a separate parking area.

"How do you want to handle this?" the officer asked.

"Surround him. Disarm him at the door. Bring him to me," Atcho replied. He moved to the shadows.

As he watched troops move into position, he experienced a curious sensation. For twenty-seven years, Govorov had stayed ahead of Atcho, knowing in advance what was going to happen to him. For the first time, Atcho was ahead of Govorov.

Atcho imagined the relief the general must feel, believing himself in sanctuary. He would open the door and step out, expecting a friendly welcome. Instead, he would face the muzzles of many rifles. His biggest surprise would come when he was brought before Atcho.

The jet coasted to a stop. Two soldiers moved to either side of the door, weapons raised and aimed toward its center. Moments later, Govorov emerged.

The moon was high, casting shadows that sharply contrasted against the objects that created them. In the eerie light, Atcho saw only Govorov's narrow forehead and strong jaw. His heart beat fiercely as he watched soldiers take the general's arms and jostle him forward. His attention alternated between the man struggling indignantly against his captors, and images of the same figure standing over him just a few miles from this place, where Atcho had lain on the ground peering through tortured eyes.

Abruptly, Govorov stood in front of him, staring in astonishment.

Atcho stared back, disconcerted by the changed visage of General Paul Clary. Gone were the amiable eyes and stooped shoulders, as well as the air of paternal congeniality. Instead, Atcho regarded a fierce, proud face that seethed with defiance. Under the general's loose clothing, a powerful physique strained against his captors.

Govorov relaxed and laughed. The sound echoed through Atcho's mind, recalling tones that had inhabited his nightmares for years.

"I see that all my secrets are out," the mocking voice of late-night phone calls crooned. Govorov peered into Atcho's eyes. He shrugged. "I took a risk. I lost."

The general observed the Cuban soldiers surrounding him. "How did you do this?" He asked with genuine interest. "I knew you were good, but ..." He looked around again, and grinned. "Wow!"

Atcho glared at Govorov, fighting to contain the urge to end the general's life, slowly and painfully. "Why?" he asked at last. "Why did you betray your country, your friends, and your family?"

Govorov laughed. "Which country did I betray? I'll tell you. Neither." He spat out the last word. "My parents were Russian immigrants. Their mission was to produce me." He laughed at Atcho's disbelief. "My training began early—I spent summers in East Berlin and Moscow." He paused. "My life was manipulated as much as yours."

"You made choices."

Govorov smirked. "I enjoyed the pay, prestige, and privileges of an officer in each of the two most powerful countries in the world. It was a great game."

"What about your family? What about Peggy and Chrissy?"

"They don't matter" Govorov said in a jocular tone. "They served a purpose. They'll get along."

"You're a sociopath," Atcho snapped. His mind transported him to a room somewhere in Havana where he had recovered from Captain Govorov's beating. He saw again the slowly rotating ceiling fan, and the strong features of Juan.

Govorov ignored the comment. "You turned things around nicely. I blew two military pensions." He leered maniacally. "If I escape, I'll be running from the two most powerful countries in the world. A new challenge, wouldn't you say? Meanwhile, you'll reap gratitude from the leaders of both superpowers."

A screech of brakes caused both men to turn. A Jeep came to a stop on the runway, fifty feet away. Its top was down, and a massive figure sat in the passenger's seat. As Atcho watched, the platoon of soldiers surrounding them snapped to attention. Then the figure clambered from the Jeep and strode toward Atcho and Govorov. He was tall and barrel-chested. His face was bearded, and he wore a fatigue cap. A cigar protruded from his mouth.

Atcho sucked in his breath. He was about to meet Fidel Castro.

Castro stopped and observed them coolly. "This is a night of ironies," he said. "Two stolen jets enter my airspace." He looked at Govorov. "On one is an old friend who helped save my air force from American bombs during the invasion so many years ago." He paused and turned to Atcho. "On the other is a traitorous countryman who became an American citizen and represents the Soviet KGB." He faced Govorov. "You're the only man I've ever known who is wanted by the heads of state of both superpowers. You didn't tell me what you'd done when you called to request entry."

Govorov grinned and bowed.

Castro pulled on his cigar and blew a cloud of smoke into the air. He turned to Atcho. "And you are the only man, to my knowledge, who traveled under the protection of both the president of the United States and the general secretary of the Soviet Communist Party."

"I told you, Atcho," Govorov chortled. "You see? You should be grateful."

Suddenly, he lunged at a distracted guard, seized his rifle and aimed at Castro's heart. "I'm not ready to be taken," he hissed. "Tell the men to drop their weapons. Now." He stepped behind the guard and held an arm around his neck.

Castro looked at him coldly but nodded. Around them, soldiers laid their rifles on the ground.

"Tell them to move to the runway but stay in sight." The guards complied. "Now, my friend Fidel, move slowly in front of me. We're going to board my jet. Then, you're going to order it refueled. I'll need a fresh pilot, and clearance to fly to Colombia. I'm sure one of the drug cartels could use my talents."

As Atcho watched, the trio set off across the tarmac. Castro led, followed by Govorov. Weighted down by the rifle, and holding on to the guard in front of him, he walked clumsily.

On the runway, the jet stood gleaming in the moonlight, a soft glow emanating from its open door. Govorov's foot hit a pothole. He stumbled.

The guard shoved him, and the rifle clattered to the ground, out of reach. Govorov whirled. For an instant, no one moved. Then, Govorov sprinted toward the jet.

Castro lunged at him.

Govorov stepped aside and ran. He passed the jet and disappeared into the shadows on the other side.

Meanwhile, soldiers rushed to retrieve their weapons. The guard who had been hostage grabbed his rifle from the ground, pulled it to his shoulder, and fired at Govorov. He missed.

Atcho took off in a dead run after Govorov. He passed the guard just as the shot was fired, and then barreled past Castro. He cleared the jet in time to see the fugitive disappear into the deep shadows of a hangar.

Atcho reached the hangar and halted. Pressing against the front wall, he listened. A low roar of distant aircraft blocked other sounds. He looked back at the soldiers. They still gathered their weapons.

Atcho edged around the corner. This side of the hangar was dark. He paused to allow his eyes to adjust, and then surveyed the area.

The asphalt surface ended halfway to the rear. Hard, barren dirt continued to a high, chain-link fence running alongside the building. It wrapped around the rear, topped with concertina. Assuming it ran all the way around, Govorov was trapped.

Staying close to the wall, Atcho crept along the hangar. His eyes probed the darkness, searching for movement. His ears strained for a discordant sound. Blocked by the hangar, the moon was not visible. However, its glow created a long shadow that tapered away by the front corner. Most of the back, and the entire opposite side of the building, must be bathed in moonlight.

Govorov would stay in the shadows as long as possible. When found, he would fight desperately. He might have already spotted Atcho.

Atcho heard a scuffling noise. A dark form slid around the rear corner, coming his way. *He just found out there's no place to run.*

Govorov came into view, a dark figure against a wall.

Atcho stepped into the open. "It's no use. Give it up."

Govorov glared at him, panting. “It’s just you and me at last. Come and get me.” He stepped away from the wall and backed toward the rear.

Atcho advanced. “It’s over. The soldiers will be here any moment.”

“Maybe I’ll take another hostage. Maybe I’ll take you.” Govorov lunged across the short distance between them.

Atcho spun away. He felt something sharp pierce his arm. He whirled to face the general, crouching for the next assault. Behind him, he heard voices and running boots.

Govorov heard the soldiers. He circled toward the rear of the building.

“It’s over,” Atcho repeated. “Give me the knife.”

Govorov laughed. “What’s that expression they have in America? It ain’t over till the fat lady sings.” He looked around wildly. “I don’t see any fat ladies. I just see you.” He lunged again.

Atcho dodged and stepped into the moonlight. He felt extremely calm. “You always hid in shadows. Let’s see what you can do in the light. You still have an advantage. You have the knife.”

Govorov hesitated inside the shadow of the hangar. He glanced at the approaching soldiers. Then he stepped into the moonlight, leering.

While their shadows waltzed in lurid symphony against the barren ground, the two enemies circled, sizing each other up. The moon watched, unfeeling.

Govorov lunged again, aiming the knife just below the rib cage.

Atcho dodged away and faced him.

Govorov grinned savagely. He wiped his mouth on the back of his wrist and lunged again. Atcho pivoted to his left, kicked with his right foot, and caught the general’s wrist. The knife flew across the ground.

Govorov swooped it. He was too late.

Atcho dove after it and wrapped his fingers around its handle.

Govorov landed on him. The two men rolled in the dirt, sweat streaming from their bodies. Their lungs heaved.

Govorov pushed Atcho onto his back and sat on his abdomen. He forced Atcho’s hand down, with the knife.

The wicked blade gleamed. Atcho felt the point prick his skin. Desperate, he clubbed Govorov’s head with his left fist, and rolled onto his right side. He continued to roll and sat on top of Govorov, the knife still gripped in his hand. He pushed against the general's upright arm and felt it weaken. Then he added the weight of his upper body, pressing down on the handle.

Govorov's arm gave way. A scream wrenched the night.

Atcho felt the knife crunch its way through bone and sinew. A spurt of thick blood gushed into his face. Govorov writhed beneath him.

Atcho pushed the knife harder and turned it inside Govorov's chest. "Do you feel that, you son-of-a-bitch?" He raised the knife high over his head to strike again. A hand closed around his wrist. He heard a voice.

"It's over, Atcho. It's over."

Atcho struggled against the restraining hand, but felt strength slipping away. He turned his head, panting, and peered up at Ivan.

"Let's go," the KGB officer said. "There's no more you can do here."

Atcho nodded. He breathed deeply and struggled to his feet. Beneath him, Govorov ceased to move. Atcho looked around.

The soldiers surrounded them, their rifles trained on Govorov's limp figure. Castro stood at their center. He studied Atcho. "It's a shame you don't work for me."

Atcho glared at him, his chest still heaving. "Not a chance."

Castro peered at him but remained silent. Then, he grunted, pulled heavily on his cigar, and blew smoke rings in the air. "Fortunately for you, the Soviet general secretary requested—respectfully—that I expedite your return to Washington."

He started toward the front of the hangar and motioned for Atcho to walk with him. Atcho turned and looked at Govorov lying on the ground. "Is he dead?"

"I don't know. We'll let the doctors worry about that." Fidel started off again. Atcho joined him. "As I said, a night of ironies. I, of all people, was asked to relay an invitation to the White House. One of my MiGs is ready to fly you to DC. You'll be met *en route* by US fighters to escort you into Andrews Air Force Base." He shook his head. "Unbelievable. Maybe this is what they call détente." He chuckled at his own joke.

They arrived at the front of the building where two Jeeps stood waiting. "*Adios*, Atcho. This was interesting." Fidel climbed into his Jeep and drove away.

Ivan stood at Atcho's side. "Your night isn't over."

Atcho looked at his watch and gasped. Only five and a half hours had passed since he had left the safe house. It was now just past nine thirty.

"I enjoyed working with you," Ivan said, shaking his hand. "Maybe we can work together again."

"Nothing personal," Atcho replied dryly. "No thanks."

EPILOGUE

Atcho awoke with a start and glanced at his watch. He had slept through the entire flight. It was now eleven o'clock.

The Cuban MiG settled onto a runway. A utility truck met the fighter on a ramp and led it to a massive, well-lit hangar. Through blurred eyes, Atcho watched. When the aircraft halted, the canopy lifted, and he climbed down. Two Marine guards, barely able to contain their curiosity, guided him through a door to a waiting helicopter.

Moments later, Atcho watched the soft, twinkling lights of Washington, DC. The rhythmic vibrations of the whirring blades relaxed his sore muscles. There had been no opportunity to clean up, so he still wore bloody, sweat-stained clothes, and he stank. Someone had given him a moist cloth to clean his face and hands, but blood still caked his hairline.

He leaned back, not knowing what to expect at the White House. Even if he were in trouble, his ordeal was finally over.

The helicopter floated to the White House lawn, and Marine guards hurried Atcho across the grass into a rear door. He looked around tiredly as he followed through a maze of halls and corridors. They climbed stairs and passed offices to a wide foyer.

A courtly, Southern gentleman met them and introduced himself to Atcho as the president's chief of staff. He motioned Atcho to follow and proceeded along a portico and through a door. "Mr. President, General Secretary Gorbachev," he announced. "Mr. Eduardo Xiquez."

Atcho entered in a daze. He was in the Oval Office.

Reagan crossed the room. Gorbachev followed him.

The president extended his hand. "It's so good to see you again. Sorry to bring you here so quickly after your trouble, but the general secretary wanted to meet you. He leaves tomorrow."

Speechless, Atcho looked at his grimy hands and filthy clothes, then back at the president.

Reagan took his hand and shook it. A mischievous smile formed at the corners of his mouth. "Why weren't you around to make me duck back in '81?"

Gorbachev also shook Atcho's hand. "I owe you a personal debt. So does my country. A simple thank you is inadequate. Is there anything I can do?"

Atcho stared numbly, his gaze resting on Gorbachev's birthmark. "Yes sir. You can accept my resignation from conscripted service with the KGB."

The general secretary reddened and smiled uneasily. "Anything else?"

Atcho shook his head. "I'm sure the president will want to ask you a few questions about General Clary."

The two heads of state exchanged forced laughter. Reagan guided Atcho to the door. They shook hands again, then Atcho followed the chief of staff out to a waiting Marine escort, who led through more halls and down more stairs.

They rounded a corner and Atcho saw a group of men gathered at the end of a hall. One of them saw Atcho and nudged the others. They started toward him.

Atcho stared in disbelief. Bob was there, and Burly, Rafael, and Mike Rogers. They surrounded him and clapped arms over his back.

"Hey Atcho," Rafael said, "when I suggested at the reception that we might do something together, this isn't what I had in mind." He grinned, clasped Atcho's shoulder, and steered him through another door leading onto a terrace. Above them, the moon bathed the area in soft light. A group of men had gathered there. They applauded when they saw Atcho and surrounded him.

He turned slowly, taking in their crumpled clothes and their faces, which bore several days' growth of whiskers. He glanced from Burly to Rafael. "Who are they?"

"Veterans of Brigade 2506," Rafael replied. "They were brought to DC for questioning after the FBI took over protective custody of your family. The president cleared us of charges a few minutes ago."

Atcho looked at the faces around him. They were rugged, unpretentious, and bore a quality of quiet confidence and competence. One of them had a bandaged jaw.

"What happened to him?"

"Your son-in-law is very protective," Burly laughed. "Bob wouldn't let anyone near Isabel, and when this man tried to explain what was happening, Bob busted him in the mouth. He fractured his jaw."

Bob looked sheepish. "I already apologized," he said, walking over to the man and putting an arm over his shoulder. The man grimaced but shook his head good-naturedly. Bob turned back to Atcho. "Come over here. Someone wants to meet you."

The group parted as Atcho followed to the center of the terrace.

Isabel sat there in a chair, tears streaming over a broken smile. She held a bundle wrapped in blankets. As Atcho leaned over her, she threw an arm around his neck. "I know what you went through for me," she sobbed.

A hush descended. Around them, the men stood back at a respectful distance.

Atcho held Isabel. Then, he felt something move by his waist. He pulled back and stared into the blankets in Isabel's arm.

Two tiny eyes peered up at him. Wonder crossed his face.

"Meet your granddaughter, Kattrina." Isabel lifted the infant into Atcho's arms.

Aware of his grimy condition, Atcho protested. Isabel prodded. Atcho held his tiny granddaughter, pulled her close to his face and hugged her as tightly as he dared.

No one cared to break the quiet, but after a few moments, Burly coughed. "You stubborn Cuban. I tried to tell you. When Bob and Isabel rushed away from their house, they went to the hospital. The baby arrived early."

Atcho whirled around to Isabel. "Should you be here?"

She nodded. "The doctor said we would be okay for a while. The president's physician is monitoring."

Atcho looked around at the members of Brigade 2506. "I can't thank you enough." His voice broke.

"Then don't," someone quipped. "We can't stand sappy." Deep-throated laughter filled the air as Atcho walked around to shake hands with each man. He held the baby to his chest while Isabel looked on.

A soft hand touched his shoulder. When he turned, Sofia stood there with an expression that was both somber and impish.

Atcho sucked in his breath.

Burly stood next to her. "I'm no fool," he blurted. "Why do you think I did so many things without question? Sofia came to see me after you broke up with her. She knew something was wrong. She needed help."

Atcho continued gazing at Sofia. Then a puzzled look crossed his face. He remembered that Sofia had told him, "I don't sit around and let things happen."

With his eyes locked on Sofia's, he said, "Burly, a pretty lady asks you for help involving national security, and you just do it?"

Burly's face reddened. He looked flustered. "Well, ah. Uh, we've worked together before."

Atcho looked over sharply, but before he could say anything, Sofia tugged at his elbow. Bob moved in, scooped up the baby, and put her in Isabel's arms.

"You won't escape me again," Sofia whispered into Atcho's ear.

His heart raced as he embraced her. Holding her, he glanced at Isabel and Bob. They stood together cooing at their baby—*my grandchild*. Behind them, Atcho's friends milled about.

Sofia's face rested against Atcho's. He touched her forehead with his own and pulled back to gaze at her. Then he raised his eyes to view the night sky.

The moon in its full splendor continued its impassive observation. Atcho lifted his hand to give it a thumbs-up.

ACKNOWLEDGMENTS

Writing thrillers full of twists and turns is not difficult—doing so against a backdrop of known historical events is much tougher. The outcome is known. To tell a rapidly paced story that entertains the reader requires detailed research and insertion of elements to raise conflict and add suspense without altering the facts of history. Surprising readers without confusing them or insulting their knowledge of history or procedure is the real art. Then there are the characters.... I'm grateful to the Editors and Beta Readers of *The Reluctant Assassin* (formerly *Curse the Moon and The Atcho Conspiracy*) for their guidance with the finer points of plot and character, and for their assistance in fighting my natural inclination toward typos: Michelle Browne, Tom Mitchell, Mac Warner, Candy Silcott, John Shep-hard, John Dinnell, Randy Morris, Jim Vaughan, Lance Gatling, Christian Jackson, Stuart Stirrat, Anita Paulsen, Margee Harwell, Barbara Hall, Clinton Herriott, Sam Stolzoff, Rich Trotter, Al Fracker, Michael Chritton, Rich Trotter, Ralph Massi, and friends who cannot be named.

ABOUT THE AUTHOR

Lee Jackson is the Wall Street Journal bestselling author of The Reluctant Assassin series and the After Dunkirk series. He graduated from West Point and is a former Infantry Officer of the US Army. Lee deployed to Iraq and Afghanistan, splitting 38 months between them as a senior intelligence supervisor for the Department of the Army. Lee lives and works with his wife in Texas, and his novels are enjoyed by readers around the world.

Sign up for Lee Jackson's newsletter at
severnriverbooks.com

LeeJackson@SevernRiverBooks.com

Printed in the United States
by Baker & Taylor Publisher Services